Also by M.A. Bennett

The Butterfly Club series:
The Ship of Doom
The Mummy's Curse

Series for older readers:
STAGS
DOGS
FOXES
TIGERS
HAWKS

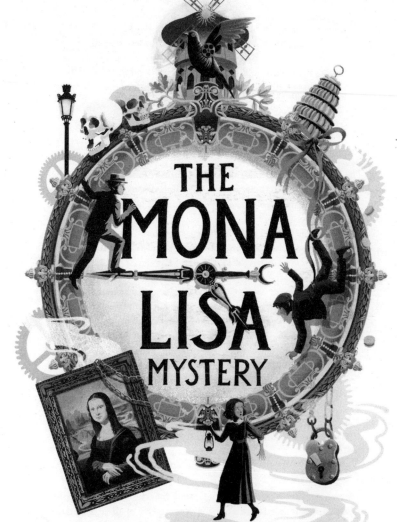

THE
MONA
LISA
MYSTERY

M. A. BENNETT

WELBECK
FLAME

First published in 2023 by Welbeck Flame
An imprint of Welbeck Children's Limited, part of
Welbeck Publishing Group.
Offices in: London - 20 Mortimer Street, London W1T 3JW
& Sydney - 205 Commonwealth Street, Surry Hills 2010
www.welbeckpublishing.com

A CIP catalogue record for this book
is available from the British Library.

ISBN: 978 1 80130 038 4

Printed and bound by CPI Group (UK)

10 9 8 7 6 5 4 3 2 1

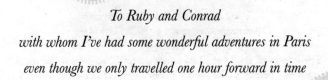

To Ruby and Conrad
with whom I've had some wonderful adventures in Paris
even though we only travelled one hour forward in time

Dear Reader,

If you are reading this you are already a time traveller, because this is the year 1894 and Queen Victoria is on the throne.

And if you are reading this you must be a friend, so I feel all right about sharing the secrets of the Butterfly Club with you.

Let me begin at the beginning. My name is Luna, and I suppose you would call me a time-thief. I live in a rather smart part of London with my Aunt Grace, who's been looking after me ever since my father disappeared. One Thursday Aunt Grace took me with her to her secret society, the Butterfly Club.

The Butterfly Club meets every Thursday afternoon in Greenwich, at the famous Royal Observatory, which is the Home of Time. It's called that because there is a long brass line running through the courtyard of the observatory called the prime meridian, the point from which all time is measured.

Deep in the belly of the observatory is the Butterfly Room, a secret twelve-sided chamber where the Butterfly Club meet. It's called the Butterfly Room because there are butterflies on the walls – those dead ones pinned to little cards – in all the colours of the rainbow. The members of the Butterfly Club are the finest minds of Victorian society, people you might even have heard of in your time – people like Charles Dickens, Charles Darwin and Florence Nightingale.

And that's where I met my fellow time-thieves. You see, there are three of us.

Konstantin is from Prussia. He has loads of brothers who are all soldiers, and his father, Dr Tanius Kass, is a very clever inventor. Konstantin loves everything military, but because he was so ill when he was little, he couldn't be a soldier himself. But Konstantin is special in his own way, because he has a mechanical heart. His own heart didn't work so his father replaced it with a clockwork one.

The third time-thief is Aidan. Aidan is Irish, and he is a navigational engineer (or navvy) who's been working on the railways since he was ten. Aidan knows everything there is to know about machines, and sometimes I think he loves them better than people. And, like Konstantin, Aidan has a secret too, which he keeps very close to his chest.

The three of us are called time-thieves because we've been travelling in time, carrying out missions for the Butterfly Club. We use a contraption called the Time Train, which was designed by H. G. Wells, one of the club's members. We travel forward in time to collect inventions and treasures from the future. We never go backwards - no Tudors or Romans or even dinosaurs for us! The point is to bring back things which our age doesn't have yet, to speed up progress. Aunt Grace says our thieving is for 'the betterment of society'. I hope she's right. The Butterfly Club certainly seem to get a lot of money - and prizes - out of it.

Well, dear reader, Aidan, Konstantin and I have had quite a few journeys through the decades since the day we met, and we've faced many dangers. We've been to the freezing Atlantic Ocean in 1912 to try to steal a wireless radio from the good ship *Titanic*, and to the arid deserts of Egypt in 1922 to uncover the lost tomb of Tutankhamun. You can read all about our exploits in our earlier chronicles, *The Ship of Doom* and *The Mummy's Curse*.

I hope you enjoy this adventure too! I wonder where it will take us...

Yours until the end of time,
Luna Goodhart x

LONDON

5 FEBRUARY 1894

5 FEBRUARY 1894
9.15 a.m.

Aidan was the first to see the strange man walking down the railway track.

He was working with his father, Michael, and a gang of navvies on the new railway snaking out of King's Cross Station – an iron way into the north which was to span rivers and burrow under mountains, a miracle of the modern age.

It was a bitter February morning. Aidan's breath smoked and his fingertips were numb. As much as he loved the work, and the music of the steel picks sparking on the iron rails, he couldn't help thinking of the arid sands and burning sun of Egypt. Even though to his father he'd been gone no time at all, in Aidan's timeline he'd spent months in the Valley of the Kings with Luna and

Konstantin, following the historic discovery of the tomb of Tutankhamun. Funny – when he was there, he'd have given anything to feel this cold, and now he'd give the Crown Jewels to be warm again. Aidan stopped work to blow on his fingers, and that's when he caught sight of the man.

He was an odd-looking fellow; a creature of contradictions. He was boxy and bow-legged and short in stature, but somehow impressive. He was wearing a frock coat and an opera cloak that bellied like a sail as he walked, as if he was moving unnaturally slowly: however, he seemed to cover the distance very swiftly. He seemed a man of importance, but as he came closer he looked no more than twenty. He had that crinkly hair that refuses to do as it is told. It puffed out on either side of his head like a clown's, but his face was serious, and his eyes had a strange silvery quality to their gaze.

'It must be Christmastide already,' murmured Aidan's father, who always had a joke ready. 'The pantomime's on.'

As Aidan and his father were working nearest to the station, the man arrived at them first and stopped. 'You are naffies?' he said in a strong accent which Aidan recognised, from his travels, as being from somewhere in the east of Europe.

'Navvies,' confirmed Michael O'Connell. 'Navigational engineers.'

'You haf chins?'

Instinctively Aidan put his hand to his face.

'Strong chins?'

It was an odd question. True, Aidan's jawline was not quite as masculine as he would like, but Da's chin was covered in a glorious black beard. 'I suppose so,' said Da, leaning on his pick and pointing to his beard. 'One here and one there. We have cheeks and noses too.'

'No, no,' said the odd little man, with a chuckle dry as tinder. '*Chins*.' He performed a little mime, circling his forefinger and thumb on each hand and locking them together. Aidan and his father found themselves watching his hands. They were extraordinary – uncommonly white and delicate compared to their own rough working hands, and they moved in an exceptionally fluid way, graceful and swift.

'Chins,' the man said again. 'One link, two link, three link…'

'Oh *chains*,' said Aidan, light dawning. 'You want chains.'

'Yes, zat is what I said,' said the man patiently. 'But they must be *strong* chins.'

4

As if he was addressing a Martian, Michael O'Connell said, 'How long?' He held out his hands like a fisherman boasting of his catch.

'Oh, not long, not long,' said the man. 'Only long enough to tie pair of feet together and dangle grown man over water tank.'

Aidan and his father exchanged a glance. They had uncannily similar blue eyes. They were both, separately, convinced that the stranger was, in fact, a Martian.

'Come with me,' said Aidan to the stranger. Then, to his father, 'I'll show him the offcuts.'

He beckoned to the stranger, who followed Aidan, picking his way over the tracks in his shiny black shoes. In an overgrown siding Aidan showed the little man various lengths of chain, left lying beside the tracks. Some had links as big as a man's fist; some had links as small as a thumbnail.

The stranger looked down at them speculatively. 'Are they strong chins?'

'None stronger,' said Aidan. 'Good Sheffield steel. These large-gauge ones...' He pointed to the biggest. 'They can pull a locomotive.' He mimed the pistons of a train with his arms, and made the sound of a train's whistle for good measure.

The man nodded with satisfaction. 'I take those.' He pointed to the length of chain with the biggest links. Then he fished out his pocketbook. 'I pay you for chins.'

'No, no,' said Aidan, goggling at the sheaf of banknotes. 'These are offcuts. Scrap.'

The man looked confused.

'Chain too long for purpose,' said Aidan, doing a little mime to explain. 'Spare bits cut off. Throw away. You take.'

The man smiled for the first time, a rather charming expression which transformed his serious face. 'I am very much obliged to you.' He got ready to pick up the chains, first donning a pair of gloves to protect those exceptional hands.

Aidan looked at him doubtfully. He didn't think his new friend had the muscle to carry the chains away. 'They're pretty heavy,' he said. 'I'll help you to carry them.' He coiled the chain expertly and heaved the bundle into his arms. The steel was so cold, it leached the warmth from his body and burned his hands. He led the stranger back down the track and through the bustling concourse of King's Cross Station. The cloaked stranger and the young navvy carrying a huge serpent of chain caused the fine ladies in their crinolines and the city gentlemen in their bowler hats to stare. Outside on the street a hansom cab was waiting. The man got into the carriage and Aidan passed the chain up to the driver, to travel beside him on the box.

The stranger put his arm on the windowsill and leant out. 'You are very kind boy,' he said. 'What is your name?'

'Aidan O'Connell,' Aidan replied.

The stranger looked at Aidan. His eyes were curiously intense, and seemed to have a light all of their own, almost as if they were made of mirrors. 'You come to the Egyptian Hall tonight. You know it?'

'*Do* I?' said Aidan. 'It's the big fancy theatre in Piccadilly.'

'The very one,' said the man. 'Come at seven o'clock. Bring some friends. I put your name on door.' He reached behind Aidan's ear and brought out a shiny new sixpence. 'You will see quite a show.' Then he tapped on the roof to signal the driver to go.

Aidan stood for a moment, looking at the coin the man had dropped into his hand. Then he went back through the station and trudged back along the iron track to rejoin his father.

'What was all that about?' asked Michael O'Connell, when Aidan reached him.

'He's in the theatre business, far's I can make out,' his son replied. 'Works at the Egyptian Hall. Maybe he needed the chains for security – to lock the doors at night or something.' Aidan picked up his shovel. 'Must be doing well, though. Fella had more money than sense. Pocketbook full of fivers, he had.' He didn't mention the magic sixpence.

Michael O'Connell brought his pick down on the pinion with a ringing spark. 'Must be nice.'

Aidan shovelled some gravel to shore up the sleeper. 'He wants me to go to his play tonight, and to bring a couple of guests. You want to come?'

His father laughed. 'You know me, son. I'd rather be inside a coffin than a theatre. Besides…' His blue eyes twinkled. 'I can think of company you'd much rather take – two young folks you've been panting to see again like a dog on a hot day.'

5 FEBRUARY 1894
6.50 p.m.

The time-thieves had planned to meet just before seven in the evening, outside the splendid Egyptian Hall theatre in London's smart Piccadilly. Aidan waited at the entrance, in the centre of a façade constructed of Egyptian pillars crawling with hieroglyphics. He thought it funny that only that morning he'd longed to be back in Egypt – and now he felt like he was.

Aidan was excited to see Luna and Konstantin, even though it had only been a matter of days since they had seen each other at the Butterfly Club. There the talk had all been about stealing some painting from a gallery in Paris. This was widely believed to be impossible and as the meeting broke up it was decided that everyone should go away for a week and come back the following Thursday with ideas. The time-thieves hadn't really been listening. For one thing, they thought it highly unlikely they would be sent on a *third* Butterfly Mission. For another, they had been much more interested in catching up with each other. So this night at the theatre had been a welcome chance to see each other twice in a week, instead of only once.

Aidan could pick out his friends straightaway, even in the crowd of smart theatre-goers forming a crush at the entrance. Luna wore a frock with fluttering skirts which resembled a butterfly, as all her dresses did. This one was a stinging green colour with black trim which went very well with her auburn hair. Because it was a cold February night, she had her hands plunged into a black muffler and wore a cloak of the same fur. Konstantin wore a Prussian-blue wool coat with an astrakhan collar. The coat was done up with gilded buttons, which gave it a military appearance. As he wore no hat on his straw-coloured hair, he was easy to pick out. Aidan was proud of his friends, who looked just as smart to his eyes as the gathered ladies, night-sky-bright with diamonds, or the gentlemen, sleek as seals in their opera cloaks. He only hoped that his navvy gear was up to the occasion – cogs were his diamonds, and an old Norfolk jacket his cloak.

The time-thieves were delighted to see one another – after camping together in the Valley of the Kings for months, they missed each other keenly. Aidan rapidly recounted what had happened that morning at King's Cross Station – the stranger, the chains, and the invitation to the theatre.

'What are we going to see?'

'No idea,' confessed Aidan. 'I only know that it's free of charge, and that's good enough for me. I'm just hoping it isn't Shakespeare. I'm sure I wouldn't understand a word.'

Of course they had no tickets, so there was a sticky moment when an usher, in the livery of the theatre, looked down his nose at Aidan. 'Tradesmen through the stage door,' he said.

Aidan wasn't having that. 'You should have been given my name,' he said cockily. 'Aidan O'Connell?'

The usher consulted the list in his gloved hand. What he read there transformed his attitude completely. 'Ah yes. Please accept my apologies, Mr O'Connell. I'll show you and your honoured guests to your seats myself. If you'll come this way?'

The time-thieves followed the usher through a grand marble atrium and up stairs that were covered with such a thick red carpet that their feet made no noise at all. They were ushered through the crowds as if they were royalty, and Aidan looked about him the whole time for the man he had met that morning. He was convinced he must be some sort of theatre manager – even the theatre owner, seeing as he had all those fivers. But the strange little man was nowhere to be seen.

It was a jewel box of a theatre. As they entered the auditorium the time-thieves saw rows upon rows of velvet seats and ornate gilded boxes, all lit by modern electric bulbs backed by silver scallop shells. The stage was an enormous arch, presently covered by a curtain, with the name of the theatre emblazoned on it in letters each taller than a man. From the dizzying heights of the dome above hung a dazzling chandelier, and chubby painted cherubs rode on fluffy clouds as if they were roundabout horses. A thousand faces looked down in anticipation, a thousand excited whispers gathered into a boiling hubbub. Every seat in the place appeared to be filled, except for three, right by the stage – the best seats in the house.

'Mr O'Connell. Sir, Miss.' The usher thrust out a white-gloved hand to indicate their seats, and the time-thieves took their places in the tip-up chairs which were upholstered in the colour of blood. The friends exchanged glances of delicious excitement – however dull the play might prove to be, the night was already a treat.

The lights dimmed twice, then the third time they didn't brighten again.

Somewhere a bell sounded.

The performance, whatever it was, was about to begin.

A voice spoke from the blackness, loud and dramatic, and several members of the audience jumped off their velvet seats.

'Ladies and gentlemen. Prepare to be amazed by the most powerful young magician in the world. Erase from your mind the Skilful Sorcerers of India, the Mighty Mages of China and the Eminent Enchanters of Africa. Here, for your delectation and delight, is the Handcuff King, Prison Breaker, Death-Defying Dematerialist and Master of Mystery himself: THE GREAT HOUDINI!'

And the little man who walked on to the centre of the stage, wearing a silk hat and a frock coat and carrying a cane, was the stranger Aidan had met at King's Cross that morning.

He had never been so surprised in his life.

5 FEBRUARY 1894
7 p.m.

Konstantin rubbed his hands together. 'Oh good, it's magic. *Much* better than a play.'

Aidan ignored him. 'That's him!' he exclaimed. 'That's the fella!'

Luna said, 'What fella? I mean, fellow?'

'The man who came to King's Cross to buy some chains. I wonder what he needed them for.'

'I suppose we'll see,' said Konstantin, and then there was no more talking, for the little man in the spotlight banged his cane on the stage. The cane instantly transformed into a raven, which flew, cawing hoarsely, over the heads of the audience.

From that moment, the time-thieves were quite literally enchanted.

The Great Houdini performed illusions such as they had never seen. Aidan had met navvies along the canals and railways who could do a card trick or two, and Luna had seen conjurors in the drawing rooms of family acquaintances. Konstantin was the only one who had seen magic performed onstage, in the gilded opera houses of Prussia, but even he had seen nothing like this. From that first flight of the raven, when the ebony and ivory of a cane turned into living feathers and a beak, Houdini went on to perform a dizzying array of parlour magic. He pulled a whole bunting of coloured handkerchiefs from his sleeve, red roses from his ears, and juggled billiard balls that turned into eggs and smashed on the stage.

Then there was more elaborate fare: a trick cabinet which swallowed up a lady, only to deposit her at the other side of the stage; shadowgraphs with a mind of their own; mirrors that stubbornly refused to reflect their subject; and a trick (which had the friends exchanging knowing glances) called the Mummy's Tomb. And all the time Houdini talked, in the thick Eastern European accent Aidan remembered from that morning: a steady stream of narration, telling the audience everything, revealing nothing.

The time-thieves were particularly interested in a trick called the Phantom Painting. A blank canvas was brought on to the stage to rest on a golden easel. Houdini merely waved his hand before it, and an exquisite portrait of Queen Victoria appeared on the canvas, as if by magic. The trick was not particularly showy, and involved no fancy props, but it was by far the most impressive of the night.

This time the applause was deafening, but Aidan couldn't help feeling a little disappointed. The hour grew late; the miracle of the Phantom Painting was obviously the climax of the show, and there had been no tricks involving his chains.

Houdini walked into the wings for some moments. The audience, believing the show was over, began to applaud again and call for an encore. But then the disembodied voice that had introduced him at the start was heard again. 'And now,' it boomed, 'the Great Houdini will perform a feat of escapology never before seen on these shores. Ladies and gentlemen, the Egyptian Hall presents the Chinese Water Torture Cell.'

The light seemed to somehow thicken, and Aidan's fingers tightened on the arms of his prickly velvet chair. Two Chinese gentlemen with long black plaits, wearing long oriental robes and square hats, wheeled an enormous tank on to the stage. The tank was made of glass, reinforced with steel, and was brim full of water, which overflowed and sloshed over the stage. The orchestra now began to play music from the Far East, all beautiful discords and plucked strings.

Then Houdini himself walked on to the stage, also wearing an ornate robe, embroidered with writhing dragons. He carried in his arms a pile of chains, links gleaming dully in the spotlight. He threw the chains dramatically down on the stage, where they landed with an enormous clash, making the audience jump in their seats.

The magician walked to the front of the stage and shaded his eyes against the footlights. 'Is there a Mr Aidan O'Connell in the audience, from King's Cross Station?'

Aidan's heart began to thump. He had never been inside a theatre before, so to become part of the performance was a bit much. But he gamely got to his feet and whipped off his cap and goggles. 'Here, sir.'

'My ffriend,' said Houdini warmly. 'Could you tell these good ladies and gentlemen what iss your profession?'

'I'm a navigational engineer, sir. Currently engaged on the Great Northern Railway.'

'Ant now, could you tell them a little about these chins you so kindly bestowed on me this morning?'

'Strongest chains in the Empire, sir,' said Aidan confidently. 'Sheffield steel.'

'Ant iss it true what you told me – that such chins can pull a locomotiff train?'

'Yes, sir. And they have.'

'Fery good. Ant now, my ffriend, you will perhaps assist me?'

Houdini beckoned Aidan with one of his elegant white hands, and Aidan reluctantly weaved among the seats and stepped on to the stage.

It was hot up there, under the lights, and he could feel every eye in the place upon him. He knew his cheeks were reddening, but he tried to concentrate on what he was being asked to do.

The two Chinese men stripped the robe from Houdini's shoulders with a flourish, to show him standing in a humble bathing suit. The little man seemed even smaller without his magician's costume. Then his assistants proceeded to wrap him in the chains like a chicken on a spit, so tightly that his pale flesh bulged through the links. Once this was done one of the Chinese gentlemen produced a padlock.

'Mr O'Connell,' said Houdini, in a voice slightly muffled by discomfort, 'could you check the padlock iss sound?'

It was a good mortice lock, such as the navvies used on the tool sheds in the sidings. 'Yes, sir.'

'Ant now can you lock me up?'

Aidan linked the padlock expertly through the two ends of the chain and locked it. He made to hand back the key but Houdini said, 'No, no. Show it to the audience, ant then put it in your pocket.'

Aidan did as he was bid, then stood about, feeling a bit like a spare part.

'You may return to your seat with my thanks,' said Houdini, 'ant I bid you enjoy the show.'

Aidan, still red-faced, found himself on the receiving end of a polite round of applause, and ducked back into his seat as quickly as possible. Of course, Luna and Konstantin clamoured to see the key, which was a solid piece of British brass – a less magical object you couldn't imagine.

Back on the stage the Chinese men laid Houdini down on the floor, and the prone magician had his ankles locked into a square frame. A crane clip on a long cable descended from above the stage, and was attached to the frame, and then the audience watched, aghast, as Houdini was winched up like a sack of rubble, upside down, and dangled over the tank. It was only when he started to pant and then took in a huge breath that Aidan understood the awful truth of what was about to happen.

Houdini was lowered head first into the water and secured in place. He was submerged from head to toe. There was no air to support his life, for the water he displaced overflowed over the stage. He had to escape from Aidan's chains, or die.

As the minutes ticked by, the time-thieves watched in agony as Houdini twisted and struggled with the chains that bound him, writhing like the dragons on his robe. His flesh was a whitish blue, bleached by the water, and little silvery bubbles escaped from his nose and mouth.

Aidan realised he was holding his breath alongside his new friend, but soon he had to let it out. His lungs were bursting, and red spots danced before his eyes.

The audience began to murmur in consternation, somehow mixed with ghoulish glee.

'They've come to see him die,' exclaimed Aidan furiously. 'They *want* him to drown.'

And it looked increasingly likely that Houdini *would* drown. He wasn't going to escape; they were watching a tragedy unfold. No one could hold their breath for that long. Now the magician's body seemed to be undergoing strange convulsions. Were these the death throes?

Suddenly Houdini's arms burst from the chains, then his legs. His feet slipped from the frame and he performed a dolphin-like twist in the water so that he stood upright. His hands scrabbled at the glass and he launched himself up in a sort of inverted dive until he was free, scrambling over the top of the tank to land with a triumphant thud on the stage. Water streamed off him.

The two Chinese assistants carried a beautiful robe over to Houdini to cover his modesty, and Houdini bowed as the audience clapped and clapped. Every man and woman in the place had jumped to their feet, their seats swinging back in place, stamping in the aisles, shouting until they were hoarse. They wouldn't let Houdini go, and for perhaps a quarter of an hour the magician was forced to bow and smile, bow and smile, before he finally left the stage. As the heavy curtains swung closed, Aidan was left with an impression of the chains he had carried just that morning, coiled like the shed skin of a snake, lying grey and useless at the bottom of the tank.

5 FEBRUARY 1894
9.15 p.m.

It was as they flooded out into the cold night that the idea came to Aidan. Perhaps it was the freezing February air that gave him a moment of clarity, but he wanted to share his notion with his friends at once.

'Hear me out,' he said. 'I think my Mr Houdini might be the key to the Butterfly Club's next mission, to steal the painting in Paris that they seem to want so badly. And if we bring him to them, maybe they'll let us travel again, which I don't think they would otherwise.'

'Why wouldn't they let us go?' asked Luna.

'Because we never do as we're told,' said Konstantin wryly. 'We left the Marconi radio on the *Titanic*, and we left Tutankhamun in his grave.'

'What can Houdini do for them?'

'You were there tonight,' said Aidan, pointing back inside the theatre. 'You saw. He can move solid objects, create something from nothing, and, crucially, *make things disappear.*' He adjusted his cap and goggles. 'If the Butterfly Club want something stolen, Houdini's their man.'

Luna and Konstantin looked at each other and started to smile.

'It can't hurt to ask,' said Konstantin. 'How would we get to see him?'

Aidan's cocky reply was not the reply of a boy who had never been inside a theatre before that night, but one of a seasoned theatre-goer. 'Stage door, of course.'

The three of them trooped around the side of the theatre, assuming this was where the stage door would be. The glitz and glamour of the theatre's frontage abruptly ran out as they turned the corner into a dark side alley, but there were plenty of theatre-goers here who had obviously had the same idea, blocking the way in their eagerness to meet the great man.

Luna noticed that many of them were women, who had been clearly thrilled by the young magician's feats and were anxious to meet him. Some of them were waving their lace handkerchiefs or hair ribbons, anxious to give their tributes to the great man.

A man leant against the stage door smoking a cigarette, seemingly oblivious to the clamour. Aidan pushed through the crowd, Luna and Konstantin in his wake. He went up to the man.

'If you please, sir, may we see the Great Houdini?'

The man took his cigarette out of his mouth just long enough to answer. 'No visitors,' he said shortly, and the time-thieves recognised the voice that had introduced the magician on stage: much quieter now, and less dramatic, but undoubtedly the same. 'The Great Houdini is very tired.'

Aidan drew himself up to his full height. 'Tell him Aidan O'Connell is here. From King's Cross Station. Reckon he owes me a favour.' He pulled the padlock key from his pocket and held it up.

The man took the key and studied it for a second. 'Wait here.'

In a moment he was back, and considerably more polite. 'Please come in.'

The time-thieves filed through the door and all at once they were in the belly of the theatre, behind the scenes. This was not a world of lights and glamour, but of whitewashed corridors, fire buckets and old rope. As he led them swiftly through the maze, their guide spoke over his shoulder.

'I am Mr Houdini's manager, Martin Beck.' He stopped at an unmarked door. 'I must ask you not to recount anything you see or hear in this room. Mr Houdini is fond of saying that "we must not daylight in upon magic".'

'We promise,' said Luna earnestly.

And there would certainly be much to tell. The chamber was not at all what you would expect from a theatrical dressing room – true, there was a mirror surrounded by electric lightbulbs, but there the ordinary ended and the extraordinary took over. The room was so crammed with interesting objects, the time-thieves didn't know what to look at first. It was positively stuffed with trick cabinets, collapsing bird cages, fake flowers, brightly coloured reams of handkerchiefs, dummy fingers, breakaway handcuffs, elasticated packs of cards, phantom portraits, rubber swords, sponge oranges and stuffed doves. The time-thieves felt like the only things in the room that were real.

The jumble was so fascinating that it took them some moments to realise that the Great Houdini was actually present. The magician looked quite different. He was seated in front of the illuminated mirror, still a little damp and wearing a towelling robe. The heavy stage make-up of quizzical brows and white pancake greasepaint had been rinsed from his face in the water tank. He looked pink and healthy, and about twelve years old. His irrepressible curls were beginning to dry and fluff up in those curious wings over each ear.

'Ah, Mr O'Connell,' said Houdini, seemingly delighted to see Aidan. 'I am indebted to you for your assistance, both this morning and tonight.' He nodded to Luna and Konstantin. 'And these are your guests?'

Luna and Konstantin were duly introduced, and Mr Houdini expressed himself charmed. 'I do hope you enjoyed the show.'

'Oh *yes*,' gushed Luna, and then, conscious that she was being a little too like all those silly women outside, said more soberly, 'I mean – yes, it was most diverting.'

'I'm most gratified,' said the magician. 'My mission is only to amaze and delight. If I have achieved that, I have achieved everything. Do make yourselves comfortable.'

The time-thieves crammed themselves on to an old settee partly covered with a Chinese shawl.

'Your English is a lot better,' said Aidan suspiciously as he settled himself. Houdini only had a slight middle European lilt now instead of the heavily accented speech he'd employed on stage and at King's Cross.

'It's all part of the act,' said Houdini airily, fluttering those amazing hands. 'I mean, I *am* Hungarian, but I have been living in America for many years. I do "Hungary it up" a bit for the audience – makes the whole act more exotic.'

'So this morning, when you met me, was *that* part of the act?' asked Aidan, studying Houdini closely.

The magician shrugged. 'I wanted some free chains, and you were good enough to help a clueless foreigner. You have to admit that it worked.'

Aidan narrowed his eyes. 'Did you "Uncle Edwin's Watch" me?'

Houdini gave his tinder-dry chuckle. 'How do *you* know about Uncle Edwin's Watch?'

'Another great man explained it to me once,' said Aidan loftily. 'A great man who *didn't* take me for a fool.'

'Come, come, don't be angry,' Houdini pleaded good-naturedly. 'You should be thanking me, for I've taught you a valuable life lesson. You should question everything you see, for there's a good chance that it is a trick.'

'Well, look, if you'd like to do me a favour in return for the chains,' said Aidan, who was never afraid to push his luck, 'we have a proposal for you. We are part of a society of… friends… who need to make something disappear.

And on the evidence of this evening, we thought you were the man to ask.'

Houdini looked interested.

Konstantin, who had been paying a little more attention – but not much – at the Butterfly Club meeting, said, 'They want to steal a painting. Straight off the wall of a famous gallery.'

'A painting, hey?' said Houdini, looking mildly interested. 'It might be an intriguing challenge. What do you think, Beck?'

The manager shook his head. 'You are very busy with your tour. Another week here and then we go to Manchester. How would you find the time?'

'Oh,' said Luna with a slight smile, 'you'll find that time won't be a problem.'

Houdini was silent for a moment.

'Pity,' said Aidan, who had learned a thing or two about the art of persuasion from Mr Arthur Conan Doyle. He got up to go. 'But it's probably just as well. It's considered to be an impossible feat.'

That did it. The little man's coin-bright eyes lit up with that strange intensity they had when performing, whether he was pulling a sixpence from a navvy's ear or breaking free of the chains that would kill him. That single word 'impossible' had captured Houdini's attention; he was like a dog who had just scented his dinner.

'Impossible?' said Houdini softly. 'Why?'

'Twenty-four-hour security,' said Konstantin, improvising.

'*Fearsome* guards,' said Luna, joining in.

'And,' said Aidan, '*unbreakable* locks.'

Houdini was silent. Aidan fancied he could see the cogs turning in the magician's brain.

Aidan played his trump card. 'If you don't think you can do it…' he said, letting his voice trail off.

The little man puffed up like a pouter pigeon. 'Of *course* I can do it. The Great Houdini can do *anything*. No door is closed to me.'

'That's what I thought,' said Aidan, grinning with relief. 'I said you were the fella for the job.'

'What must I do?'

Konstantin took out his pocketbook and picked up a pencil from the magician's bench. 'Come to this address on Thursday.' He began to write but the pencil, at the merest pressure, collapsed in his hand, soft as a noodle.

'Try this one,' said Houdini, pulling a pencil from his own ear with a half-smile. Konstantin took the pencil suspiciously, but it was firm and functional, and he wrote

Royal Observatory, Greenwich on the pad, tore out the page and gave it to the magician.

'Just ask for the Butterfly Club,' said Aidan. 'Come at noon.'

Houdini looked at the page, and then at Aidan. 'What's the magic word?'

Aidan screwed up his face, thinking. 'Abracadabra?'

The magician laughed. 'I meant *please*,' he said. 'I'll be there.'

6 FEBRUARY 1894
10 a.m.

It seemed an awfully long time until Thursday, so the morning after Houdini's show, straight after breakfast, Luna took herself off to the National Gallery.

The connection with Mr Houdini had fired her with the hope that the time-thieves might be allowed to go on another Butterfly Mission, despite their rather unusual past results. She crossed Trafalgar Square, with its fountains guarded by four crouching lions, and Nelson's column in the centre like the pointer of a sundial. Everything was silver-grey that winter morning, from the sky to the pavings, and even the pigeons she scattered as she walked. Egypt – and Papa – seemed very far away.

Of course, one of the reasons she wanted to travel in time so dearly was so she could once again see Papa. He seemed to have a strong dislike for his own time these days, but if he was somewhere out there in the future – well, she'd just have to seek him there.

Entering the gallery, with its grand dome and pillared portico, very much reminded her of Papa. Although Aunt Grace was very much a woman of science and didn't seem to have much love for the arts, Daniel Goodhart had taken Luna to see the paintings here many times. Today, however, Luna was not as interested in learning about the Old Masters as she was in the workings of the gallery itself. She wished, now, that she had paid more attention at the last meeting of the Butterfly Club; but if the members wanted a painting stolen off a gallery wall, then the National might provide some valuable research.

She walked through the marble atrium and paid her penny at the reception desk. She hardly noticed the grandeur, but looked instead at the security. Apart from the gentlemen on the desk, there were four guards at the door watching the visitors come and go. Their navy uniforms made them look like peelers – London's police force – and even though she hadn't done anything wrong, their very presence made Luna feel strangely guilty.

The walls in the National Gallery were the colour of raw meat, and the gilded frames stood out from the red beautifully. There were large skylight windows above to illuminate the paintings. As she wandered around the gallery gazing at all the Marys and Josephs and Jesuses and kings and queens and landscapes and cityscapes, Luna had no idea if this was at all like the gallery the Butterfly Club wanted to steal from. Once again, she cursed herself for not paying more attention at last week's meeting, but then she imagined that all grand galleries in capital cities were somewhat similar. And if that was the case, security was fairly tight. True, the paintings just hung on the wall, untethered and unlocked just as they would in a house: there was simply a red silken rope set about a yard from the wall to keep people back. No higher than a hurdle, it would be simplicity itself to step over. But one burly guard sat, arms crossed, in a chair by the door of each grand room, and at least one more patrolled the parquet floor on silent feet, looking beadily at the visitors and telling people off if they got too close to the pictures.

As it was early on a weekday, the gallery was not too crowded, and Luna could have a really good snoop around. She had just reached the point when she felt like she really couldn't look at another picture when she found herself in a little side room, totally alone with the artworks. The guard for that particular room had obviously stepped out for a moment, and Luna began to tingle. Had she been brave enough, she could have taken one of the smaller paintings off the wall, hidden it under her cape, and walked right out of the gallery. Perhaps art theft wasn't quite so impossible after all.

She resisted the temptation and was just turning to go when she caught sight of a curious painting. It wasn't especially large or colourful, but the image it portrayed chilled her to the bone.

It was of a man and a lady in olde worlde costumes walking in twilight through a tangled wood. A couple who looked exactly like them, except for the fact that they were glowing with a supernatural light, were walking the other way. The twin couples were destined to meet, and the picture captured the moment when they caught sight of each other. The man reacted by drawing his sword, and the lady seemed to be fainting in terror at the sight of her own likeness.

Luna was suddenly aware of a presence standing close to her – too close for a stranger. For one petrified moment she dared not turn her head for fear that she should see her own double, and look into her own face, just like the lady in the painting. But then a warm hand closed round her shoulder, and a voice hummed a familiar refrain. '*Yesterday*.'

'I thought this is where you would be, my darling Luna.'

She heard Papa's voice with a rush of relief, and the cold fear fled. She wrapped her arms around him. 'You're here!' Of course, to Luna the word 'here' meant two things. It meant here in London, and here in 1894. She had not seen her father in this time and place since he had left her in the care of Aunt Grace without a word.

'For now,' he said. 'And I dearly hope, after next Thursday, for ever.'

'Next Thursday?'

'The 15th of February.' He spoke in a deadly serious voice.

Of course. The attack on the observatory. 'But Papa, I am due to go there *this* Thursday, on the 8th. Will that be safe?'

'Perfectly,' he said. 'And if you are asked to go on a Butterfly Mission, go. The farther away you are, the better.'

'Well, I'm hoping we might be asked.' She told Papa all about the Great Houdini, and the Butterfly Club's plans to steal a painting.

'Speaking of paintings,' he said, 'I am glad you saw this one. Do you remember when you and I used to come here, and we used to talk about the paintings, and I would tell you the stories behind them?'

'Of course.' She leant into his shoulder. 'I was thinking of it this very morning.'

'This one is called *How They Met Themselves*,' said Papa, 'and it is by Dante Gabriel Rossetti. It is one of my favourites.'

'Really?' Luna looked back at the image. 'It scares me.' She considered. 'You never showed me it before, did you? When we used to come here?'

'No. It wasn't important then. But it is important now.'

'Why is it important?'

'The story goes that Rossetti painted it on his honeymoon. It depicts him and his wife. It is said that an encounter in a dark wood terrified him – that he and his wife met themselves.'

'Well, but they can't have,' said Luna with a little laugh. 'You mean, surely, that they met a couple that looked very *like* them? You said yourself… the wood was dark, and I know that sometimes…'

'Luna,' Papa interrupted gently. 'It was them. They *did* meet themselves.'

'But…' she stuttered. 'That's impossible.'

'Is it?'

Luna began to be afraid again.

'Wouldn't you have said, before this year, that travelling through time to 1912 and 1922 was impossible? That saving doomed passengers and an ancient mummy were impossible? What does your friend Conan Doyle say?'

Luna thought back to the first time she had gone with Aunt Grace to the Butterfly Club. She remembered her aunt quoting Mr Conan Doyle: *That when you have eliminated the impossible, whatever remains, however improbable, must be the truth.*

'Exactly that,' said Papa. 'The same factor that made your travels possible makes this picture possible. Time.'

And then Luna remembered, in a flash. 'Is this about what Professor Lorenz told us aboard the *Titanic*?'

'I don't know,' said her father guardedly. 'What did he tell you?'

'It was when we wanted to help Signor Marconi escape in the Time Train, but he said that we couldn't. He said no one but a time traveller could take the Time Train, because they didn't already exist in another plane. If we took Marconi back to 1897, he would already have existed there.' She looked at Papa, wide-eyed. '*He could have met himself.*'

'Precisely,' said Papa. 'I could not have expressed it better myself.' He looked back at the painting. 'The

Germans have a word for it. *Doppelganger*. It means double-walker.'

'Doppelganger,' Luna repeated. 'What a funny word.'

Papa smiled, but the next thing he said wasn't funny. 'In German folklore, to meet yourself means your own death is close. And for good reason.' He gave a small sigh. 'It is time to understand a little more about time travel, since you are now so experienced. And it is as serious a warning as I can possibly give you. To meet oneself, on another plane, is to meet death.'

Luna went very still, her eyes on the swooning woman in the painting. She could feel her heart thudding.

'And therefore,' Papa went on, 'you must *not* go back to *before* when you *first* travelled. Not on any account. And Luna, this is important.' He swung her round to face him and cupped her face in his hands. 'Not even if I ask you to.'

She frowned a little. 'You're scaring me.'

He looked serious. 'I mean to, a little. I only have a week to make things right.' He drew her to him and kissed her forehead. 'Go, enjoy your mission, but remember what I said.' Papa looked around him, as if he was being pursued. 'I'll see you soon, my dearest darling.'

'When?' she said, knowing the answer as she always did.

'Yesterday.'

And Luna was alone with the painting. Without Papa by her side, it began to frighten her again, so she hurried from the gallery as fast as if she really *did* have a painting under her cloak.

8 FEBRUARY 1894
11.50 a.m.

It was a sparkling winter day as Luna and Aunt Grace bowled up the green hill of Greenwich Park in their hansom cab.

Luna wriggled around in her seat so that she could fix her gaze on the Royal Observatory at the top of the incline. The elegant red building decorated with white brickwork like the icing on a cake seemed such a fixture – so strong and certain, just as the Home of Time should be – that it seemed impossible that it could be turned to rubble just one week from today. She prayed that whatever Papa was up to, it would work.

'Sit still, Luna,' admonished her aunt. 'Ladies do not fidget.' Aunt Grace was sitting bolt upright, immaculate in her searing yellow gown, the exact shade of a Cloudless Sulphur butterfly.

The cabbie reined in his horse and helped the ladies down from the footplate. Luna, who since her visit to the National Gallery had been thinking about security, began to consider how hard it would be for a stranger to gain access to the Butterfly Club. As she followed Aunt Grace past the various obstacles, she counted them off on her gloved fingers. First there were the ten-foot railings. Second, the only break in those railings: the wrought-iron gate. This was constantly attended by bowler-hatted guards, all of whom seemed to know Aunt Grace and admitted her at once with a tip of their hat. Third, you had to know to follow the copper meridian line through the right door (another guard), then track it all the way through the building to where it disappeared under the grandfather clock.

Fourth, and most awkwardly of all, you'd have to know, as Aunt Grace did, to open the casement of the door/ clock and turn the hands to 4.45 for the portal to the Butterfly Room to swing open.

Even though Luna always found this little journey tremendously exciting, this time her heart sank a little.

She'd been hoping against hope that the Great Houdini would remember his invitation and attend the meeting, but it was clearly impossible to get inside the Butterfly Room without being escorted by a member of the club. She now realised, mentally kicking herself, that the time-thieves should have offered to meet Houdini outside. Oh well, she would just have to suggest this to Konstantin and Aidan when she met them.

She spotted them almost at once, standing together, and her heart warmed. Konstantin stood straight and still with his almost military bearing – Aunt Grace would no doubt approve. And Aidan, half a head taller, fidgeted about as if he was a machine, buzzing with so much kinetic energy that he could hardly keep still.

The grandfather clock which was also a door struck noon, for of course the side of the clock that was in the Butterfly Room told the true time. Luna looked around anxiously. Some of the gentlemen present she recognised; some she didn't. Luna waved at Mr Conan Doyle, who smiled and gave a courteous little bow. Beyond him stood a group of gentlemen she couldn't remember seeing before. They seemed to be dressed rather differently to the other gentlemen present, who were mostly clad head to toe in sober black. The new group were all clothed in vivid colours and fabrics: one of them wore a smoking jacket that seemed to be made out of curtain material, while another wore a coat of some sort of tapestry. They all seemed to have prodigious beards. 'More writers?' she asked her aunt.

Aunt Grace shook her head. 'Artists,' she replied. 'William Morris, Sir Frederic Leighton and William Holman Hunt. And the lady standing with them is Evelyn De Morgan. They are some of the foremost painters of our age.'

Luna was impressed. She remembered seeing some of those names etched into little gold plaques below the paintings she had seen in the National Gallery. But interesting though the artists were, none of them was the Great Houdini.

'We will now call the meeting to order,' announced Aunt Grace.

Luna took hold of her sulphur-yellow arm. 'Could we wait a moment, Aunt? We are expecting a rather special guest who will be able to help with the next Butterfly Mission. The magician I told you about?' For Luna had enthusiastically told her aunt all about their night at the theatre.

Aunt Grace's gaze flickered to the clock and she frowned slightly. 'Does your guest know that we begin at noon?'

'We did tell him,' put in Aidan.

'I even wrote it down for him,' added Konstantin.

Aunt Grace sniffed. 'Then we must assume your guest is deficient in reading, or timekeeping, or both.'

Luna looked at the others and voiced the fear she'd felt on the way in. 'It's possible that he is waiting outside,' she said. 'You see, it would be impossible to gain access to this room if you did not know its secrets.'

'Not so,' said a voice. There was a flash of light, and a smell of matches, and suddenly Houdini was there in the room, standing right in the middle of the company, one foot either side of the Greenwich meridian. 'For the Great Houdini, nothing is impossible.'

He walked right up to Aunt Grace, took her hand and kissed it gallantly. 'The Great Houdini, madam, magician and escapologist extraordinaire.'

Aunt Grace looked faintly surprised, as well she might. Luna was convinced that a moment before, Houdini had not been in the room.

'You are most welcome, Mr Houdini. My niece told me all about your… theatrical extravaganza,' said Aunt Grace. 'But how on earth did you get in here?'

Houdini bowed his head. 'Dear lady, we must not daylight in upon magic. Let it just be said that I am a man who always seeks a challenge, and to that end you may help me, as much as I may help you.'

Aunt Grace inclined her own head graciously. 'Then perhaps you would like to hear what our next mission is all about. William? If you would be so good?'

One of the artists – the one who looked like he was dressed in curtains – stepped forward. He looked quite elderly: he had wild and woolly hair and his magnificent beard was quite white.

'Which William is that?' whispered Luna.

'Holman Hunt,' hissed her aunt. 'Now pay attention.'

'In the art world,' said William Holman Hunt in an impressive, rolling voice, 'it has long been rumoured that there is a missing painting so precious that its worth is beyond price.' Every tongue fell silent, every ear listened. 'Its name is *Salvator Mundi*, which means "The Saviour of the World", and it is by an obscure Florentine artist called Leonardo da Vinci.'

The time-thieves looked at each other and performed a little pantomime of shrugs. They'd never heard of this artist with the funny name. Even Luna, who considered herself quite the art expert after her trips to the National Gallery, had never heard the name before.

'I myself have been searching for the *Salvator Mundi* for many years, but to no avail,' said Mr Holman Hunt, shaking his noble head.

Aidan, with the new-found confidence that came from securing the Great Houdini, piped up. 'Why don't you just ask the fella?'

Mr Holman Hunt laughed a snuffly laugh, a little muffled by his beard. 'My dear young fellow, Leonardo da Vinci lived over three hundred years ago, in that great time we call the Renaissance.'

Aidan stepped back, deflated, and the artist continued. 'It is a period of art that I and my brotherhood have attempted to recreate for our times – the ones who are still working.' He nodded to his fellow artists. 'And the ones who are gone from us – like our dear departed friend Dante Gabriel Rossetti.'

Luna made a little sound, like a parrot's squawk, and everyone turned to look at her. Dante Gabriel Rossetti was the artist who had painted the frightening picture – *How They Met Themselves*.

Mr Holman Hunt ignored this unmannerly shriek and continued. 'And then, recently, a breakthrough. Through our late and *very* successful association with the British Museum' – he smiled at Mr Conan Doyle and the children in turn — 'Professor Flinders Petrie, the director of the museum, allowed me access to Leonardo's papers and notebooks which are held there. And in one of them, I found a clue.'

He gently eased a paper from his curtain-coat and held it up for the company to see. 'This, ladies and gentlemen, is one of Leonardo da Vinci's sketchbooks. It is called the *Codex Arundel*. Hidden in its pages is an invaluable clue to an invaluable painting. As you will see' — he leafed through the book — 'Leonardo covered the pages with drawings, but there are also notes in the margins. One such note, on this page here, is a poem or riddle.' He turned to the page in question. 'And I believe it is the vital clue. I will now pass the book around the company, but I must beg you to be careful, for the paper is over three hundred years old.'

When the fragile book came around to the time-thieves, they peered at the writing.

Konstantin said what they were all thinking. 'But it's just squiggles!'

'Indeed, my boy. Dr Kass, if I may trouble you?'

Dr Tanius Kass, Konstantin's father, brought forth something square and heavy, covered in a velvet cloth. Luna was convinced he was going to reveal a painting, but when her aunt took the cloth away she could see it was a mirror. Clear and bright, it reflected all the important personages in the room, the bright butterflies on the wall, and the time-thieves themselves. Mr Holman Hunt reclaimed the book from Konstantin, carried it to the mirror and held it up. All the important ladies and gentlemen of the Butterfly Club huddled close as urchins round a fire, and the time-thieves had to jostle for a place. They saw, as everyone saw, the words resolve into letters that they understood – regular letters of the alphabet. But the writing still made no sense to Luna. 'Is it in a different language?'

'It's in Italian,' said Konstantin.

'It is indeed, young sir,' said Mr Holman Hunt. 'Luckily, through my dear departed friend Rossetti, I have a smattering of the language. It translates as this:

The saviour of the world is in her smile,
The saviour of the world is in her eyes,
The saviour of the world is behind her back.
If you would find what you now lack,
The answer lies in just one dame
The Mona Lisa is her name.'

'All right,' said Aidan, seemingly recovered from his humiliation. 'Where do we find this Lisa woman? I'm assuming she is dead too.'

'She never lived,' said Holman Hunt. 'For she is not a woman, but a painting.'

Aidan, squashed again, gave up.

'The *Mona Lisa* is an unknown canvas, also by Leonardo da Vinci And from the riddle of the *Codex Arundel*, it seems that Leonardo hid vital clues as to the whereabouts of his missing masterpiece – the *Salvator Mundi* – in a much more obscure and unimportant work.'

Aidan tried one more time. 'So the *Mona Lisa* is like a key, and the *Salvator* thingy is like the treasure chest?'

'Precisely, young man,' said Mr Holman Hunt. 'I could not have put it better myself.'

Aidan, beaming all over his face, felt redeemed. 'All right. So where do we steal the *Mona Lisa* from?'

'Ah, now there is the rub,' said the painter. 'It is in the best-known and most closely guarded art gallery in the world.'

'The National Gallery?' offered Luna, hoping to share in Aidan's glory.

Holman Hunt smiled sadly. 'How I wish it were – for I or any of my brotherhood could practically walk in and take it off the walls, for there we are known and respected,' he said. 'No. The matter is far more complex than that. One might almost say, *impossible*.'

Aidan shot a look at Houdini, just in time to see the little man's eyes light up.

'Dr Kass?' The artist beckoned to Konstantin's father. Dr Kass brought over the little twelve-sided table the time-thieves remembered from past meetings. Their old friend Chronos the brass cuckoo sat upon it. Dr Kass wound the bird's little golden key. The bird's beak opened, its ruby eyes shone, and the hologram from the future sprang into being. There was Professor Edward Lorenz, in his own time of 1969. He looked the same as ever, in a checked suit, with thinning hair and the peculiar watch strapped to his wrist, instead of in his pocket where it belonged.

'Hello, old friend,' said Konstantin. Although it was odd to call him 'old', because he had not yet been born, and it was odd to call him a friend, as they had never met. But the greeting felt true all the same.

'Hello, kids!' said the hologram cheerfully. 'Good to see ya.'

Mr Holman Hunt addressed the image. 'Professor Lorenz. Please tell us everything you know about the Louvre Museum in Paris.'

8 FEBRUARY 1894
12.10 p.m.

'Okay, folks, so you find me in the library as usual.'
Professor Lorenz smiled. He was wearing a suit of
an even nattier check and a tie of even wider proportions
than usual. 'Just let me get you an overview from the good
ol' *Encyclopaedia Britannica*.' He took a big book from a low
shelf and began to flick through it. 'Lorry… loudspeaker…
lounge… Ah, here.' He began to read.

**Louvre Museum or Musée du Louvre,
national museum and art gallery of France,
housed in part of a large palace in Paris that was
built on the right-bank site of the 12th-century
fortress of Philip Augustus. It is the world's most
visited art museum, with a collection that spans**

work from ancient civilisations to the mid-19th century.

It was not clear how much of this Houdini heard. The magician was busy waving his hand through the image of the professor. 'This is incredible!' he said. 'How is it achieved?' He walked from Chronos over to the hologram, then back again. He clamped his hand over Chronos's beak, so the hologram disappeared, then took his hand away again so the professor reappeared.

'It is not Mephistopheles' Mirror, nor Pepper's Ghost, nor yet a Phantom Portrait,' he muttered to himself. 'Remarkable.'

Aunt Grace didn't seem to know what to make of the strange little Hungarian man. 'This is no trick, Mr Houdini. The professor is speaking to us from the state of Texas in America, in the year 1969.'

'You are saying that this apparition is speaking to us from the future?' asked Houdini, wide-eyed. 'You have found a way to travel forward in time?'

'Yes, indeed. This club's mission is to… borrow from the future for the betterment of society,' explained Aunt Grace briefly, sounding anxious to focus the club's attention on the problem at hand. She turned back to the hologram. 'So what period would be best for us to attempt our… extraction?'

'Well, ma'am, if you're planning a heist I'd avoid the period when the museum is run by a guy called Theophile Homolle,' said the professor. 'When he was director of the Louvre Homolle prided himself on the security of the museum. He even boasted that it would be easier to steal the towers of Notre Dame than break into the Louvre. Notre Dame is the great cathedral in Paris, kids,' he said to the time-thieves, 'so obviously stealing the towers would be impossible.'

Houdini barely let him finish. 'Then. I want to go then. When this person, this Homolle fellow, was in charge. His words are a challenge. He has thrown down the gauntlet, and the Great Houdini shall pick it up.'

Luna didn't fully understand these words, but she understood the sense behind them. Houdini wanted the theft to be as difficult as possible, for only then would he feel he had won a true victory.

The professor peered through the layers of time at the magician. 'Is that Houdini? *The* Houdini?'

'The one and the only,' said the gentleman proudly.

'Well, it's a gosh darn pleasure, I'm sure,' said the professor, beaming all over his pleasant face.

Houdini bowed. 'The honour is mine. Tell me, do your magic tomes tell you when this Homolle was at the Louvre?'

'He was in charge from 1904 to 1911,' said the professor, 'so any time in that range will do you if you insist on smacking this specific guy in the eye.'

'Capital. Take me there,' said Houdini, as if the spirits of time would transport him instantly to Paris.

'A moment, Mr Houdini,' said Aunt Grace. 'We have not yet agreed to your acting as an agent for our society.'

'Although there's no doubting your confidence, sir,' said Dr Kass.

'He's a wizard, Father,' said Konstantin enthusiastically. 'He can do anything. And,' he said slyly, 'we'd be happy to go along and help.'

'I don't know, *lieber Sohn*,' said Dr Kass. 'Your heart…'

'Never mind that,' said Houdini, in return for Konstantin's compliment. 'These three young people and I will go. It is settled.'

'Wait, whereabouts is the *Mona Lisa*?' said Luna, remembering her concerns about security. 'You've said the Louvre is a palace built on a fortress, Professor. That sounds big.'

'Good point,' said the hologram. 'Let me have a look.'

The professor walked over to a bookcase, reached up to a shelf and took down a book. He leafed through it and said, 'I've found a photo from 1911. I'll try to show it to you.' He turned the book around. The members of the Butterfly Club were able to see a black and white photogram printed in the pages of the book. It was a gallery wall, reproduced over two pages. The wall was crowded with paintings, some huge, some tiny. 'This is the Salon Carré, one of the major rooms in the Louvre.'

'Which one is the *Mona Lisa*?' asked Aidan.

The professor moved his ghostly forefinger over the page. 'This one.'

The time-thieves crowded in to peer at a fuzzy blob, barely bigger than a postage stamp. It seemed to be a portrait of the head and shoulders of a woman.

'At least it's small,' said Konstantin, 'but I must say she doesn't look very impressive.'

The professor scanned the next few pages of the book. 'If you want to make it particularly hard for yourselves, it says here that in August 1911 all the paintings were being reframed, so there were many more people working at the Louvre. Lots of people milling around, even when it was closed.'

'Then August 1911 it is,' declared Houdini. 'Prepare the magic.'

He stood in front of the professor, closed his eyes and took several deep breaths, just as he had before he plunged into the Chinese Water Torture Cell.

'Yeah, I don't really do that bit, sport,' said the professor, smiling at him wryly. 'I'm not a conjuror like you. You'll need the Time Train.'

'Mr O'Connell,' said Aunt Grace. 'Bring the machine, if you please.'

Aidan's father rolled the Time Train – all twinkling brass, blood-red velvet and bone-white ivory – along the meridian line.

'One moment,' said Mr Holman Hunt, as the time-thieves were about to climb aboard. 'Take the *Codex Arundel*. You may have need of it.'

Luna accepted the sketchbook reverently. 'Thank you,' she said. 'We'll take good care of it.'

'And here,' said Mr Conan Doyle, stepping forward with a purse full of sovereigns from the Gabriel Medal. 'You will definitely have need of these.'

'Make yourself comfortable, Mr Houdini,' said Aidan, jumping into the passenger seat. 'Professor, got an address for the Louvre?'

'Sure thing, chief,' said the professor. 'Rue de Rivoli, Paris, France.'

Aidan set the ivory dials. 'Rue de Rivoli, Paris, France,' he repeated. '1911. August the what?'

'Let's go for the fifteenth,' suggested Luna. 'That's right in the middle.'

Houdini climbed in with them. 'Amazing,' he pronounced, testing the sides of the Time Train for solidity, just as he had with his magic boxes on stage. 'I have never seen a trick cabinet like it.'

Aidan engaged the ignition. Butterflies began to break away from their cards and flutter around the room in a rainbow maelstrom. 'Incredible!' exclaimed Houdini. 'I have only ever been able to train two at a time.' Then the blue forked lightning began to dance around the Time Train. 'And now electricity,' marvelled Houdini. 'Extraordinary.'

'If you like that,' said Aidan, 'this is going to blow your boots off.' And he threw the lever forward.

The Time Train speeded towards the grandfather clock, the brass meridian line sparked under the wheels, and Houdini witnessed the greatest trick of his life as the ladies and gentlemen of the Butterfly Club, and the Greenwich Observatory, simply disappeared.

PARIS

15 AUGUST 1911

15 AUGUST 1911
12.30 p.m.

After the usual sick heaviness of time travel had passed, the passengers clambered unsteadily out of the Time Train, stretched their legs, and looked about them.

On past journeys the time-thieves had emerged into the cargo hold of the *Titanic*, the bustling harbour of Southampton and the arid deserts of Egypt.

This was quite different. Paris was a dizzying sight – massive sandstone buildings with blue-grey slate pitched roofs buttered with sunshine, wrought-iron balconies like twisted liquorice, and elegant mint-green plane trees lining the avenues. In the distance an ornamental iron tower stood out blackly against the pale blue summer sky. This, they knew, was the famous Eiffel Tower, which had just been finished in their own time. On this particular street arched colonnades stretched in each direction as far as the eye could see, so the genteel citizens did not have to be troubled by rain or sun as they peered into the smart shop windows. And here, unlike at their other destinations, there was no need to worry about concealing the Time Train, for it was neatly parked at the side of a vast thoroughfare, in a row of other outlandish vehicles. More of these vehicles were racing up and down the road, and the visitors from 1894 were forced to jump back in a cacophony of honking horns and squealing tyres.

'Are they all Time Trains?' asked Konstantin, bemused.

Aidan was in heaven. He whistled, low and slow. 'Motor cars. They're all motor cars. In our time they're already being made here in France and in America. But look how good they get!' Next to the Time Train was another machine, with two lamps, four black rubber wheels and metallic red paint. Aidan ran his hand over the shiny bonnet and touched the badge, which read *Renault*. 'Jesus, Mary and Joseph! Wouldn't I just like to take this back to show Da!'

Meanwhile Luna was captivated by a magnificent display in the shop window next to them. It was a cake shop, but it was unlike any cake shop Luna had ever seen before.

The window itself was very grand, with diamond-bright plate glass and a gilded curlicue frame, but what was inside was even more magnificent. There were the most beautiful decorated pastries and gateaux, but the greatest glory was a tall tower, not unlike the one on the skyline, but built entirely of beautiful little biscuit-cakes. It was constructed in decreasing circles from a broad base to a single biscuit-cake at the top, and all the sweetmeats were a beautiful pastel colour – from rose pink, to baby blue, to pistachio green. There was a little card sign with gold writing propped at the bottom of the tower and Luna spelled out the word:

Macarons

She made a mental note not to leave Paris until she'd tasted one. Just the sight of them made her mouth water, but as she licked her lips she saw a shape resolve in the reflection of the tower of cakes.

A dark figure, dressed in some sort of cape, was watching them from across the street.

She spun around, searching the pavement opposite, but the figure was gone.

She looked so peculiar that Aidan actually tore his eyes away from the Renault. 'You all right, Duch?'

'Perfectly,' she said. There was no need to scare the others over something she had imagined. 'Just thinking how much I'd like to steal one of those biscuit-cakes.'

'Let's steal the painting first,' said Houdini, who seemed to have adjusted to his new surroundings quite quickly, perhaps because he was well used to magical happenings. 'We need somewhere to stay, somewhere to use as a base.'

Konstantin looked around. 'How about there?' he said, pointing.

Across the road, one of the buildings had a name affixed to its grand balconies, each gilded letter as big as a man.

HOTEL DU LOUVRE

'Must be a good omen,' said Houdini. 'Come on.'

'Wait,' said Luna. 'Should we cover up the Time Train, like we did on the *Titanic*?'

'Might attract more attention than it does now,' said Konstantin. 'Parked here, it just looks like one of the other motor cars.'

'Yes, but I tell you what,' said Aidan. 'Just to be on the safe side, I'll take the crystal columns. It won't work without them.'

'Good idea,' said Luna, and Aidan unscrewed the long twisted crystals that powered the Time Train.

'And what about Chronos?' asked Konstantin. 'We should take him too.' He set the hands of the console clock to 4.45, and out the cuckoo popped. Konstantin gently disengaged him from his spring and nestled Chronos in his jacket pocket. The time-thieves and the magician crossed the road, carefully dodging the speeding cars, and entered the Hotel du Louvre.

Luna had a good look at all the ladies and gentlemen in the hotel's fancy marble atrium. They all wore the same colours of rose pink, baby blue, pistachio green and soft mauve. There were ribbons and parasols and straw boaters with the same pastel bands, and in style the clothes were very much like those on the *Titanic* in 1912 – which was to be expected, as they were just one year before that great maritime disaster. It gave Luna a chill to think that the *Titanic* hadn't even been launched yet. It was in her mind to tell someone, to warn them, but how would she even begin such a conversation? And besides, she now knew enough of Professor Lorenz's Butterfly Effect to know that you could only change small things. Stealing one unknown, insignificant painting would have to be enough.

Houdini made his way to the grand mahogany reception desk, and the time-thieves gathered about him. Too late, it occurred to Luna how odd they looked in their heavy Victorian winter clothes. They looked so dark and old-fashioned and frankly bizarre next to the elegant guests in the lobby in their macaron pastels. A boy in a military greatcoat with no hat on his blonde head. A girl in a crinoline frock the colour of a Green Hairstreak butterfly. A boy dressed in cogs and chains and goggles. And a peculiar little man with silvery eyes, in a loud checked suit, with fuzzy, crinkly hair standing out on either side of his head in two wings. Too late, Luna realised that they must look like a troupe from the travelling circus.

The same thought had clearly occurred to the snooty-looking man behind the desk. He took one look at them down his long nose, and said something incomprehensible in French.

'Forgive me,' said Houdini, smiling and fluttering his white hands apologetically. 'I don't understand.'

'I said,' hissed the man in English, conscious that all his fancy clients were watching, 'that you and your... *associates* will have to leave. This is one of the premier hotels in Paris.' He beckoned to two burly doormen in hotel livery and top hats, who came to stand threateningly on either side of the time-thieves like a pair of policemen. 'Perhaps *now* you understand me?'

Houdini drew himself up to his full height, which wasn't saying much. But he had that odd magical power about him, and there was something stagey about the way he produced the enormous bag of sovereigns and flung it on the reception desk. The lip of the bag opened neatly to reveal the gold within.

The transformation was remarkable. The man behind the counter was suddenly wreathed in smiles. 'Maurice. Gaspard,' he barked. 'Get back to your posts at once and cease harassing this very *special* guest. Four rooms on our penthouse floor, I trust, will suffice? And the Presidential Suite for monsieur?'

Houdini inclined his head graciously, and the time-thieves exchanged a look. They were all thinking the same thing: that although magic was miraculous, money was even more powerful.

'Could you also give us directions to the Louvre?' Houdini asked the smooth gentleman as he signed the register.

'Most assuredly, monsieur,' said the man, now all politeness. 'You may see the Musée du Louvre from the windows of your suite.' He handed over four heavy brass keys, and nodded at a bell boy to lead them upstairs.

After all the excitement of choosing rooms and – of course – jumping on the beds, the time-thieves gathered in Houdini's suite to gaze at the huge building just across the busy road. It had four sides to it, surrounding an immense square courtyard. The gallery was so vast that they could barely see beyond it to the broad, glittering river, slicing Paris into a left bank and a right.

'Is that the Louvre?' said Aidan in dismay. 'It looks like a palace.'

'It *was* a palace, remember?' said Konstantin. 'And a fortress before that. It doesn't look that easy to get into.'

'And it's huge,' said Luna. 'That drab little painting will take some finding.'

'Not at all,' said Aidan confidently. 'Remember, the professor told us where to look. The *Mona Lisa* hangs in the Sally Carry.'

'Salon Carré,' corrected Konstantin, who was better at languages than the rest of them.

'Well, let us go and pay the lady a visit,' said Houdini. 'There's no time like the present.'

'What shall we do with the notebook?' said Luna as the others were heading for the door. 'Do we need to take it?' Carefully she turned the pages of the *Codex Arundel*. 'All the notes are in mirror writing,' she said, and carried it over to a large looking glass over the bureau. It made no more sense forward than backwards. 'Even right way round, it's all in Italian.' She met Konstantin's eyes in the mirror. 'You were the one who recognised the language back at the Butterfly Club. Could you read it?'

'No,' he said. 'I know a little – Prussia is right in the middle of Europe, so we know a smattering of many languages. I know a little French and Russian because they sit at our borders. I believe I might even know a little Hungarian, Mr Houdini. *Jo napot! Hogy vady?*'

The magician bowed, his hand on his heart. '*Köszönöm jól.*'

'But Italian?' Konstantin shook his fair head. 'To be honest, I only know the swear words.'

Houdini gave his dry chuckle. 'Very well. Then until we find a friendly Italian, I suggest we leave the *Codex* here. There might be a safety deposit box – there are such things in great hotels sometimes.'

And indeed there was. The safe was tucked discreetly inside the grand mahogany wardrobe. Aidan jiggled the dial of the strongbox, but it would not give. 'Perhaps you have to get the combination from reception.'

Houdini snorted scornfully. 'Stand aside,' he said. He applied his ear to the dial, turning it in little increments and listening to the tiny metallic sounds of the tumblers within the mechanism. In roughly three seconds the heavy door swung open. He had cracked the safe.

'Let's put Chronos and the crystals in there too, just to be on the safe side,' advised Aidan, and as they left the suite Houdini locked the door securely too.

'We might not be the only thieves in Paris,' he said darkly. 'Ready?'

'Wait,' said Luna, who had been thinking about all those curious glances in reception. 'What about our clothes? We don't exactly fit in. For one thing, it was winter at home, and for another, everyone here is dressed like…' She struggled to find a word, and found the newest one she knew. 'Like macarons.'

'What on God's green earth,' said Aidan, 'are macarons?'

'Those little cakes in the window. Near where we stopped the Time Train. They're all pastel colours. Baby pinks and blues and greens. That's how everyone dresses here.'

The boys both looked scornful – they couldn't care less about clothes. But Houdini came down firmly on Luna's side. 'She's right, you know. One of the first rules of magic is to hide in plain sight.'

'What do you mean, sir?' asked Konstantin.

'Well, that if you are hoping to pull off a trick, you have to look as innocent as possible. You have to make everything look ordinary, in order to perform the extraordinary.'

'All right.' Aidan groaned. 'Seems a shame to waste time shopping.'

'Why bother?' said Konstantin. 'Why don't I just take a trip to the laundry?'

They all looked at him as if he was mad, until he said, 'It's all right. I've done it before. Or rather, I'll do it in a year's time. On the *Titanic*.'

And then of course Luna and Aidan remembered when Konstantin had gone to the vast laundries on the lower decks of the *Titanic* to steal 'modern' outfits for them all. Before they could explain this to Houdini, Konstantin had slipped out of the door.

In no time he was back, almost hidden by a huge bundle of clothes.

'Was it all right?' asked Aidan, as Konstantin dumped his burden on the fancy hotel carpet.

'Fine,' replied Konstantin. 'A polite smile and a uniform go a long way. I just helped myself.'

The time-thieves all scattered to change. They went into their rooms as one thing and came out as another, transformed as completely as if they had emerged from one of Houdini's magic cabinets. They gathered in the magician's suite, examining each other with delight. Konstantin was in a powder-blue suit with a straw boater and a hat band that matched his suit. Houdini was in a light pistachio suit, and his hat band was green to match. Aidan was in a suit of dove grey, with a flat cap of the same material, while Luna's dress was baby pink, a colour that clashed magnificently with her auburn hair.

Luna turned to Houdini. 'How do we look?' she asked.

He smiled. 'Parisian. They won't know what's hit them. Let's go.'

15 AUGUST 1911
3 p.m.

Entering the Louvre Museum was just like entering a palace.

Luna had thought the National Gallery in London terribly grand, with its lofty pillars and grand dome, but it was nothing compared to this. The Louvre was not one palace but four – an identical quartet of exquisite buildings facing each other across a beautiful square. Like the other buildings, it had blue-grey roofs and golden walls, but the carving of the stone frontages was incredibly fancy, with all kinds of leaves, statues and curlicues. It was incredible how, in the right hands, stone could be made to behave like water. Many elegant Parisians as well as tourists from all over the world were wandering across the square, enjoying the summer sun. They didn't seem in a hurry to go inside and peruse the artworks – clearly the outside of the Louvre was considered just as much a work of art as the inside.

With Konstantin's help, they managed to work out where the main entrance was, and they walked under an impossibly grand archway out of the sun and into the shadow of the entrance hall. Mr Houdini had exchanged some of their English sovereigns for French francs at the hotel reception, which Luna thought clever – she would never have thought of such a thing. He paid for four tickets, and they were inside the Louvre.

Luna noticed – just as she had in the National Gallery, and again at the observatory – just how many guards were on the door. There seemed to be a great deal more in Paris than she had seen in London. Here they were dressed in the same blue-grey as the slate roofs outside, and they all seemed to have rather splendid moustaches, and the same military bearing as Konstantin. They did not smile, but gazed unblinking at all the visitors with flinty eyes.

Houdini ignored them. 'Right,' he said. 'The Salon Carré.' He opened the paper pamphlet he'd been given at the same time as the tickets, and located a floor map of the gallery. 'This way.'

The Salon Carré was a breathtakingly beautiful room. Big as a cathedral, it was painted a coffee colour, and from floor to ceiling the walls were covered with paintings, some as big as a hackney carriage, some as small as a looking glass. All the paintings were in gilded frames, giving a golden richness to the room. The gallery was topped with a vaulted gilt ceiling and lit by wide crystal windows set into the roof. At that time in the afternoon the summer sun streamed through to illuminate the canvases. The paintings were so splendid and numerous that it took the time-thieves and Houdini some moments to locate the Leonardo. When they finally found it, not one of them was impressed.

The canvas was about the size of a small coffee table. It was of a woman, with brown hair and eyes, wearing a brown dress and sitting in front of a brown landscape. Her hands were crossed in front of her, the right hand holding the left. Behind her was a brown valley, a muddy-looking winding river, arid trees, and a few arches of a bridge under a dull sky. The only features of note were the lady's smile, which seemed to suggest that she kept a secret, and her eyes, which seemed to watch the viewer as much as the viewer watched her. But the whole was rather dull and uninspiring, and hanging on the coffee-coloured walls she all but disappeared.

'She's a bit… muddy,' said Luna, trying to be kind.

'Too small to be truly impressive,' pronounced Konstantin.

'But too big to put under your coat, dammit,' said Aidan.

Houdini rubbed his remarkable hands. 'No, no, this is marvellous. It's going to be *much* harder than I thought.' Clearly, the odd little man relished a challenge.

Luna went as close to the canvas as she dared with the beady guards staring at her, and peered closely at the canvas. 'I can't see any hidden clues to the whereabouts of the *Salvator Mundi*,' she said.

'Possibly they can't be seen by the naked eye,' said Houdini hopefully. 'We'll just have to study it properly once we get it to the hotel room. Probably with a magnifying glass.'

'Just like Sherlock Holmes!' Luna burst out.

'Exactly so. No, we'll definitely have to steal it,' Houdini said with satisfaction. 'Now, let us take a turn about the room and see if anyone else is interested in our *Mona Lisa*.'

A quick survey of the salon told them that at that particular time there was only one other person looking at the *Mona Lisa*. He was standing about twelve feet away from the painting, totally still, just gazing and gazing at the woman's face. He was a young man, with black hair and a neat black moustache that turned up at the ends. His soulful brown eyes were fixed on the canvas and didn't seem to blink.

His stance wasn't the only odd thing about him. He was wearing a white coat. The sight of white coats always made Konstantin feel funny inside, as he'd spent his childhood surrounded by doctors, looming over his sickbed, placing cold stethoscopes on his failing heart. But this man didn't seem like a doctor. For one thing, his coat was more creamy than white, and for another it was more blousy than fitted. In fact, the man looked more like a craftsman than a physician – an artist, even.

The time-thieves and Houdini circled the room, looking at all the other far more impressive paintings. There was an enormous canvas by a painter called Veronese, which seemed to be drawing all eyes to it. Houdini's bright eyes watched the visitors, rather than the paintings, his vivid gaze darting from one face to another.

When they finally left the room, Konstantin looked back at the man in the white smock. He was still staring at the *Mona Lisa*, and he didn't seem to have moved at all.

19 AUGUST 1911
9.30 a.m.

Over the next week the time-thieves went to the Louvre every day.

After the first time, they made sure they were never seen together. They went at different times of the day and, taking their cue from Leonardo, wrote down their research in leather-covered sketchbooks that Houdini bought from a stall on the left bank of the river. Afterwards, they shared their notes seated at a pavement café in the sunshine, and formed a very high opinion of French food. Breakfast was a particular highlight: they enjoyed warm hunks of French bread and jam, gulped down with huge bowls of milky coffee or creamy hot chocolate. They wolfed down flaky, buttery croissants – delicious crescent-shaped pastries that exploded when eaten, showering them with crumbs.

And their great favourite was pain au chocolat. 'Whoever thought of melting a bar of chocolate inside the nicest pastry in the world,' pronounced Luna, 'is a genius.'

At these café sessions they would all practise their French. Houdini thought it important that they were all – himself included – able to communicate a little in the native language, and so they attempted to read menus and order food, with sometimes hilarious results. Aidan was desperate to try an odd fruit he'd never seen before, with knobbly toad-green skin. He asked the waiter for an *avocat* and couldn't understand why Konstantin creased up with laughter. 'You just asked for a lawyer,' he said.

While they ate, the time-thieves were mesmerised by Houdini's incredible hands as he talked – he would pass a sugar lump across the back of his knuckles, from finger to finger, fluidly and flawlessly, as he talked, or make the silver spoons disappear up his sleeve. He would do these things almost without thinking, and it made it quite difficult to concentrate on what he was saying. Luckily the magician's instructions were simple.

Notice everything.

Nothing, Houdini insisted, was too trivial. They noted down how the light fell on the *Mona Lisa* at different times of day, how many guards were in the room, when and what time the guards switched over, what time the gallery closed, what time it opened again. They noticed how many visitors there were, and on what days of the week. They noticed that the numbers ebbed and flowed like a tide. Around ten o'clock was very busy; then, as the Parisians liked their luncheons, the gallery emptied out and did not fill again until four o'clock, when there was another peak until closing time. They noticed which other paintings were in the room, who they were by, and which ones interested the visitors most.

They noted too that no one seemed much interested in the muddy little Leonardo. Only the man in the white smock was there day after day, staring longingly at the canvas, staring into the woman's eyes.

Back at the hotel, the time-thieves became increasingly interested in the *Codex Arundel*. They would take the notebook from the safe and peruse it in their quiet hours. Luna was captivated by the incredible drawings of people – ladies' heads, men's hands, close-ups of hair and eyes and feet. Aidan was fascinated by Leonardo's engineering prowess – there were diagrams of inventions: flying machines, pump systems and even diving suits. For Konstantin, it was the mirror writing. One day he spent the entire afternoon holding the *Codex* in front of the mirror above the bureau, trying and failing to decipher a single complete sentence of the backwards script. 'Da Vinci's keeping secrets,' he muttered.

'It's like I always say,' called Houdini from the couch. 'We must not daylight in upon magic. Leonardo knew that too.'

'Hmm,' said Konstantin. 'What we need is an Italian. But where would we find one in Paris?'

The next morning they had a council of war over a café breakfast. 'We've found out as much as we can on our own,' declared Houdini. 'We need a breakthrough. And I think I know how to get it.' He pointed at them with a pair of sugar tongs. 'Think of it. We are visitors, outsiders. We are only seeing the gallery as everyone else sees it, anyone who can pay a franc at the entrance. We need the perspective of an insider.'

'And how do we get that?' asked Luna.

'We go and see Monsieur Theophile Homolle.'

'Who?' said Konstantin.

'The director of the gallery,' said Houdini. 'The man who claimed that nothing could be stolen from his gallery.'

'And how exactly are we going to get to see him?' asked Luna.

'Easy,' said Houdini. 'We donate something.'

'What?' asked Konstantin. 'We are not exactly in the habit of carrying round works of art like Leonardo did.'

'Well,' said Houdini, scratching his head under the crinkly hair. 'That's the hard part.'

'Not necessarily,' said Aidan, his blue eyes beginning to twinkle. 'I think I might have an idea.'

19 AUGUST 1911
10 a.m.

'**A**bsolutely *not*,' said Chronos, and shut his little brass beak with a snap.

Back at the hotel, they'd extracted Chronos from the safe, wound him up and set him on the coffee table in the middle of the suite. The three time-thieves and Houdini sat in a row on the couch in front of him.

'Oh, come *on*, Chronos,' wheedled Aidan. 'Don't be so *wet*.'

'I am *not*,' said Chronos, 'remotely sodden, drenched or watery. I am a sophisticated, sentient clockwork mechanism. I am here to assist you with my considerable knowledge bank. I am the latest in a long tradition of wise birds which stretches right back to Athena, the wise owl of ancient Greece, and as such I absolutely decline to participate in a piece of grubby subterfuge designed to reduce me to the status of a mere artefact.'

'English, please,' said Konstantin.

'I won't do it.' Chronos hopped round furiously until his back was turned to the time-thieves.

'Remarkable!' Houdini chuckled. In the half-darkness of the Butterfly Room he had been more interested in the hologram of the professor than in the source of his image, but now he got to his knees and peered closely at the mechanical bird, fascinated, touching the filigree feathers with his fingertip. 'And I thought my stuffed doves were ingenious.'

Chronos's ruby eyes sparkled angrily. 'I don't know what's worse,' he said. 'Being revered like a religious relic, or being prodded and pushed by a performing prestidigitator.'

'*Dearest* Chronos,' wheedled Luna. 'Mr Houdini is paying you a compliment. He is saying you are a work of art.'

Chronos harrumphed and ruffled his feathers with a metallic chime. 'Well,' he said, thawing slightly and hopping back round to face them, 'I *have* been described as a miracle of automaton engineering.' He coughed modestly.

'There,' said Luna, stroking the little brass head. 'And that's *exactly* what you are. Any museum would be lucky to have you. And we aren't going to *leave* you there. You'd be a pivotal part of the plan, and we'd rescue you when we steal the painting.'

'He needs a trick, though,' said Houdini. 'Everybody needs a trick. I mean, the workmanship is remarkable, but his speech is the real magic.'

'We could just get him to natter to Homolle,' said Aidan. 'He'd talk the hind leg off a donkey.'

'I am here, you know!' screeched Chronos.

'Sorry,' said Aidan. 'But no, we shouldn't let Homolle know that Chronos can think for himself, otherwise we'll never see him again. He'll be down the funfair for a penny-a-throw. No, we just have to make him think he's just a very sophisticated – sorry, Chronos – toy.'

'What we need,' mused Houdini, 'is a song or a rhyme…'

'I am *not* a performing budgerigar…' interrupted Chronos.

'…ideally in French,' Houdini continued as if the bird hadn't spoken. 'Something that will appeal to Monsieur Homolle – and, even more importantly, will appeal to his visitors.

'Konstantin?' Luna turned to him. 'You said you knew some French.'

'Hmm.' He thought for a moment. 'I did have a French nursemaid once. And she taught me this song. It's about a bird actually, but it is pretty foolish.'

'Sounds perfect,' said Houdini. 'Teach it to this pigeon.'

'Cuckoo!' screeched Chronos. 'I'm. A. Cuckoo. Cuckoos are traditionally associated with time, specifically the coming of spring in the agricultural calendar, an association that was strengthened with the invention of the cuckoo clock in 1730 by clock-master Franz Anton Ketterer from the Black Forest, who—'

'Yes, yes,' said Aidan. 'Beak closed, ears open. Go on, Konstantin.'

Rather shyly, Konstantin cleared his throat. 'All right. Here goes. It's called *Alouette*, by the way.'

The song had a pretty lilting melody, and Konstantin's voice was surprisingly sweet.

Alouette, gentille alouette
Alouette, je te plumerai…

'What does it mean?' asked Luna, impressed.

'It means, "Lark, nice lark, I will pluck you." And then it goes on to say which bits of the bird gets plucked first – the head, the throat, etc.'

'That's the *stupidest*...' began Chronos.

'Yes, but it's perfect,' said Houdini. 'It showcases your speech and song, without letting Homolle know that you have your own intelligence. Aidan's right. If he knew that, he'd be showing you at every fair and carnival in Europe.'

Aidan remembered how he'd managed to persuade Houdini to be a part of the heist. He spoke to Chronos as if to a child. 'But if you don't think you can remember one little song...'

The ruby eyes flashed. 'Nonsense,' Chronos said. 'One more time, if you please, Mr Kass, and I'll have it committed to my memory bank.'

19 AUGUST 1911
11 a.m.

Theophile Homolle was a distinguished-looking gentleman who looked a little as if his hair had slipped down from its proper place on his head, for he had very little on his crown and rather a lot on his chin. When they entered his office he wasn't actually seated at his desk, but seemed to be packing up his things into a large carpet bag.

At the sight of them he stopped packing and smiled rather distractedly. *'Bonne journée,'* he said. *'Puis-je vous aider?'*

Everyone looked at Konstantin. *'Parlez vous anglais?'* he said.

'Yes, yes,' said Monsieur Homolle. 'Of course I speak English.' And he did it very well. 'How may I help you?'

'Ve vish to make a donation to the museum,' said Houdini.

Aidan noticed that Houdini's Hungarian accent was back; and that meant the magician was putting on a performance.

'Ah. That is most kind. Please, take a seat, Mr…?'

'Houdini. Just Houdini.'

Aidan shot him a sharp glance. He thought it risky of Houdini to use his real name. Considering the magician's success in London in 1894, it was possible that he was even more famous in 1911 Paris. But the museum director did not show a flicker of recognition at the name.

'These are my associates,' Houdini went on, waving a hand at the time-thieves who remained standing behind him. 'And this is the artefact I wish to donate.' He unwrapped Chronos from the towel they'd carried him in, concealing by sleight of hand the words *Hotel du Louvre* stitched into the hem.

Monsieur Theophile Homolle studied Chronos closely with a practised eye. 'The workmanship is exquisite, but we don't usually take automata. We are more about paintings and statuary and such.'

'Well, just wait,' said Houdini. He nodded to Konstantin, who turned the key to his father's invention.

Chronos began to animate and, looking deeply annoyed, began to sing:

Alouette, gentille alouette
Alouette, je te plumerai…

Monsieur Homolle's eyes seemed to mist over at the sound of the simple little nursery rhyme. 'My mother used to sing that song,' he said in a strangled voice, almost to himself. 'It is incredible – almost as if there is a human intelligence within.'

Chronos glared at him with his ruby eyes, but said nothing.

'Quite like a real voice. Remarkable, quite remarkable. How is it achieved?'

'Clockwork,' Houdini replied briefly, for more than that he didn't know.

'And its provenance?'

The time-thieves weren't familiar with this word, but fortunately Houdini seemed to be. 'Craftsmen from Greenwich, London, we think. Around 1894.'

'Well.' Monsieur Homolle actually rubbed his hands together. 'I congratulate you on your choice. We at the Louvre pride ourselves on being at the very centre of Western art. It is a claim that other galleries – such as the

National in London – simply cannot make.' He opened his desk drawer, flipped out a form, scribbled a few lines on it and laid it in front of Houdini. He seemed in somewhat of a hurry.

'What is dis?' asked the magician.

'An acquisitions form to declare that you gave this bird automaton to the Louvre of your own free will.'

Chronos ruffled his filigree feathers at this description, and the brass gave off a little chime like a tuning fork.

Homolle took a pen from his pocket, unscrewed the cap and laid it on the paper.

'Thank you, but I haff my own,' said Houdini, bringing out a pen from *his* pocket and unscrewing the cap. Looking over his shoulder, Aidan was surprised to see that Houdini gave his own name instead of an alias, and gave their address correctly as the Hotel du Louvre.

Luna, who always felt rather affectionate towards the prickly little bird, felt a small misgiving at signing Chronos away like this, even though she knew it was all part of the plan to steal the *Mona Lisa*. She kissed the bird's little brass head and said, 'We'll see you soon, Chronos.'

Chronos gave a little nod, but then he slowed and stilled – he'd run down.

'Could you tell us where he vill be displayed?' said Houdini. 'My young ffriends here would be most gratified to see him in the gallery.'

'Unfortunately you have caught me at a somewhat awkward time,' said Monsieur Homolle. 'I am afraid I am preparing to take a short leave of absence. I am due to take my annual vacation tomorrow – I'll be away for a week with my family.'

'Somewhere nice, I hope?'

'Very. We're going to Brittany on the coast.'

Houdini made appreciative noises, then looked significantly at the time-thieves. There was now a ticking clock. They had one week – just one week – to perform the heist of the century, one week when the director was on holiday and security could be expected to be a little looser.

'Unfortunately, I will not have time to think about the matter of this artefact's placement until my return,' said Homolle. 'So for this short time your bird will be in the stores.'

Houdini feigned a worried look. 'And you are sure he will be secure there? He is of considerable value.'

'My dear sir, the Louvre is like a fortress,' said Homolle. 'Indeed, it *was* a fortress. The stores are perfectly secure –

in fact, there is only one place more secure than the stores, and that is the gallery itself.'

Houdini gave his dry chuckle. 'I hope so. For only this morning my young associates and I met a suspicious-looking gentleman, who was boasting of his intention to steal something from the Louvre.'

Monsieur Homolle went as white as the paper Houdini had just signed.

'Indeed?' he stuttered. 'What manner of gentleman?'

'A foreign gentleman, by his accent.'

Homolle looked like he was struggling to breathe. 'And what manner of theft?'

'That is not known to me. It was in your Salon Carré, I think.'

Homolle laughed, seemingly relieved. 'Well, I wish your foreign gentleman good luck. It would be easier to steal the bell towers from Notre Dame than to steal a painting from the walls of the Louvre.'

'Yes,' said Houdini, his bright eyes veiled. 'I think I heard that somewhere.'

'It is true, my dear sir. We have over two hundred guards patrolling the galleries of the Louvre day and night, when it is open and when it is closed. They change shifts every four hours so they are always, *always* alert. We also have eighty conservators, who are in charge of making sure all the paintings are where they should be.'

'Why would they not be where they should be?' asked Houdini. 'Why would they move?'

'Because the paintings are occasionally removed for photography. Our own photographer takes colour plates of them for postcards and catalogues. Then they must be replaced, and if any of them are misplaced, the conservators rectify this, or return any paintings that should not be on display to the stores.' Homolle folded Houdini's form and placed it in a filing cabinet. 'Added to this, we are currently having the shadow boxes on each painting replaced. Each frame is being redressed and the paintings placed behind glass to better conserve them. So in addition to our usual personnel we have also eighty glaziers working in the gallery. You may have seen them – they wear white smocks.'

Konstantin opened his mouth to speak, then shut it again.

'So if your "foreign gentleman" can avoid all of those watching eyes, then he *deserves* a painting.' Homolle laughed. 'No, I feel I can go on my holiday with absolute confidence. Speaking of which, if you will excuse me, I really must finish clearing my desk in order for my deputy to take over.' He rose from his desk.

They were clearly dismissed. As soon as the door closed behind them, Aidan turned on Houdini. 'What,' he hissed, 'did you just *do*? Now we've warned him someone's planning to steal from him. Now it will be *twice* as hard.'

'Not at all,' said Houdini mildly. 'We found out much more from him than he found out from us.'

'And how do you work that out?'

'We found out how many guards there are, and when they change shifts. We found out about the conservators and the photographer. We found out about the glaziers and the shadow boxes, which may be our most significant discovery yet. *And*,' he finished, 'we found out that Homolle's going to be in Brittany for a week from tomorrow, so whoever else we're dealing with, it won't be him. While the cat's away' – he winked one bright eye – 'the mice will play.'

Aidan had a much freer relationship with Houdini than Luna and Konstantin, who were a little cowed by the magician. Aidan challenged him now. 'And you don't think that when a "foreign gentleman" actually *does* steal the painting, namely you, he'll put two and two together? You just wrote down your particulars on his form, and signed your name to them.'

'That won't be a problem,' said Houdini as they walked out of the gallery into the sunshine of the Place du Louvre.

'How d'you mean?' asked Aidan. But the magician's mouth was clamped shut.

'Oh, won't you tell us?' pleaded Konstantin.

Houdini looked at him. 'What's the magic word?'

Konstantin remembered the joke answer Aidan had given at the Egyptian Hall. 'Abracadabra?'

The magician laughed this time too. 'I meant *please*,' he said. Houdini gave his devilish smile. 'I used disappearing ink to fill in the form,' he said, checking his pocket watch. 'By now, that page will already be blank.'

19 AUGUST 1911
4.45 p.m.

Houdini had a plan.

He no longer came to the gallery, but spent his time perusing the pages of Leonardo's sketchbook. This was a frustrating business as he didn't know any Italian, but he could understand the diagrams. 'A man after my own heart,' he declared of Leonardo. 'Look at all this planning, and measuring, and all these diagrams. It is exactly how I work. The man was a true artist.'

Aidan looked over his shoulder. 'More than that,' he said. 'He was an engineer.'

When he wasn't studying the *Codex*, Houdini was off spending time in the Latin Quarter of Paris, buying strange chemicals and bits and pieces of equipment with which he covered the floor of the hotel suite. Luna,

Aidan and Konstantin looked at these preparations and scratched their heads – the bits of wood and metal and rubber tubing and sheets of glass and chemicals didn't seem to fit together. When he wasn't messing about with chemicals, the magician was drawing in one of the buff-covered sketchbooks, practising faces and hands and figures. An accomplished artist, he filled page after page with his sketches, as if he was trying to rival Leonardo and create a new *Codex Arundel*. He obsessively checked the evening paper for the weather report, asking Konstantin for his help in decoding the little symbols.

'So long as there is no cloud,' he would mutter. 'Cloud may undo us.' They had no idea what he was planning, and nor would he tell them. 'Let not daylight in upon magic,' he would repeat over and over – his favourite way of saying that the Great Houdini would never, *ever* reveal how his tricks were done.

Meanwhile the time-thieves still went to the gallery for the purposes of research.

Houdini's instructions became more specific. Inspired by all the diagrams in the *Codex* about lenses and prisms and how light behaved, his questions were all based around the sun – when it rose, when it set, how and when its beams flooded through the glazed skylights of the vaulted ceiling, and how and when those beams hit the paintings. For Aidan, the magician had a very specific instruction. 'You are an engineer, and you have an engineer's eye,' he said. 'I want you to find out the size of the *Mona Lisa*, as accurately as you can.'

Aidan duly visited the Salon Carré and did his best, skulking around the *Mona Lisa* and trying to get an accurate reading of her measurements. 'Well, that was no easy task,' he reported back to the others at dinner. 'Although everyone completely ignores the *Mona Lisa* herself, she happens to hang underneath a painting by a fella called Veronese. Phew!' He blew a lock of black hair out of his eyes. 'If I had to guess, I'd say he'll be the one to stand the test of time, not old Leonardo. Anyway, that Veronese – well, you've seen it. As long as a coach-and-four and as colourful as a rainbow. Since everyone comes to gawk at that, it was pretty difficult to get the measure of the *Mona Lisa*. You should've seen me.' He giggled. 'Yawning and stretching right next to it, so I could see if it was an arm's length or a hand's breadth.' He nodded confidently. 'I reckon we're talking thirty by twenty inches.'

'It's good, but not good enough,' said Houdini, turning a table napkin into a white rose. 'I require her dimensions down to the last fraction. I need one thing above all,' he declared. 'I need to find one of those glaziers, and fast.'

It was Konstantin's turn to patrol the Salon Carré at closing time, and once more he saw the man in the white smock, standing statue-still, gazing into the *Mona Lisa*'s eyes. As usual he was the only one paying her any attention. As Aidan had said, everyone else only had eyes for the Veronese. And at last Konstantin understood. He'd seen the man half a dozen times and it had taken him this long to interpret the look in his dark eyes. It was how you looked at someone you knew – how you looked at a photogram of someone you held very dear.

Then he understood. The man looked at the *Mona Lisa* the way his father looked at Luna's Aunt Grace.

It was how you looked at someone you were in love with.

He was watching the man carefully, marvelling at his stillness, when another man approached.

It was the director of the Louvre, Monsieur Theophile Homolle.

Monsieur Homolle went right up to the watching man and gave his shoulder a little shake. He was clearly angry and began to scold the man, whispering a volley of furious French into the watcher's ear.

The watcher tore his eyes from the canvas and began protesting, gesturing expressively with his hands. Konstantin edged closer. His French was not fluent at the best of times, but it was doubly hard to understand angry whispering. He thought the gist of it went like this.

HOMOLLE: Have you been idiot enough to blab about stealing the Mona Lisa in front of the visitors?

WATCHING MAN: Of course not, what do you take me for?

HOMOLLE: Well, just make sure you don't, that's all. I'm away for the next week — can I trust you not to mess everything up?

WATCHING MAN: Of course, don't worry. Everything will be well.

HOMOLLE: Well, you'd better hope so. For your sake.

Homolle began to walk away, then he turned and shot the man a look of utter contempt, and he said a very curious thing. '*Sal macaroni.*'

That was when Konstantin knew that his French had failed him. He'd definitely misheard that bit. *Sal macaroni?*

Although the word sounded a little like the name of Luna's favourite cake, the macaron, macaron*i* meant something quite different. It was a kind of short hollow noodle they ate in Italy. And *sal* meant dirty. Why would anyone call anyone a dirty macaroni? Apart from being mean, it was just bizarre.

However silly the insult, it seemed to bother the watching man. He looked very upset and said an extremely rude thing under his breath as Homolle walked away. This time Konstantin was not so much struck by the terrible word as the language it was in. It was a beautiful language, of which Konstantin unfortunately only knew the swear words.

It was Italian.

19 AUGUST 1911
4.49 p.m.

Konstantin was by the man's side in a trice. On closer inspection he could better see the noble features, the neatly parted black hair, the black moustache flipped up at the ends, and the soulful brown eyes fixed on the *Mona Lisa*. The Italian words he did know were not nearly polite enough to introduce himself, so he spoke in English.

'Excuse me. Are you Italian?'

The man looked guarded. 'Yes.' He sighed, in a weary sing-song voice. 'What have we done wrong now?'

Konstantin was puzzled by the question. 'Nothing. It's just… well, I've been longing to meet one of your countrymen.'

The Italian's face was transformed by a charming smile. He seemed surprised to be spoken to so courteously.

'My name is Konstantin Kass,' said Konstantin, holding out his hand.

The Italian looked at the hand, and then back at Konstantin, as if he had forgotten what to do. Then he took Konstantin's hand and shook it. 'Vincenzo Peruggia.'

'Delighted.' Konstantin smiled back warmly. 'Tell me, Vincenzo. Are you a physician? Or perhaps a surgeon?'

Vincenzo looked down at his white smock and laughed. It was a pleasant sound. 'No. I work here, at the Louvre. I am a – how do you call it – I put the glass on the pictures.'

Konstantin's clockwork heart leapt. It was almost too good to be true. 'You're a glazier?' he said, his voice cracking with hope.

'Yes, that. I am that.'

A bell began to ring – a familiar sound to Konstantin after all his time in the gallery. It meant the Louvre was about to close. Konstantin was due to meet the other time-thieves and Houdini at one of their favourite restaurants on the banks of the Seine, and he had a sudden idea.

'Vincenzo. Would you like to dine with my friends and me? I am sure they would love to meet you.'

Vincenzo actually looked like he might cry. 'Truly?'

Konstantin smiled. 'Yes. We'd be delighted.'

Vincenzo smiled shakily. He took Konstantin by the shoulders and, much to the boy's surprise, kissed him heartily on both cheeks. 'You don't know what this means to me,' he babbled. 'I live alone. I have no friends. You are the first person to use my given name since I left Italy. They all call me "macaroni" here. I would welcome, so much, some friendly company.'

By the time they reached the restaurant, right by a beautiful bridge arching over the sparkling Seine, the others were already there.

Konstantin introduced his new acquaintance in a manner not unlike Houdini producing the correct card at the end of a card trick.

'This is Vincenzo Peruggia. He's a *glazier*. And...' – his pause was worthy of the magician himself – 'an *Italian*.'

Vincenzo found himself on the receiving end of a rapturous welcome. The time-thieves and Houdini pressed him with Paris's finest food and drink. The younger diners ordered their favourite dish, beef bourguignon with potatoes dauphinoise – a rich, savoury beef stew with creamy slices of potato. They drank citron pressé, a kind of lemonade you made yourself at the table from crushed lemon juice and water and sugar, and the grown-ups had wine. For dessert Luna fulfilled her long-held Parisian dream when the waiter brought a plate of pastel macarons. 'Like eating a coloured cloud made of sugar,' was her description. They all enjoyed themselves immensely. It was a lovely warm summer night, and the sun set over the Seine, painting the sky in rose and gold. The ornamental iron tower in the distance stood out black against the colours, creating a scene worthy of a canvas in the Louvre. The time travellers took to Vincenzo at once. After a glass of good French wine he forgot to be shy, and told them all about his childhood in a poor region of northern Italy, and how he came to France, like many of his countrymen, to seek work. 'What I really want is to make my family proud of me,' he said. 'And beyond that, my country. But the French don't like us Italians. They call us "dirty macaroni". I told your friend.' He nodded at Konstantin. 'No one has called me Vincenzo for years.'

Houdini was silent for a moment, turning the stem of his wine glass in his hand. 'I know what it is to exchange one name for another,' he said. He held out his hand, and the Italian took it. Houdini shook his hand and said, 'Vincenzo Peruggia, I am very pleased to make your acquaintance. I am Ehrich Weisz.'

The time-thieves stared at Houdini with wide eyes. This was the first time they had heard his real name.

'I was born in Budapest, and my father was a rabbi – a Jewish priest. I loved my city, but my city did not love Jews. We had to move to a place where our people were not numerous enough to be hated, so we went to America. But still, to be safe, I renamed myself Harry Houdini. An American first name, and a second name borrowed from a French magician, Robert Houdin. From that day Ehrich Weisz no longer existed. For the very first time in my life, I disappeared.' Houdini's strange mirrored eyes looked even more reflective, as if they held unshed tears. 'But though I am now Houdini, I will never forget little Ehrich Weisz, and the names he was called in the streets of Budapest. So you see, I do understand how it hurts when you are called "dirty macaroni" by your co-workers.'

'That wasn't just his fellow workers,' put in Konstantin. 'It was the director of the Louvre.'

'*What?*' Houdini's distinctive eyebrows shot up. He looked at Vincenzo. '*Homolle* called you that?'

'Yes.' Konstantin was fired up now, and answered for his new friend. 'When I met Vincenzo, our friend Homolle was telling him off. He thought he'd been talking about stealing a painting from the Louvre.'

'Ah,' said Houdini, a flicker of guilt in his eyes. 'That might have been my fault. I told Homolle that a foreign gentleman had been considering stealing a painting,' he said to Vincenzo. 'I meant myself, of course. It was a trick to get him to reveal his security arrangements. Why he concluded that the foreign gentleman was you, I don't know.'

'I do,' said Vincenzo. For a moment he didn't meet anyone's eyes, but then he looked up. 'What he said was true. I *do* want to steal a painting. I want to steal the *Mona Lisa*.'

19 AUGUST 1911
8.10 p.m.

'**Y**ou want to steal the *Mona Lisa*?' Houdini leant in, as if he had not heard the Italian correctly. 'The Leonardo?'

'Yes,' said Vincenzo, very definitely. '*La Gioconda* must come home with me. Where she belongs. To Italy.'

'La…' Luna queried. 'What did you call her?'

'*La Gioconda*. It means "the happy one". Because of her smile.'

'If you can call it a smile,' muttered Aidan.

Vincenzo shot him a chilly look – clearly, criticism of the *Mona Lisa* was not appreciated.

'I mean,' blustered Aidan, 'her smile is beautiful, but so… small.'

Vincenzo thawed. 'You are right. It is a subtle, secret smile. As if she knows something she will not tell.'

The time-thieves exchanged a look. They knew each other well enough by now to agree, without speaking, that it was too soon to share with Vincenzo that the *Mona Lisa* did indeed know a *very* valuable secret – the whereabouts of a much greater painting – the *Salvator Mundi*.

'That painting contains magic,' Vincenzo said.

Houdini sat up. 'What do you mean?'

'The eyes,' said Vincenzo. 'They follow you around the room. And that smile? If you look at it long enough, it disappears. The phenomenon cannot be explained. It is some trickery of Leonardo's.'

Houdini looked thoughtful. Clearly he'd never thought of Leonardo as a magician.

'The *Mona Lisa* is a piece of genius,' stated Vincenzo, 'and entirely underrated. One day it will be considered the greatest painting in the world. Leonardo used to carry her around, so she was certainly *his* favourite painting.'

The time-thieves and Houdini looked at each other. They thought it far more likely that Leonardo carried the *Mona Lisa* around because she held the key to the whereabouts of his greater work.

'But Napoleon looted my nation and brought the *Mona Lisa* to France,' continued Vincenzo.

'Who's Napoleon?' whispered Aidan to Konstantin.

'French fellow,' Konstantin whispered back. 'Small man; great general.'

'That very bridge was built under his reign,' said Vincenzo, pointing to the elegant iron walkway arching over the river. 'But as much as he built from the ground up, he stole. The *Mona Lisa* was looted when he conquered Italy. She does not belong in a French gallery. She belongs in Italy's greatest gallery – the Uffizi in Florence.'

Houdini nodded slowly, thinking. He stroked his chin with one of his extraordinary hands. 'Tell me. What exactly is it that you do at the Louvre?'

'Homolle, the director, is embarking on a programme to replace the glass on every picture. It's a huge undertaking, and that's why the Louvre is full of… what did you call us?' Vincenzo looked at Konstantin.

'Glaziers.'

'That's it. I cut and fit the glass for the frames,' said the Italian.

'And it's you who will replace the *Mona Lisa*'s glass?'

'I would not let anyone else do it.' Vincenzo's chest puffed out like a pigeon's. 'I do not trust anyone else to touch her.'

Once again Konstantin got the feeling that, to Vincenzo, *Mona Lisa* was a real woman.

'But if I take the painting,' Vincenzo went on, 'they will know it is me. I have already made so much fuss about replacing the glass myself. The French already hate me. I will be arrested.'

'My dear fellow, you won't be required to take her anywhere,' said Houdini. 'Someone else will do it for you. All I want you to do is your job – replace the glass on the painting. But the only difference will be that you will replace the glass with a special pane which *I* will give you. Or rather, *you* will give *me*.'

Vincenzo frowned a little. 'I am sorry. Perhaps it is my English which is not so good. But I don't understand at all.'

'It's not your English,' Konstantin reassured him. 'I don't understand either.'

'Let me ask you this,' said Houdini. 'When are you due to replace the glass on the *Mona Lisa*?'

'This coming Monday, the 21st, that is the day,' said Vincenzo.

'Very well,' said the magician. 'Tomorrow I will come to your glaziers and purchase a piece of glass. You will sell me a piece exactly the right dimensions to fit the *Mona Lisa*. I will take the pane away and work my magic on it. Then I will bring the pane back to the shop, saying it is cracked. It will not be cracked. You take the pane into the Louvre on Monday next, and place it on the *Mona Lisa*. Can you do that?'

Vincenzo licked his lips. 'Yes.'

'If you play your part, we will do the rest. I will pay you well for your service, and you and your beloved *Mona Lisa* can travel home to Italy.'

The Italian jumped from his chair and kissed Houdini on both cheeks. '*Grazie, grazie, gentile signor.*' Then he stood straight and noble, tears standing in his eyes, fists clenched at his sides. 'I'll show them who's the macaroni.' And he strode off into the night, along the banks of the Seine.

It was Aidan, once again, who took Houdini to task once Vincenzo had safely gone home. 'You sailed off course again, didn't you?' he said. 'What in the name of all the saints possessed you to tell him he could take the painting back to Italy?'

'Well, he can,' said Houdini, bright eyes open wide. 'We only need the *Mona Lisa* to look for clues to the whereabouts of the *Salvator Mundi*. Once we have found the clues, it doesn't really matter what happens to the painting. It is such an obscure work, I doubt it would be much missed. If Signor Peruggia wants to take it home to Italy, let him take it.' He sniffed. 'Besides, I didn't particularly care for Monsieur Homolle, did you? I think he needs teaching a lesson.'

'I agree,' said Konstantin fervently, 'especially since he called Vincenzo a dirty macaroni.'

Luna looked at Houdini. Even in the dark, his eyes shone like mirrors. She could tell he was excited about his plan. '*Dear* Houdini,' she wheedled. 'Won't you tell us what you are planning to do?'

Houdini looked her. 'What's the magic word?'

Luna remembered the well-worn joke. 'Abracadabra?'

Houdini laughed, as he always did. 'I meant *please*,' he said. Then his face grew thoughtful. 'I keep saying we must not let in daylight upon magic,' he said, taking a sip of his wine. 'Well, maybe now we *should*.'

20 AUGUST 1911
9.15 a.m.

Houdini's preparations moved up a gear.

The time-thieves were no longer required to go to the gallery. Each of them was sent on a very strange and inexplicable errand, away from the Louvre to other parts of Paris. Before they departed on their separate missions, Houdini shook a stream of gold sovereigns into their hands like bon-bons. Luna remembered that this was still the prize money the Butterfly Club had won alongside the Gabriel Medal, with the help of Signor Marconi's radio.

Luna left the hotel first, a little afraid to be on her own in a strange city and in a strange time. Her discomfort was heightened when she got the strong impression that someone was following her. Footsteps dogged her all the way along the rue du Louvre. She remembered the first day in Paris, when she'd seen a shadow behind her in the bakery window, and used the same trick again. Pretending to stop to look at some very smart hats, she could see an imperfect reflection of the man who was following her. She registered that he was wearing a Hotel du Louvre uniform and breathed a sigh of relief. Of course the staff would be sent on errands that took them away from the hotel. This man had nothing to do with her.

Her errand took her to the sunny left bank of the Seine, where there were rows of little stalls with pretty leaf-green awnings. Here the artists of Paris could be found. They stood, in their paint-covered smocks, enjoying the sun and calling out to passers-by to purchase their wares. Their paintings were arranged on their stalls, a riot of colour and light, a little Louvre-by-the-Seine. Some of the artists had set up stools and easels, and almost all of them called out to Luna to sit for them. She didn't speak French, but she could tell by their enthusiastic gestures that their raptures were due to the colour of her hair and eyes. She wondered, just for a moment, what it would be like to be the object of an artist's eye, like the *Mona Lisa* had been for Leonardo, to feel that absolute focus of attention, to see yourself recreated in paint.

But Luna wasn't there to model for a painting.

She was there to buy one.

'What would you like me to buy?' she'd asked Houdini that morning.

'Doesn't matter,' the magician had replied. 'So long as it measures around twenty to thirty inches. Here, take this.' He'd thrown a rolled-up tape measure across the room and Luna had caught it deftly.

Now she took that tape measure from her pocket and unravelled it. She took a good look at all the paintings – there were waterlilies, opera-goers, picnickers on grass, bathers on the beach. But the one that seemed to be the right size didn't seem to be a painting so much as a poster, recreated on a wooden panel. It had a handsome black cat on it, and some swirly lettering that read *Chat noir*, and it seemed to be advertising some sort of cabaret. The stallholder watched her measure the panel indulgently, obviously happy to humour his more eccentric customers if it meant he made a sale. The poster was exactly twenty by thirty inches – around the same size, according to Aidan, as the *Mona Lisa*. Luna shrugged to herself. If the black cat was the right size, then the black cat she would buy. She was pleased to see that the painting was on wood, not canvas, just like the *Mona Lisa*. 'Wood?' she asked, pointing at the painting and doing her best mime of a tree.

The stallholder did a more complicated mime back, which she eventually understood to mean the panel was made out of old wine boxes. That was good enough for Luna. She paid the money and walked with her prize back to the hotel, humming to herself in the hot sunshine with the pleasure of a job well done.

Aidan was dispatched to the Post Office, or *le bureau de poste*, as Konstantin called it. It was a huge, elegant building on the rue du Louvre, and even Aidan, who had been in the turbine room of the *Titanic*, found the bustling interior a little disorientating. Clerks and postmen ran hither and thither with trolleys and parcels, customers queued in snaking lines, chattering in French, and the ringing of tills echoed in the marble halls.

Having even less French than Luna, Aidan trusted the evidence of his own eyes and joined the queue for envelopes and packing supplies. Using an expressive mime and flashing his gold sovereigns, he managed to purchase a quantity of brown paper and string. Hurrying back out into the fresh air and sunshine with considerable relief, he headed back to the hotel, his mission accomplished.

Back in the suite, Houdini gathered the fruits of Luna's and Aidan's labours and put them together. He wrapped the wooden panel of the *chat noir* in the brown paper and string that Aidan had bought, cocooning it in reams and reams of packing, and tying the parcel with a firm knot.

He inked a direction clearly on the parcel:

DELIVER TO:

La Gioconda

Little Italy

New York

USA

'Just my little joke,' he said, with his familiar tinder-dry chuckle. 'Now for Konstantin's task – and as you speak the best French, yours is the most difficult mission.'

Konstantin made his way down the left bank of the Seine to the Port of Paris. There he could see the masts of the tall ships huddled against the summer blue like a quiver of arrows, and the funnels of the steamships belching out their white clouds to join their cousins in the sky. Konstantin mingled with the crowds of passengers, feeling nervous that Houdini had placed too much trust in his French. He wasn't at all sure he had the language skills to do what the magician had asked. He walked along the quay to the New York steamer, as Houdini had instructed, and heard, with relief, some English voices. Or rather, two young men who were conversing with each other in accents very like Professor Lorenz's.

Americans.

Mr Conrad Perry and Mr Ruben Schwartz were students at Princeton University in the state of New York. They had spent their summer on a grand tour of Europe and were buying tickets for Monday's voyage, so that they could return in time for the start of their fall term. Yes, they would be glad to courier Konstantin's parcel to Little Italy in Manhattan. Well, that was most kind of him to offer to pay for their passage. They sure would make sure his package was safely delivered.

Konstantin didn't have much time to judge their characters, but they were well-spoken and bright-eyed, and he thought he'd chosen well. He handed over the parcel and the sovereigns, and wished them, in the only French he had left, a *bon voyage*.

None of the time-thieves really understood why they'd been asked to do those tasks that day, but nor did they understand the mission Houdini had given himself. It seemed to be to go to the Louvre's gift shop to buy a postcard.

It must only have cost a couple of centimes, but he waved it in front of the time-thieves as if it was the most precious image in the world.

It was not even of the *Mona Lisa*, but another woman. She wore a black dress and a white lace veil secured by an oversized pink ribbon or flower. The image was odd, because she partly looked like she was wearing a mourning gown, and partly looked like she was wearing a wedding veil. The image was dark and rather grim.

'Who is it?' asked Konstantin.

'This,' said Houdini, 'is the Countess del Carpio, a portrait by the Spanish artist Goya. And by the end of the night, I shall know her image better than I know my own.'

'Why did you choose that particular postcard?' asked Aidan, bemused.

His answer was absolutely bizarre. 'Because it was the simplest.'

For the rest of the evening, Houdini asked to be left alone. He had been to the glazier's shop where Vincenzo worked, to collect the piece of glass that had been cut for the *Mona Lisa*'s frame. He laid it gently on the coverlet of his bed and sent his young associates out to dinner without him.

When they returned some hours later, they expected the glass to have been transformed in some magical way. But although Houdini was fast asleep in an easy chair, clearly exhausted by his labours, and although the paraphernalia he'd collected over the last week lay strewn across the bed – the chemicals, the brushes, the pumps and the rubber tubing – the glass pane still lay on the coverlet, pristine, blank and transparent. It did not seem to have changed at all.

21 AUGUST 1911
6 a.m.

On the big day Houdini was up before daybreak, his obsession with the weather alive and well. He stood on the wrought-iron balcony of his suite, staring skywards like those ancient peoples who lived in doubt that the sun would rise in the morning. But he saw the cloudless sunrise with relief, and as the sky brightened so did his expression.

Before they'd even finished breakfast, Vincenzo Peruggia was at the door of their suite. He was paler than usual, and dark circles under his eyes told the tale of a sleepless night, but his mouth was set in a determined line.

He and Houdini spoke few words, but exchanged a glance and a nod as Vincenzo carefully slipped the special glass pane into a leather portfolio he'd brought for the purpose.

'You know what you must do?' asked Houdini.

The Italian gave a single nod.

Konstantin laid a hand on his shoulder. He did not know what was going to happen today, but he was getting the idea that, whatever it was, it required considerable courage. 'Good luck, Vincenzo Peruggia,' he said.

At the music of his given name the Italian gave the ghost of a smile, not unlike the *Mona Lisa*'s, and left.

'Now what do we do?' asked Aidan when the door had closed behind Vincenzo.

'We wait,' said Houdini. He took out his pocket watch. 'What time does the sun hit the Salon Carré?'

Konstantin consulted his notebook. 'At 10.15.'

'And what time does the sun hit the frame of the *Mona Lisa*? I need an *exact* time.'

'At 10.27,' said Aidan promptly.

Houdini looked at him with those curiously bright eyes. 'You're sure? You didn't write it down.'

'Can't,' said Aidan simply. 'I'm not Leonardo. I don't scribble everything down. But I'm an engineer like he was, and engineers live by numbers. I'll swear by Mary, Joseph and all the saints that those sunbeams will hit that frame at 10.27 precisely.'

Houdini nodded, 'I believe you. Very well. Then we're ready.' He took out his pocket watch and unhooked the safety chain from the buttonhole of his waistcoat. He looked at the three of them in turn, then gave the watch to Luna. 'My dear,' he said, 'you are young, and female; the eye of suspicion will not fall on you. Go to the Louvre like an ordinary visitor. Look at what you like, but be in the Salon Carré at ten o'clock. At a quarter past the morning sun will reach the skylights. Watch, and mark, and *do not let your eyes leave the Mona Lisa.* I want you to observe most particularly what happens to the painting at 10.27, and then I would like you to remain and note the consequences of these occurrences. Then return here and report to me. Have you got that?'

Luna swallowed nervously, but nodded.

Houdini smiled. 'Don't be afraid. Think of it this way. You are not unlucky; rather, you are lucky to be chosen.' His gaze flickered up to the blue sky. 'If the sun continues to smile upon us, then you, Luna Goodhart, will be an audience of one to the Great Houdini's greatest trick.'

21 AUGUST 1911
10 a.m.

Luna paid her franc at the entrance to the Louvre and followed the very familiar pathway to the Salon Carré.

She noted that the gallery was reasonably quiet – not surprising, really, as it was first thing on a Monday, and apart from the tourists all of Paris would be at work or school.

The salon itself was all but empty. A guard sat, as he always did, on a chair by the door. She did not recognise him, which was good – that meant he would not recognise her. Inside the room a lone priest gazed at the vast and colourful *Wedding Feast at Cana* by Veronese, obviously wishing he'd been there. But apart from him Luna was alone in the room. No one was looking at the *Mona Lisa* but her.

That lady gazed back at Luna calmly from her frame, her white hands placidly crossed, that secret smile playing across her lips. The gallery was in shadow, and rather cold. Luna glanced at Houdini's pocket watch and then up at the skylight. A fingernail of sun was beginning to show at the very edge of the crystal windows.

10.15 a.m.

In the silence the ticking of the watch seemed deafening, and Luna's heart kept pace. If only no one else came into the room, things would be all right.

Then: disaster. A group of schoolchildren filed into the room, herded by a harassed-looking female teacher. They were all dressed in a school uniform that resembled a sailor suit, holding hands, walking in two by two like the animals coming into Noah's ark. They were chattering excitedly in French and their poor teacher constantly shushed them, to no avail.

Luna's heart sank. Children noticed everything, and would be far too beady-eyed to be hoodwinked by whatever Houdini had planned. The priest took one look at them, nodded politely to the young teacher and scuttled from the room. The class gathered around

Wedding Feast at Cana, gazing up at the massive canvas, their attention momentarily held by the size and colour of the painting.

Luna fixed her eyes on the minute hand of Houdini's watch.

10.18…

10.20…

The young teacher began to deliver a lecture about the giant painting, and the children began to whisper and fidget as the teacher's voice droned on. Luna looked up and saw the sun working its own magic trick: the beams were making their way down the walls, warming the brown paint to a creamy coffee, gilding the picture frames, brightening the colours on each canvas.

10.25.

One of the children broke rank. He dropped his partner's hand and began to dance around in an agitated fashion. His hand shot up, the fingers reaching skywards in agony. Luna knew what the little dance meant. He needed the toilet.

Luna inwardly blessed the child, and whatever he had drunk that morning. The teacher spotted his discomfort and hurriedly ushered the class from the room, presumably in search of the nearest toilets.

With the room to herself again, Luna was able to walk over to the *Mona Lisa*. She pretended to gaze, like the priest and the children, at *Wedding Feast at Cana*, but in reality her eyes never left the smaller, dull-as-ditchwater painting below.

Slowly, almost imperceptibly, the *Mona Lisa* began to change.

At first Luna thought her eyes were deceiving her – that some trick of the light on the glass was making the painting beneath difficult to see. But as she moved – casually – closer, she could see that the image was disappearing.

No… not disappearing. Being replaced.

She darted a glance towards the guard. His chin was lolling on his chest – he was either dozing or asleep.

She looked back at the *Mona Lisa*.

The bluish yellowish sky was bleaching to a silvery grey. Something pink began to replace the woman's smooth forehead – something like a ribbon or a rose. Then her watchful eyes disappeared, to be replaced by a much smaller, wan, waifish face, a woman with even darker hair and eyes, wearing a lace shawl crowned by a pink rose. As the slab of sunbeam crawled down the picture, more of it changed – the *Mona Lisa*'s secret smile was replaced by the lady's hands, holding a folded fan, and her torso by a black dress – perhaps a mourning dress, in contrast to the almost bridal veil.

A sound from the doorway. An elderly couple, very elegant, very upright, entered the room. Their presence woke the guard, who sat up, snorting a little. Luna felt a thrill of fear – they couldn't be allowed to see the rest of the metamorphosis. She manoeuvred her body so that she stood between the door and the painting, but she need not have worried. The elderly couple had come – like everyone else – to see *Wedding Feast at Cana*. The enormous canvas was fully and gloriously illuminated by the morning sun and stood some yards away from Luna, who was peering up at it.

For the third time that day she cursed the fact that such an important painting hung just above the *Mona Lisa*, but it should be all right – the trick, if it was a trick, was almost done.

Luna watched the *Mona Lisa*. It looked most peculiar. The painting was almost entirely of the Countess del Carpio – the image on the postcard Houdini had bought from the gift shop. Only the *Mona Lisa*'s pair of crossed hands remained at the bottom. Then the sunbeam crept down to the bottom of the painting and, as if by magic, the hands were replaced by a neat pair of button boots.

As if by magic. Luna had heard the phrase all her life, had read it in books, had it read to her by her father. It ran like a thread through all the fairy tales she'd ever known. Here the transformation wasn't from a princess to a frog or from a beggar to a king, but it seemed just as fantastic. In this unlikely setting of the Louvre, magic, real-life magic, was happening in front of her eyes.

Luna breathed a sigh of relief. The painting was now entirely transformed. And the relief was soon replaced by respect – she was immensely impressed by Houdini's skill. She looked at the magician's watch. It said 10.32. In a little under five minutes he had been able to exchange one painting for another, he was nowhere near the gallery, and she hadn't the faintest idea how he'd done it.

21 AUGUST 1911
10 a.m.

I would like you to remain and note the consequences of these occurrences.

Houdini's words echoed in Luna's mind. She knew she had to move away from the *Mona Lisa* and the *Wedding Feast of Cana* now. Even the most dedicated art lover could not remain in the same place for much longer. She turned her attention to the other walls of the gallery, but she knew that anyone who entered the room might notice the switch.

How long would it take until someone realised that the *Mona Lisa* by Leonardo da Vinci was gone, and had been replaced by the Countess del Carpio by someone called Goya? She felt incredibly nervous that someone would see the change, then as the minutes passed she became worried that no one would see it. One dark, dreary painting had been exchanged for another. Since they hung beneath the glory of the Veronese painting, the switch could surely go unnoticed for many hours, if not days. How long did Houdini want her to stay?

But luck was on Luna's side once more. Just as she had decided that she must leave the room before she began to look suspicious, a gentleman walked discreetly into the room. He was wearing a smart navy suit, and on his lapel he wore a badge bearing a gold C.

A conservator.

Conservators, Luna knew from Houdini's conversation with Monsieur Homolle, the director of the gallery, were the gentlemen who patrolled the Louvre making sure that all the pictures were in the right place.

This one spotted the Goya. His footsteps stuttered.

He stopped.

Stared.

Frowned.

He peered closer, then rocked back on his heels, looking at the picture. Then he left the Salon Carré, walking much faster than he had walked in.

Luna waited, heart pounding, for what she knew would come. The conservator came back with another of his number – a conservator dressed just like him – and another man, who was dressed in a craftsman's smock. For a moment she thought it was Vincenzo, but this man was shorter and blonder – a glazier, certainly, but not the one she knew. The two conservators had a murmured conference, heads close together, then gave the man in the smock an order. The man in the smock carefully lifted the canvas from the wall and the three of them left the room. The gap where the *Mona Lisa* had been stood out from the other paintings like a gap in a row of perfect teeth.

After a moment Luna followed them on silent feet. She kept at a discreet distance, then lost them when they disappeared through a private door that almost seemed like part of the panelling.

She stood for a moment, staring at a blank wall, then she turned to go. There was no more she could do that day – the magic painting, Leonardo, Goya, whatever it was, was safely in the Louvre's stores.

21 AUGUST 1911
1.15 p.m.

'How *did* you do it?'

The time-thieves and Houdini were having lunch at their favourite bistro by the Seine.

Houdini was silent, playing with the salt and pepper cellars, his bright eyes veiled. Somehow he managed to get the salt to shake out pepper, and the pepper to shake out salt.

Luna looked at the mess he'd made on the white tablecloth. She'd spent the first part of the meal recounting, word for word, what had happened at the Louvre that morning, repeating every detail for Houdini's satisfaction, and she felt that it was his time to talk.

'Come on,' she said. 'You let daylight in upon magic this morning. Can't you do it again?'

'Very well,' he said, waiting until the waiter had cleared the table and moved away. 'Just this once. Do you remember, when you came to see me at the Egyptian Hall, that I created a portrait of Queen Victoria on a blank canvas, with just a wave of my hand?'

All three time-thieves nodded. They had loved that trick.

Houdini looked over his shoulders and leaned in before he spoke. 'That is a trick called the Phantom Painting. You paint an unbleached canvas with certain chemical solutions that appear invisible when dry. You use sulphate of iron for blue, nitrate of bismuth for yellow, copper sulphate for brown, and so on.'

'But how do you make the painting appear on stage?' asked Aidan, who was very interested in the mechanics of magic.

Houdini looked around again. 'The magician has an atomiser concealed in his sleeve, which sprays out a fine mist of a compound called prussiate of potash. As the magician waves his hand dramatically over the painting he is, in reality, gradually spraying the whole of the canvas so that the chemical reaction takes place. In front of the audience, as you witnessed, the portrait of Queen Victoria – or whoever it is - magically appears.'

'But... but... you weren't *there* this time,' said Konstantin. 'You couldn't spray the *Mona Lisa* with anything. You weren't actually *in* the Louvre. You were in the hotel with us.'

'Ah,' said Houdini, mirror-bright eyes twinkling. 'That is because this variation on the Phantom Painting uses not liquid but *light*.' He took a sip of wine. 'I've been experimenting for some years with a compound called Sol Tinctura. It means "sun dye". It's a water-based paint and its colour develops and binds permanently when it's exposed to the sun.'

'Like photography,' said Aidan.

'Exactly,' said Houdini. 'First I copied the postcard of the Countess del Carpio on to the glass.'

'How did you recreate it so accurately?' asked Konstantin.

'I am a poor artist,' confessed Houdini, 'but I used Leonardo's own method, which he details in the *Codex Arundel*. I divided the glass into a net of squares, and mapped the postcard on to the glass, one square at a time. This way, it's possible to enlarge a work of art to the correct size. And just as in the Phantom Painting,' he went on, 'you can see the paint as it goes on, because it is wet, otherwise it would be impossible to see your own work.

But it dries invisible, so you have to work quickly. Once I'd finished, the glass was completely clear and transparent again. I gave the pane to our friend Vincenzo this morning to put on the frame of the *Mona Lisa* before the gallery opened at nine, and he must have done his work well – for, according to Luna, the act worked perfectly.' He smiled happily. 'In the theatre the limelight is enough to develop the image, so I was confident that a strong summer sun would do the trick.'

Luna was trying to get things straight in her mind. 'So the *Mona Lisa itself* didn't change?'

'No,' said Houdini, 'the glass did. The *Mona Lisa* is still there, untouched underneath. The genius of the trick is that none of us had to steal the painting. That poor innocent conservator took it down and put it in storage until it can be rehung. All we have to do now is get it from the stores, and that will be much less troublesome than taking it from the walls of the Louvre. The only thing is,' he went on, 'that I don't know how stable the process is. I usually test and retest my tricks before I take them to the stage. My experiments in the hotel suite seemed to hold their colour. But you never know.'

'What do you mean, stable?' asked Aidan, his blue eyes narrowed.

'I mean,' the magician said, 'that I hope she doesn't change back.'

The rest of that day, and the whole of the night, was agony. No one got much sleep knowing the *Mona Lisa* was in the stores: not being able to get at her, not knowing if she would be discovered, or moved, or whether the Sol Tinctura would fade in the darkness, was dreadfully worrying. But Houdini insisted. 'We must hold our nerve,' he said. 'Sooner or later they will realise that the *Mona Lisa* is missing, and anyone attempting to get back into a closed gallery on the day of the theft will naturally fall under suspicion. I told Vincenzo to stay right away from the Louvre, and we must too.'

22 AUGUST 1911
9 a.m.

On Tuesday morning the time-thieves were up early and in the queue for the Louvre to open, so they could be among the first to enter the gallery.

The atmosphere was quite different that day from the usual calm. The Louvre was buzzing like a beehive, with an atmosphere of barely concealed chaos. Although the public were allowed to enter, the guards were distracted, and the gallery was full of strange men. The strange men were either in royal-blue uniforms, or looked military, as if they used to wear a uniform before they were promoted into different clothes.

'Gendarmes,' murmured Konstantin. 'French police. We need to avoid them,'

'On the contrary,' said Houdini. 'Let's find out who's in charge.' He grabbed a passing royal-blue uniform.

'Excuse me, my good man,' he said. 'Could you point me to your commanding officer?'

The young policeman looked busy. He didn't seem to have time to talk, but he jabbed a gloved finger at a tall man wearing a hat and an overcoat. Houdini strode up to the man, the time-thieves in his wake. 'Just what on earth is going on?' Houdini had a strange power: although he was little, you would never mistake him for anything other than a man of consequence.

The police chief seemed to feel it at once. 'Monsieur, there has been a small theft.' He was clearly trying to play the situation down. 'Nothing that Chief Inspector Le Pine, the finest detective mind in the world, will not soon be able to solve.'

'Isn't the finest detective mind in the world Sherlock Holmes?' said Luna, on behalf of her friend Arthur Conan Doyle.

The policeman's lip curled, and Luna got the feeling he'd had the name of Sherlock Holmes thrown in his face before.

'Mademoiselle,' he said coldly, 'Mr Sherlock Holmes is a fictional character. Chief Inspector Le Pine is very real indeed.'

'And who is this Chief Inspector Le Pine?' Aidan chimed in.

'*Moi*,' said the man, thumping his thumbs into his chest, and the time-thieves realised that Inspector Le Pine was one of those annoying people who talk about themselves in the third person, as if they are telling a story. 'And I assure you, I will not rest until this case is solved.'

Houdini's brow furrowed with concern. 'The theft. It was not... please tell me it was not... of a brass bird?'

Le Pine looked at him as if he had lost his wits. 'A brass b—? No. No. It was a painting. The *Mona* something. A minor Leonardo.'

Dramatically, Houdini pressed one hand to his forehead. 'This is intolerable.'

Le Pine narrowed his eyes. 'You seem troubled, monsieur. Perhaps you have a particular... connection to the painting?'

'I never heard of it in the whole of my life,' lied Houdini. 'My concern is that only the other day I myself donated a precious artefact to the Louvre. How do I know it won't be stolen too?'

'I beg you not to worry, sir,' said the detective soothingly. He bent closer and lowered his voice. 'Between you and me, Le Pine has already had a huge breakthrough.' said the policeman, smugly. 'It just so happens that we have already found the painting.' He paused, as if for applause, just long enough for the time-thieves and Houdini to go cold with horror. Had the *Mona Lisa* been found in the stores?

'Two gentlemen were apprehended as they boarded the steamer from Paris to New York,' said Le Pine.

It was then that the time-thieves began to appreciate the genius of Houdini's planning. Just two days ago he had sent Konstantin to the docks to find two students who were returning home to America. He had given them the cost of their passage in return for delivering the cat painting that Luna had bought, wrapped in the brown paper and string which Aidan had purchased. Now the police were following the wrong painting out of Paris. 'The gentlemen were carrying a picture addressed to La Gioconda. Of course, you couldn't be expected to know this,' Le Pine added patronisingly, 'but *La Gioconda* is the Macaroni name for the *Mona Lisa*.'

'Don't you mean the *Italian* name?' put in Konstantin pleasantly.

'Yes, yes, of course,' said the detective with a wave of his hand. 'The two fellows – students, of course – had some *coq au vin* story about delivering the painting to New York.'

'They won't get in trouble, will they?' asked Konstantin nervously.

'No, no,' said Le Pine airily. 'They were pawns in a larger chess game. The word is…' He looked all around, just as Houdini had the night before when he explained the Phantom Painting. 'The word is that they were hired as couriers by a mysterious foreign gentleman. Mark my words, we will track him down, for he knows far more than they do.'

Konstantin began to fidget a little at this. The finest detective mind in the world had that 'foreign gentleman' right under his noble nose, for of course it was Konstantin who had paid the American students to take the fake parcel to New York.

'So you have already found the *Mona Lisa* then?' he said.

'Yes. We are no longer looking for the painting, but the perpetrator.'

'You're sure you have the right painting?' asked Aidan casually.

'Well, she looks a little different at the moment,' admitted the detective. 'We have reason to believe she was over-painted – a crude cat design covers the original. But we have our best forensic archivists working on the picture right now, painstakingly removing the top layers of paint so as not to damage the masterpiece below.'

At this point Luna had to bury her face in her handkerchief to stifle her giggles. She knew that once Inspector Le Pine's fancy experts had finished cleaning off *le chat noir*, they would likely find nothing more than a wooden panel made of wine boxes.

'Our task now,' Le Pine went on, 'is to find the *real* criminal – the person who stole the *Mona Lisa*.'

Only Houdini and the time-thieves knew that the *Mona Lisa* was still in the Louvre, safely nestling in the stores, and that the theft that Le Pine was investigating hadn't happened yet. Luna, Konstantin and Aidan looked at the magician. The hardest bit was yet to come. If this was a chess game, what would be Houdini's next move?

They could never have guessed what he would say. 'I am most displeased with the security here,' declared the magician haughtily. 'I would like to demand the return of my donation.'

Le Pine saw a way to make Houdini someone else's problem. 'I'm afraid that is not my department. You will have to speak to the director of the museum. No – not he,' he corrected himself, 'he is on vacation. The *deputy* director.'

'And who is the deputy director?'

'I believe,' said Inspector Le Pine, 'his name is Georges Benedite.'

22 AUGUST 1911
9.20 a.m.

Georges Benedite was not having a good day.

A gentle young academic who lived for Egyptology, he was now in charge of the Louvre on the day of the most daring art heist in history.

He sat in Monsieur Homolle's chair, in Monsieur Homolle's office, but of course Monsieur Homolle himself was off building sandcastles with his family on the beaches of Brittany. So it was poor Georges Benedite who had to listen to Houdini ranting, while nervously twitching his tie the whole time. When the magician had finished, Benedite spread his sweaty hands. The time-thieves noticed that his fingers shook a little.

'I'm afraid what you suggest is impossible, monsieur. You cannot just ask for your artefact back. You donated your – brass bird, is it? – in good faith. You will have signed a form to that effect.'

'I signed no such form,' lied Houdini. 'I told your superior that I would lend my bird for a short period while I investigated the efficacy of your security. And as you can see' – he spread his own hands – 'that has been sadly lacking.'

Georges Benedite ran a finger around his collar, as if it was a size too small. 'But, monsieur, you must be mistaken. We do not take loans from private persons without paperwork. You must have signed *something*. What day did you come to see my superior?'

'Wednesday, I think it was,' said Houdini, who knew perfectly well what date it had been.

Georges Benedite crossed to the filing cabinet and opened a drawer, riffling through the files. He frowned. 'There *is* one new form in here from Wednesday last, but it is blank.' He pulled out the paper and showed Houdini both sides, as if he were the magician.

'Then, I'm afraid, your gallery must render me my property.'

On any other day Georges Benedite might have argued. Artefacts were his life. But museum procedures were the rules by which he lived that life, and if the Louvre didn't have the paperwork, then the Louvre didn't have the paperwork. 'Very well. I'll find someone to take you to the stores. They will help you find your donation.'

Handily, Vincenzo Peruggia was hanging around outside the office, just as he'd been told to.

'You,' said Georges Benedite, recognising the glazier's smock. 'Take these people to the stores.' Hurriedly he scribbled on a permission slip and handed it to Houdini. 'They may take their bird automaton away with them.'

The time-thieves and Houdini, showing no sign of having met their guide before, followed Vincenzo down the parquet-floored corridors of the Louvre. As they walked, Luna, for the second time that morning, appreciated the cleverness of Houdini's plan. Donating Chronos to the gallery reminded her of a story her father had told her when she was little. It was a story from the time when Troy was at war with Greece, and the Trojans gave the Greeks a huge wooden horse as a peace offering. The Greeks accepted the horse, but that was a huge mistake: a regiment of Trojan soldiers was hiding inside the horse's belly, and they defeated the Greeks from inside their own citadel.

What Houdini had given the Louvre was their own blunt-speaking little brass Trojan horse. And it had worked.

Within a few minutes, the magician and the time-thieves had been admitted to the secret heart of the world's most secure gallery: the stores of the Louvre Museum.

22 AUGUST 1911
9.30 a.m.

It was dark in the stores and for a moment the time-thieves stumbled around. Vincenzo switched on an electric light, but it didn't make much difference.

'Dim light protects the paintings,' explained Vincenzo. 'Now, let's find your bird. And, more importantly, *La Gioconda*.'

There were paintings everywhere: propped against the walls, piled high in corners, stored flat in map drawers. Also artefacts, decapitated stone heads, sarcophagi like the ones they'd seen in Egypt, and marble statues staring out of blank eyes.

Aidan gave a long, low whistle. 'There's so much in here. They must have tons more than they display.'

'Only 5 per cent of what the Louvre owns goes in the gallery,' said Vincenzo as they walked through the stacks. 'Sometimes they swap pieces around, or put on special exhibitions, but not often. Monsieur Homolle would like to expand, but the Louvre doesn't have the money. Visitor numbers have been dropping like a stone. There are other more modern attractions to claim the public's attention – like moving pictures.'

'What are moving pictures?' asked Luna.

Vincenzo looked at her oddly, as if suspecting a joke. 'Why, kinetoscope films shown at public exhibitions. Have you not seen Georges Méliès' *A Trip to the Moon*?'

Luna shook her head. 'Moving pictures – or movies – are films that come out of a projector. A modern miracle.' She thought that movies were a little like the professor.

The little group split up so they could search more effectively. They looked around for some time, without success. Vincenzo did find his leather portfolio, though, which he had used to bring the magic glass to the Louvre. 'Might be useful,' he said, picking it up. And Luna found Chronos, standing alone on a little plinth. She gathered him up fondly and kissed him on his little brass head. But as for the *Mona Lisa*, they could not see the painting – or, rather, the Countess del Carpio, for that was the disguise she wore – anywhere among the stacks.

'This is hopeless,' said Konstantin. 'She could be anywhere.'

'No,' said Houdini. 'We just need to think about this logically. She's probably right at the entrance where we came in. Think about it. The conservator who took the painting off the wall and brought it to the stores had bigger problems than worrying about where to keep the Goya. He would have been too preoccupied with finding the missing *Mona Lisa*. I bet he propped the Goya just inside the door and went to get help. We probably walked right past it before Vincenzo found the light switch.'

This seemed sensible, so they retraced their steps to the entrance. And there, right by the door, was the Goya, the gloomy countess staring palely from the frame under the electric light.

The little group gathered around the painting. But, as they watched, a strange transformation began to take place before their eyes. The grey background began to fade and erode and, through the disappearing paint, trees and a bridge began to emerge. The countess's pale features retreated like a ghost to reveal the golden flesh of the *Mona Lisa*; through the mourning gown peeped those enigmatic eyes; and the button boots were replaced by that secret smile.

Houdini swore in Hungarian. '*Átkozzot!* She's changing back.'

Aidan's blue eyes were wide. 'What do you mean, she's changing back?'

'I had no idea how stable the chemicals in the Sol Tinctura would be,' confessed Houdini. '*Mona Lisa* has now been in the dark for about twenty-four hours. Then we put the light on. She's reappearing.'

And then the worst happened. Voices and footsteps approached the door, and the doorknob began to turn.

'Quick,' hissed Houdini. 'Hide!'

With great presence of mind, Vincenzo clicked off the light and they all dived behind the nearest stack of paintings – and not a moment too soon. The door opened wide and two figures stood in the doorway. In the dark they were no more than silhouettes, framed against the light streaming in from outside, but their distinctive hats gave away their identity.

Gendarmes.

'What do we do?'

The policemen began to look at the paintings and artefacts near the door. In another moment they would see the *Mona Lisa*, transforming before their eyes. The time-thieves could only hope that it was too dark to see the magical painting. But their hope was in vain. One of the men pointed down at the painting, exclaiming in French, and they both dropped down to their knees to look. Luna shifted in agony and her skirts knocked a canvas. The frame teetered and fell, with a crash that sounded like a thunderclap.

The two gendarmes sprang to their feet.

'*Qui est la?*' barked the first one.

The second held his lamp high. 'Who's there?' he said in broken English.

No one breathed, and no one moved. But the two policemen began to pick their way through the canvases and artefacts towards their hiding place. They'd seen the *Mona Lisa* and they were about to find her kidnappers. Luna felt dreadful. She'd given them away.

Then she had an idea. Desperately she turned Chronos's key clockwise – forward in time. 'Dear Chronos,' she whispered. 'Show me the professor.'

Chronos's ruby eyes sparkled, his little brass beak opened, and the bluish-whitish hologram of Professor Edward Norton Lorenz, inventor of the Butterfly Effect, appeared in the room. As it was earlier in the day than when they had visited him before, he was clutching a cup of coffee and seemed to be wearing a dressing gown. 'Hey, folks,' he said genially. 'How you doin'?'

Of course, the time-thieves were hidden behind a stack of paintings, so the professor's otherworldly eyes fixed on the two gendarmes. The policemen jumped to their feet in alarm, the painting quite forgotten.

'I don't know these two. Hi, fellas. Ain't you gonna say hello?'

The terrified gendarmes stared and stared at the apparition, mouths agape.

'What's the matter, boys?' said the professor wryly. 'Cat got your tongues?'

That did it. The gendarmes turned on their heels and fled out of the stores, banging the door behind them and turning the key.

'Right, quick,' said Konstantin, as they all stood up and stretched. 'Chronos, shut off the hologram. Professor, we'll explain later.'

The professor raised his coffee cup as if to say 'cheers'.

'Okay, sport,' he said equably. Chronos snapped his brass beak shut and the hologram vanished.

'They'll have gone to get reinforcements, so we'd better be quick. We've got to get the *Mona Lisa* out of here.'

'That's all very well,' said Aidan. 'But how in the wide world do we do it?'

'Sometimes the simplest way is the easiest,' said Houdini. 'In magic we understand well that people only see what they are looking for. They won't be looking for a person carrying a painting today. Apart from our two gendarme friends, everyone thinks the *Mona Lisa* has already gone.'

'What are you saying?' asked Aidan.

'I'm saying,' said Houdini, 'that we should just walk out of the gallery with her. We carry the brass bird first, unboxed, holding it high. If anyone looks at anything, it will be at that, and we have written permission to take it. Vincenzo will follow in our wake, carrying the *Mona Lisa* in his leather portfolio.' He looked at the Italian almost apologetically. 'The smock you wear gives you the right to be carrying a painting. You're a glazier, so it should be you. Will you do it?'

Vincenzo hesitated for a moment, clearly afraid. But then he looked at the re-emerging face of the woman he loved, her eyes pleading with him, her smile reassuring. 'Yes,' he said. 'But let's make it easier on ourselves.' He fell to his knees as if he was about to propose, then turned the painting around and turned the metal clips that held the painting in the frame. It was the work of a moment to free the panel from its gilded surround. The Leonardo was now considerably smaller and slipped easily into Vincenzo's portfolio.

But there was another problem. The terrified gendarmes, who had obviously not read enough ghost stories when they were children to know that phantoms can pass through doors, had turned the key in the lock when they had fled the store, in an attempt to keep the professor's apparition inside. Vincenzo rattled the doorknob helplessly.

The conspirators were trapped.

22 AUGUST 1911
9.45 a.m.

'Great,' said Aidan. 'Now what?'

Houdini walked over to the door. 'Get out of zee way.' He put both his hands around the doorknob, but without actually touching it, just as a medium might cradle a crystal ball. His crinkly brown hair seemed to crackle with electricity and his strange, silvery eyes became even more mirrored. He moved his hands fluidly around the knob for perhaps a minute, then he turned to Vincenzo. 'Pull zee handle,' he said.

'I beg your pardon?'

'Take eet in your hants and pull.'

Vincenzo touched the handle and drew his hand back at once. 'Ouch – it's hot. What did you do to it?'

Houdini took a breath. 'Try eet now.'

Vincenzo reached for the handle again – and the doorknob came away in his hand, leaving a hole which daylight streamed through. The door itself swung open. 'I told you once before,' said Houdini, 'that no door is closed to me.' His voice had gone back to normal – the show was over.

'Right,' said Konstantin. 'Forward march. Luna – you're in the vanguard, holding Chronos. Vincenzo, you're in the rear guard with the portfolio. Let's go.'

Walking out of the Louvre with the painting was easier than they could have imagined. The place was chaos but, as Houdini had guessed, because the crime had taken place the day before no one was looking for a man carrying a painting. The girl with the red hair, wearing a pink dress and carrying a filigree brass bird on her wrist like queens of old would carry a hawk, attracted a fair amount of attention. But the glazier in his humble smock walking a little way behind was not noticed at all, and the little party were able to walk unhindered to the exit.

Then – disaster. The guards at the door held up their hands as Luna approached, and closed ranks. They were tall, broad men, built like strongmen at the fair, their dove-grey uniforms forming an impregnable wall, their gilt buttons glinting threateningly. Luna stopped, as did the boys and Houdini behind her. And, because no one else could leave at that point, Vincenzo, a little way behind them, stopped too.

'*Arrêt!*' barked the guards, and Luna didn't need to speak any French at all to know that meant 'stop'.

'*Qu'est-ce que c'est ça?*' said the first guard.

Luna looked at Konstantin in a panic. He gave a tiny shake of his head, which she took to mean that she should speak in English. 'I'm sorry,' she said politely. 'I don't understand.'

The second guard pointed at Chronos. 'What is this? And why are you taking it away?'

Houdini stepped forward. He was a good two foot smaller than the guards, but still gave off an air of authority. 'This is an automaton that I donated to the gallery last week. But after yesterday's... incident... I'm afraid I felt that the Louvre's security left a great deal to be desired.'

'Do you have permission to take it?' said the first guard.

'Yes,' said Houdini, taking out the permission slip given to him by Georges Benedite. 'Signed by the deputy director of the gallery himself.'

The second guard looked at the form, nodded, and then glanced at Chronos. 'What does it do?'

Luna turned Chronos's brass key anti-clockwise. 'Sing, Chronos, sing,' she urged.

Chronos's ruby eyes glittered and his beak opened. He sighed huffily, shifted his brass feet on Luna's wrist, then broke into song.

Alouette, gentille alouette
Alouette, je te plumerai

Je te plumerai la tête
Je te plumerai la tête
Et la tête, et la tête
Alouette, Alouette
Oh, oh, oh, oh

Alouette, gentille alouette
Alouette, je te plumerai

The two enormous burly guards melted like ice. 'My mother used to sing me that song,' said the first, clutching his heart.

'Mine too,' sniffed the second, who actually had tears in his eyes.

Luna looked up. A little crowd had gathered. Vincenzo Peruggia was lurking by the door with the portfolio. Luna caught his eye and moved her head in a tiny, almost imperceptible movement, towards the door.

'Our apologies, monsieur,' said the first guard, blowing his nose with a trumpeting sound on his pocket handkerchief. 'As you are obviously aware, we had a theft yesterday, so we must be vigilant.'

'I think if you boys had been on the door yesterday,' said Houdini warmly, 'the unfortunate incident would not have happened.'

The two guards stood a little straighter, clearly pleased with the compliment.

'I don't know about that, monsieur,' said the second guard modestly, as he waved Houdini and the time-thieves through. 'But we have been given orders to check everyone who leaves the gallery.'

But they weren't checking *everyone*. While all this was going on, with admirable nerve and absolutely unnoticed, Vincenzo Peruggia of Dumenza, Italy, walked right out of the Louvre with the *Mona Lisa*.

22 AUGUST 1911
10 a.m.

Halfway down the rue de Rivoli the others caught up with Vincenzo. He stopped and turned, shaking with relief. It was only then that the time-thieves realised that Vincenzo was still clutching the storeroom's doorknob.

'What shall I do with this?' Vincenzo asked.

'It's evidence,' said Houdini. 'Better chuck it.' So the Italian lobbed the doorknob over some nearby railings into an alley.

The conspirators hurried back to the Hotel du Louvre in silence. At the entrance Vincenzo reluctantly passed the portfolio to Aidan, who he correctly judged to be the strongest.

'Take good care of *La Gioconda*,' he said. 'Let me know when she's ready to go home.' Looking sad, he turned to go.

'Where do you think you're going?' said Houdini.

'I thought – I mean, I assumed…'

'You're one of us now,' said Houdini. 'Get in here.'

And Vincenzo Peruggia gratefully bounded up the steps and into the Hotel du Louvre.

Houdini called for lunch to be brought to the room. The *Mona Lisa* was such an important guest that no one wanted to leave her alone, but the time-thieves did have to hide her in the wardrobe before the hotel staff brought the lunch. 'A slightly undignified hiding place,' said Luna apologetically to the painted lady, 'but it's just for a moment.'

'That's a good point,' said Houdini as a knock sounded at the door. 'We must make sure that no members of staff come into this room in future.' The magician opened the door himself, received the heavy silver lunch tray from the waiter, then closed the door firmly behind him. Partly because he was feeling so triumphant, partly because the tall, pleasant fellow had obviously had some misfortune in his life (for he had a patch covering one eye), Houdini tipped the waiter generously.

A green bottle of something fizzy had come with their lunch, and Houdini opened it with an enormous pop. 'After all, we're in France,' he said. 'And we are celebrating. I thought champagne fitted the occasion.'

The time-thieves took a sip each but none of them cared for champagne much – it was incredibly fizzy and quite sour – so it was up to Vincenzo and Houdini to toast their success. The magician was cock-a-hoop. 'Let us drink to the anonymous conservator who performed the biggest art heist in history,' he crowed. 'The poor man who took the *Mona Lisa* from the wall of the Salon Carré and placed her in the stores knew not what he did. We did not even have to raise a finger. And there is nothing to connect any of us to the painting.'

'Well,' said Vincenzo. 'Apart from me.'

Konstantin said, 'Were you seen putting the magic glass on the painting?'

'No,' said the Italian. 'We do the majority of our work before the gallery opens, and I was alone in the Salon Carré. Besides, I have no friends at the company. No one knows what I'm doing or what I'm not doing. And the glaziers don't know the names of the paintings – they have numbers and are just jobs to us. No one would know the *Mona Lisa* anyway – she has no significance to anyone but me. She is such an obscure work of art.'

'Good. So there's nothing to connect you to the painting?' asked Houdini.

'Well, if the police cared enough to contact the company,' Vincenzo replied, 'they could, I suppose, find out which craftsman worked on which painting.'

'I think they are more concerned with finding the *Mona Lisa*,' said Konstantin. 'Live your life normally, go to work as usual, and my guess is that you'll be all right.'

'From your mouth to God's ear,' said Aidan, crossing himself.

Once lunch was over and Vincenzo had made his rather tipsy way back to the gallery, Houdini was back to business. 'Right,' he said. 'Time to get to work. Now we have the *Mona Lisa*, we need to extract the secrets she holds.'

The time-thieves had been so excited by the heist that they had almost forgotten their principal mission – the treasure hunt.

'The *Mona Lisa* was never the endpoint,' Houdini reminded them. 'She is a minor work at best. The real prize is Leonardo's greatest painting – the *Salvator Mundi*. And we are no nearer to finding that.' He retrieved the *Mona Lisa* from the wardrobe. 'Time to find out what she's smiling about.'

For the rest of that day, and for many days to come, the time-thieves and Houdini examined the *Mona Lisa*. They set her upon a makeshift easel, constructed from a laundry rack, right by the big window of the suite, which had doors leading to a wrought iron balcony, because this was where the light was best. Houdini went down to reception and shook a stream of golden sovereigns into the concierge's hand in return for a promise that no maid would service the Presidential Suite.

'You may clean my children's rooms, by all means,' said the magician, 'but I am a man of peculiar tastes. I have arranged my things just so, and do not wish them to be disturbed. And if we require food or other services to that room, I wish them to be left outside the door.'

The concierge nodded discreetly. 'Of course, monsieur. I will see to it that no member of staff enters the room until after you have checked out.'

Back in the suite the time-thieves spent hours scrutinising every inch of the *Mona Lisa*, until they knew her image better than they knew their own faces, desperately seeking the tiniest clue as to the whereabouts of the *Salvator Mundi*.

And long after they were exhausted, and long after they gave up, still she smiled, as if taunting them that she would not give up her secrets so easily.

In the meantime, in the outside world the *Mona Lisa*'s image was becoming more and more famous by the day. Houdini ordered every major newspaper to be brought to the suite every morning so that he and the time-thieves could pore over them for news of the robbery. The papers seized on the story, and conspiracy theories about the theft filled column inches. The painting had been stolen by famed artist Pablo Picasso. It had been taken by notorious art criminal Adam Worth. It had been stolen to order for wealthy American art collector J. P. Morgan, who had made six copies for his various houses. It was hanging on the walls of the Russian Tsar's palace in St Petersburg.

Considering that the *Mona Lisa* was in their very own suite, these crazy theories gave the time-thieves some light relief, and they laughed until their sides ached. They had to conclude that Houdini had been right to hide out at the hotel. 'The one place Le Pine won't look,' the magician said, 'is right under his nose.'

But the press coverage was not always accurate. The *Washington Post* actually published the wrong picture beside the story of the stolen painting. It was a da Vinci, but an entirely different one – a woman with bare arms and flowing hair. Many of the smaller papers, assuming that the *Washington Post* had done its research, copied them.

'Just shows how little known the actual *Mona Lisa* is,' said Aidan.

But all that was about to change. After this major embarrassment for the world's press, the *Mona Lisa*'s true image was in every newspaper, in every nation, every day.

Aidan, whose turn it was to go out and buy long loaves of bread and squashy, smelly cheese, came back instead with a sheaf of flyers. 'Look at these,' he said, tipping them on to the table. There was the *Mona Lisa*'s face, over and over again, smiling out of the flyer. 'They're on every wall, door and lamppost.'

Luna, Konstantin and Houdini gazed at the multiple copies of the *Mona Lisa*'s face spilling over the coffee table and the carpet. The real thing, the *Mona Lisa* herself, stared at them from the easel in the middle of the room, smiling at the spectacle.

Houdini was less amused. 'They're redoubling their efforts to find her,' he said. 'We have to be very careful. This is clearly not just a humiliation for Chief Inspector Le Pine; this is a *national* humiliation.'

'How d'you mean?' asked Aidan.

'Think of it. The Louvre is the centre of Western art, and they have lost a painting. The painting they lost was somewhat obscure. But with each passing day the *Mona Lisa* becomes more and more significant, and thus more and more valuable. If she is not found, that shame belongs to France. We'd better find out what she has to tell us, and fast.'

'Let's go back to the basics,' said Konstantin, as they all sat down in front of the picture for the hundredth time. 'It's a picture of a woman.'

'Half a woman,' joked Houdini. 'She might have been the victim of one of my magic tricks.'

'She has brown eyes, brown hair and sort of sallow, yellowish skin,' added Konstantin.

'Don't let Vincenzo hear you say that.' Aidan grinned. 'He thinks she's one of God's angels.'

'She's wearing a greenish-brown overdress over a sort of old-gold frock,' said Luna. 'The sleeves are quite a different colour. And she's wearing a veil – see, you can just see the outline of it, but it's so thin as to be hardly visible. It almost looks like part of her hair.'

'Good,' said Houdini. 'What else?

'And she has her hands crossed,' said Konstantin. 'Left... no, *right* hand above.'

'Two eyes, two ears, one nose, one mouth,' teased Aidan.

'Actually,' said Houdini, pointing at Aidan as if he was picking him out of an audience, 'that's not a bad notion.

Numbers. Maps have numbers, co-ordinates and such. What numbers can we see?'

'Well,' said Luna, 'you can see eight fingers.'

'And one thumb,' added Konstantin.

'And four fingernails,' said Luna. 'The others are hidden.'

'So we have 2, 2, 1, 1, 8, 1, 4,' said Houdini, scribbling the numbers down in one of the sketchbooks they'd bought. He looked at the numbers from all angles, shrugged and threw the book on the coffee table, sending the flyers of the *Mona Lisa*'s face fluttering like butterflies. 'Meaningless. This dame is telling us nothing.'

Something tugged at Luna's memory – a word, a phrase, just out of reach. 'Maybe it's not about numbers, but letters,' she said. 'We need to go back to the poem.'

'What poem?' asked Konstantin.

'You know, the one Leonardo wrote about the *Salvator Mundi*. William Holman Hunt quoted it at the Butterfly Club. It's in the *Codex*.'

Konstantin took Leonardo's sketchbook from the safe, and found the page with the mirror writing poem on it. He held it in front of the mirror over the bureau, but after some moments shook his head. 'It's no good,' he said. 'My Italian is not great at the best of times, but what with Leonardo's handwriting and the fact that it's backwards, this has beaten me. Can anyone remember it?'

Aidan couldn't read, and he was usually good at remembering things he'd been told for that reason. But he shook his head too. 'Something about her eyes and her smile. But I can't remember the details.'

'Nor I,' said Luna. 'I think we were all so caught up with the idea of going on another Butterfly Mission, we didn't really concentrate. Was there something about "behind her back"?'

'There's a landscape in the background,' said Konstantin excitedly. 'With a winding river on the left and an arched bridge on the right. The right fork of the river looks like it's almost dried up. And there are kind of craggy hills or mountains in a misty blue.'

'It's somewhere in Western Europe, I reckon,' said Aidan, who had travelled the most. 'If you look at the trees and the terrain. Looks like France, Germany…'

'Italy!' said Konstantin, slapping his hands on his thighs. 'Where else?'

'Yes, of course!' said Luna. 'Home of Leonardo! Oh, well *done*, Konstantin.'

'Yes, grand,' said Aidan sarcastically. 'We're really cracking on here. The *Salvator Mundi* is *somewhere in Italy*. Should be easy to find.'

Konstantin ignored his tone. 'Hold on,' he said. 'Vincenzo said he was from Vinci, near Florence. That's what Leonardo *da* Vinci means – *from* Vinci. Maybe this is a picture of Vinci.'

'Perhaps,' said Houdini cautiously. 'But isn't it more likely to be where the *model* was from? I mean, otherwise, why her? What connects *La Gioconda* to the *Salvator Mundi*?'

'We could just ask the person who knows her best,' suggested Luna.

'Leonardo?' scoffed Aidan. 'That might be difficult, Duch. He's been pushing up daisies for three hundred years.'

'*After* him, clever clogs,' said Luna, rolling her eyes. 'I meant the other Italian of our acquaintance. Vincenzo.'

25 AUGUST 1911
5.30 p.m.

Vincenzo Peruggia came over most days after work. He enjoyed the company of Houdini and the time-thieves – they were his only friends in Paris and the only people who called him by his name instead of calling him 'dirty macaroni'. But he spent most of his time gazing at the *Mona Lisa* – not in the way they all did, trying to find out her secrets, but in an adoring, uncritical way. Konstantin, having formed the idea that Vincenzo was in love with *La Gioconda*, couldn't shake the theory. The Italian had visited her every day when she hung in the Louvre, and now she was in the Hotel du Louvre – well, he just carried on their strange, one-sided courtship. He talked about her constantly, just like someone talks about a person they love. It was Vincenzo who reminded them that *Mona Lisa*'s eyes followed you round the room, and the time-thieves spent a good few moments leaping about, trying to avoid her gaze, but it was perfectly true. He told them again that if you looked at the *Mona Lisa*'s smile it disappeared, and that was perfectly true too.

'It is a kind of magic,' said Houdini, the greatest compliment he could give. They all began to have a grudging respect for the painting, and the painter.

After the carpet-picnic that served as an evening meal, Luna turned to Vincenzo. 'What do you know about *La Gioconda*?' she asked. 'Who was the model for the *Mona Lisa*?'

Vincenzo gazed longingly at the portrait. 'Her name was Lisa Gherardini,' he said in a longing whisper. 'She was born in Florence, Italy, to an old aristocratic family.'

Houdini glanced at the time-thieves in turn. Luna felt very strongly that he was trying to remind them not to tell Vincenzo about the *Salvator Mundi*. Then, very casually, the magician asked, 'And are any *places* in particular associated with *La Gioconda*?'

Vincenzo furrowed his brow. 'Just Florence, really. She was born there and lived there all her life.'

'Always in the city?' asked Houdini, and Vincenzo gave a nod.

'How about… the countryside?'

'The Gherardini family owned a country house in San Donato in the Chianti region, about fifteen miles south of the city.'

The time-thieves exchanged glances. Could the *Salvator Mundi* be hidden in the Chianti countryside?

'I suppose it's very mountainous there?' said Konstantin casually. 'Lots of crags and trees?'

'Maybe a winding river?' put in Luna.

'And an arched bridge?' added Aidan, earning himself a stern look from Houdini.

But Vincenzo, still lost in *Mona Lisa*'s eyes, didn't seem to notice that the time-thieves were describing the background to her portrait. 'No,' he said. 'Chianti is all rolling hills and vineyards. Not as you describe at all.'

They seemed to be getting nowhere, so Luna made a decision. She couldn't check with the others, but she knew they had to trust Vincenzo to move forward in their quest. She rose and fetched the *Codex Arundel* from the safe, and laid it in Vincenzo's hands.

Vincenzo knew what it was at once. His eyes widened so that you could see the whites all the way around his soft brown pupils. 'Where did you get this?'

'We can't tell you. But if you help us translate *this* poem,' she turned to the right page, 'we will be able to give you the *Mona Lisa* much more quickly.'

Vincenzo clearly knew Leonardo better than they did. He knew at once that the poem was in mirror writing, and carried the book to the looking glass over the bureau. He peered at the writing and began to read. Konstantin, grabbing a pencil and a sketchpad, wrote the translation down.

The saviour of the world is in her smile,

The saviour of the world is in her eyes,

The saviour of the world is behind her back.

If you would find what you now lack,

The answer lies in just one dame

The Mona Lisa is her name.

Vincenzo turned to them. 'What does it mean?'

Luna looked at the other time-thieves and Houdini. Vincenzo clearly hadn't made the connection between the poem and Leonardo's hidden masterpiece, the *Salvator Mundi*, so her gamble had paid off. 'We're not sure,' she said, with perfect truthfulness. 'But we thank you.'

The time-thieves changed the subject and for the rest of the meal they discussed other matters. Vincenzo, as their man inside the Louvre, was able to tell them how the police investigation was going. 'Le Pine is clueless,' he said.

'*Not* a greater detective than Sherlock Holmes then?' asked Aidan.

Vincenzo laughed. 'Hardly. He strides up and down like a pair of shears, trying to look important, but in reality he is baffled. They are even more puzzled by the fact that the *real* Countess del Carpio – the Goya you copied – was hanging in another part of the gallery the whole time. Le Pine's detectives are everywhere – he's brought in sixty of them, but they're all running around like headless chickens, with absolutely no leads. The word is that the bosses of the Paris police are bringing someone in from London over Le Pine's head. A specialist from Scotland Yard, who arrives tomorrow.'

'Hmm,' said Houdini. 'Then I think we'll pay a visit to the Louvre tomorrow too.'

26 AUGUST 1911
10 a.m.

When the time-thieves and Houdini reached the Louvre in the morning, the street was transformed. The rue de Rivoli was packed with people, and the queue to enter the gallery snaked around the block. When they eventually reached the entrance the entire frontage of the museum was completely obscured by bunches of flowers. People had clearly been leaving tributes to the missing *Mona Lisa*. Aidan pushed his cap back and scratched his head. 'It's like someone has died,' he said, perplexed.

When they'd been doing their reconnaissance the time-thieves had always walked right in to the Louvre, and, more often than not, had been alone in the Salon Carré. This time, when they reached the inner gallery, they were obliged to squash in like so many sardines.

'More people have come to see the space where she hung than came to see the *Mona Lisa* herself,' marvelled Luna.

Houdini went to find Vincenzo, who was on the edge of the crowd, staring at the blank space with the rest. And as they watched, the space was filled by a tall, impressive-looking figure. The figure, who was facing the wall, wore a checked cape and a deerstalker hat, and brandished a magnifying glass. This, then, must be the great detective who had been brought over from Scotland Yard to take over from the hapless Le Pine. The people in the crowd were muttering 'Monsieur Sherlock Holmes! Monsieur Sherlock Holmes!'

'Do you think they realise that Sherlock Holmes is a fictional character?' whispered Luna.

'This one looks like a music-hall Sherlock Holmes,' said Aidan.

'Yes,' said Konstantin. 'The parody of a detective – what people who don't really know *think* a detective looks like.'

'I can't wait until he turns round.' Luna giggled, sure that this imposter from Scotland Yard would be a figure of fun.

But when the gentleman straightened up and turned round, the smiles were wiped from their faces. For from under the deerstalker stared a single eye, while the other one had been replaced by a watch.

Luna's stomach flipped over. 'Oh no,' she groaned.

'*Arthur John Priest,*' breathed Konstantin.

'I was wondering when he was going to show up,' said Aidan grimly.

Houdini came over to them, with Vincenzo in tow. 'What's all the whispering about? Is that the Scotland Yard man?'

'Yes,' said Luna. 'And no. That's actually Arthur John Priest. Time traveller, member of the Butterfly Club, and agent of chaos.'

Houdini looked at Arthur John Priest, a curious expression in his strange silvery eyes. 'He looks just like the waiter at the hotel.'

'Then he probably is,' said Aidan.

'Ought we to say hello?' asked Houdini mischievously.

'Absolutely *not*,' said Konstantin. 'We need to avoid him at all costs. He's poison.'

'Never mind what he *is*,' said Houdini. 'What's he *doing*?'

'What he's always doing,' said Aidan. 'Causing mayhem and trying to mess things up for us. I'll bet you a shilling to a hayseed that he's after the *Salvator Mundi* too.'

'No, I mean, what's he showing everyone? It looks like he's performing a trick.'

It did indeed. Arthur John Priest, with the enormous crowd around him, was still occupying the empty space that had once held the *Mona Lisa*. The four iron pegs that had held the painting were sticking out, uselessly, from the wall. Their old enemy was flanked by four peelers – police officers from London, in their familiar blue cloth uniforms with gilded buttons. By Priest's feet lay the gilded frame that Vincenzo had left in the storeroom.

'Jesus, Mary and Joseph,' exclaimed Aidan. 'They've found the frame.'

'Don't worry,' said Konstantin. 'What can it tell them? It's an inanimate object.'

Then their old enemy stepped forward to address the crowd. 'On Monday 21st August,' he began, 'in this year of 1911, a painting by Leonardo da Vinci, known as the *Mona Lisa*, was stolen from this very wall.' He pointed to the space and the four iron pegs. 'She was taken to the gallery's stores, where she was extracted from this frame.' He pointed to the gilded frame by his feet. 'The French police are baffled. A week has passed, and they are no nearer to recovering the painting.'

Luna saw Chief Inspector Le Pine on the edge of the crowd, his face like thunder. He obviously didn't enjoy being humiliated in public.

'But *somebody* knows where she is,' said Arthur John Priest, pointing at the crowd who watched him. 'Someone, perhaps, who is here today.' The pointing finger pointed skyward, turning itself into a number. 'Lesson one – the criminal *always* returns to the scene of the crime. He cannot resist the pull. He is part-egotist, part-daredevil. He is compelled to see how the investigation is going. That is his first mistake.'

The time-thieves, Houdini and Vincenzo looked at each other uncomfortably. They were the ones responsible for the theft and, sure enough, they had returned to the scene of the crime.

A second finger joined the first. 'Lesson two. Even when *people* keep their secrets, *objects* want to speak out. This frame, empty as it is, can tell us valuable things. And I am blessed with the ability to hear what it wants to say. My name is Henry Faulds from Scotland Yard.'

'Oh, so *that's* who he's pretending to be this time,' scoffed Konstantin in an undertone.

'Gosh he must just about lose track of his professions.' Luna giggled. 'Remember how he pretended to be an archaeologist in Egypt?'

'Arthur Cruttenden Mace,' Aidan grinned. 'And now he's a detective.'

'Shhh,' said Konstantin, batting away the compliment. 'I want to hear.'

Arthur John Priest, as Henry Faulds, spread his fingers as if he was a conjuror, showing that they were empty.

'I have nothing in my hands, correct?'

Some of the crowd nodded.

'Wrong. Each of your fingers, and your thumb, has a print – a series of marks on the pad of each digit. Now, the crucial thing to note is that *your fingerprints are entirely unique*. Not even identical twins have the same fingerprints. And your prints remain the same from birth until death.' He unrolled a poster from a tube and stuck it up where the *Mona Lisa* had once hung. The crowd pressed closer.

'There are broadly three types of fingerprint,' said Henry Faulds, pointing at his diagram. 'Featuring arches, loops and whorls. Arches are by far the rarest type, occurring in only 5 per cent of people. You might want to look at your own fingertips.'

Arches   Loops   Whorls

The time-thieves, along with the rest of the crowd, began to peruse the tips of their fingers, making out the tell-tale lines and loops that were etched into their flesh.

'For those of us in law enforcement,' Arthur John Priest went on, 'these prints have a crucial function. They leave their impression on everything we touch. Which means that the fingerprints of the person who stole the *Mona Lisa* are *on this frame.*'

The time-thieves turned as one to look at Vincenzo. His face was as white as his smock.

'Now – watch,' said Arthur John Priest. He held up a gadget with a little rubber bulb, like a tiny car horn. 'This,' he said, 'is an insufflator. It blows small amounts of powder on to the fingerprints. The prints are left by the natural oils in our skin. And the powder – in this case made of rosin, black ferric oxide and lampblack – sticks to the print and makes it visible.'

He bent and pointed the insufflator at the bright gilt frame, and squeezed it several times. The powder huffed out in a small inky cloud, and settled on the frame. Then 'Henry Faulds' took out a small soft brush, much like a gentleman's shaving brush, and swept away the excess powder.

What was left was as clear as a little bruise on the golden frame. A thumbprint.

'Lovely,' said Arthur John Priest with satisfaction. 'A thumbprint, clear as day. What we have found here,' he said, 'is known as a latent print. This is a print left on an object or surface. What we need in order for this to mean anything is an exemplar print. These are the prints we take from members of the public, or the criminal fraternity. Now, I am sure there are no members of the criminal fraternity present, but we do have you lovely members of the public. But since you are such clean and tidy ladies and gentlemen, let us select someone for our experiment who is better used to getting his hands dirty. A craftsman, perhaps. Yes, you.'

His finger pointed straight at Vincenzo Peruggia.

26 AUGUST 1911
10.10 a.m.

If possible, Vincenzo went even whiter. He looked about him and pointed at his chest. 'Me?'

'Yes. Would you assist me for a moment, my good sir?'

Slowly and reluctantly, Vincenzo walked forward to the front of the crowd and joined 'Henry Faulds'.

'What we are about to do here is take a set of what we call exemplar prints. One of my officers will assist me.'

One of the blue-clad officers came forward with a block of creamy paper, and the other with a pad of something spongy and black.

'Now, our friend must dabble his fingers one by one in the ink and apply them to this paper. Like so.' He helped Vincenzo place his fingerprints on the creamy card, with a curious rolling action. 'We collect the prints by rolling the fingertips from one side of the nail to the other, so that we collect a complete print. We then ask the subject to touch his finger to the paper, which we call a slap print.'

Arthur John Priest made Vincenzo repeat the process ten times, for each finger and thumb. Then he held up the card for his audience to see. 'A complete set of exemplar prints from our willing volunteer. Thank you, sir.' Then he pulled a lens of bright glass from his pocket. 'This is a very powerful little tool called a magnifying glass. The lens produces a magnified image of an object, at a resolution that cannot be seen by the naked eye.' He peered at the prints closely, with the assistance of the bright glass. The time-thieves forgot to breathe. At length the 'detective' stepped back. 'Well, this is extraordinary!' he exclaimed. 'In the normal course of things we would have to examine hundreds, sometimes thousands, of latent prints before we find a match. But on this occasion, we have hit the jackpot on our first go. Might I ask your name, sir?'

Vincenzo looked at the officers, at his inky fingers, and back at 'Henry Faulds'.

'My name is Vincenzo Peruggia.'

'Well, Monsieur Peruggia, I must tell you that your right thumbprint is a perfect match for the one on the frame of the *Mona Lisa*. Would you care to explain yourself?'

For a moment Vincenzo looked frozen with dread. None of the time-thieves dared move. Then the Italian's mouth curled into a shaky smile. He shrugged. 'But of course. I am a glazier and I work here. I put the glass on the *Mona Lisa*. Naturally my prints will be on the frame. I would be surprised if they were not.'

His brown eyes looked wide and innocent, and they held, unwaveringly, the gaze of the single eye of Arthur John Priest.

The single eye blinked first. 'Of course,' said Inspector Faulds. 'My task here is to eliminate the prints that are on the frame legitimately, and then the prints that are left will be those of the thief. Thank you for your assistance.'

The time-thieves breathed again, and the gathered ladies and gentlemen gave Vincenzo a polite ripple of applause, unaware that they were clapping for the *Mona Lisa*'s thief. The Italian, who looked as if he had escaped the hangman's noose, scuttled over to the time-thieves.

'What do I do now?' he pleaded, his eyes wide and terrified. He placed his filthy hands together as if in prayer. 'They have my fingerprints.'

Houdini spoke through clenched teeth. 'Keep calm, my friend. You made your case well – your prints had every right to be on that frame. Go and wash your hands, and continue your life as normal. And for the moment it is better that you do not come to the hotel. There can be nothing to connect you with us.'

Vincenzo looked bereft; even his moustaches drooped.

'It is only for a short time, for your own safety. We will contact you soon,' promised Houdini.

Henry Faulds began to thread his way through the crowd towards them. 'Quick, go,' urged the magician. 'We cannot be seen together.'

For a second Vincenzo clung, panicked and undecided.

Then Konstantin said, 'The *Mona Lisa* is depending on you.'

That did it. Vincenzo melted into the crowd, which had begun to disperse. But before the time-thieves could escape, Arthur John Priest was somehow by their side. 'Ah, my old friends,' he said. 'It's always nice to meet people you know when you're travelling abroad, don't you think?'

He smiled widely, showing his tobacco-yellowed teeth. 'I spotted you, Miss Luna, right away. I notice you had changed your clothes, but if you wish to remain unseen, I would wear a hat over that distinctive hair.' He touched one of her curls in a way that turned Luna's stomach. She jumped away from his hand as he turned to Aidan. 'And my friend "Aidan".' He gave the name a cruel emphasis. 'Even without *his* cogs and chains, I would know *him* anywhere.'

Houdini turned wide eyes on Aidan, taken, for once, by surprise.

'And Konstantin,' Arthur John Priest went on, 'the tin soldier with the clockwork heart. Still keeping time, is it? Tick-tock, I hope it doesn't stop,' he rhymed. He tapped his own watchglass eye. Its hands were resolutely halted at 4.45.

'And you've been forming new acquaintances, I see. Mr Houdini, isn't it?'

Luna looked at him sharply. No one else from the future seemed to know who the magician was yet. So how did Arthur John Priest know him when he hadn't been at the last Butterfly Club meeting?

Luna was rather surprised when Houdini shook their old enemy's hand, smiling pleasantly. 'Delighted to make your acquaintance, sir.'

Aidan noticed that the magician's silver eyes were shining brightly, as they did whenever he was performing. Houdini was up to something.

'I hope you enjoyed my own little performance, Mr Houdini.'

'Oh, I certainly got something very valuable from it,' said Houdini.

'Who are you working for this time?' asked Aidan bluntly. 'I'll bet a penny to a pea it's not Scotland Yard. Is it Germany again, or some other rogue nation? No offence, Konstantin.'

'None taken,' replied his friend.

Arthur John Priest laid his hand on his heart. 'I'm shocked – *shocked*, I tell you – that someone who knows me so well could think so little of me. I am working on behalf of Monsieur Theophile Homolle himself.'

'The director of the museum?' said Luna. 'He's back from his holidays, is he?'

'He is,' replied Arthur John Priest, 'and he would very much like his property back.'

There was an awkward silence. Houdini jumped into it. 'Well, we wish you good luck in your endeavours. And now I'm afraid we must leave you. I expect we will meet again.'

'Oh, I'm sure of it,' said Arthur John Priest, bowing politely.

For some reason Houdini seemed in a hurry to return to the hotel. As they walked down the rue de Rivoli, Aidan fell into step with him. 'I suppose... I suppose I ought to explain. About... why that man said my name in that way.'

'No need,' Houdini said. 'I've never met a person yet who is exactly what they seem. I once told you to expect everything you see to be a trick. And the greatest trick, of course, is to find out who you are, and be that. You are Aidan, and I am Houdini.'

'No,' said Aidan, touched. 'You are the *Great* Houdini, and you always will be.'

'Well, I hope the morning improves,' said Konstantin when they got safely back to their suite. 'Arthur John Priest is now in the mix, and he's got hold of Vincenzo's fingerprints.' He flung himself down in a chair. 'It feels like we just took a giant step backwards.'

'On the contrary,' said Houdini. 'We have gained one thing today.' He produced the Sherlock Holmes magnifying glass, and the lens winked in the morning sun. 'I relieved your adversary of this when I shook his hand.'

Aidan grinned delightedly. 'I *thought* you were up to something, as soon as you got out your Hungarian accent.'

Houdini winked. 'And I think this humble lens might just be the key to the mystery of the *Mona Lisa*. We learned today the value of close scrutiny – things that remain unseen until you peruse the detail.' He waved the magnifying glass at the smiling lady, who was gazing calmly at them from her frame. 'We've looked and looked at this painting from a distance. Now we have to look more closely.'

26 AUGUST 1911
11 a.m.

Houdini locked the door of the suite.

The *Mona Lisa* sat on the easel by the large glass doors leading to the balcony. The summer sunlight flooded in, illuminating every brushstroke of the picture. But there were still secrets to be discovered. The time-thieves crowded round.

'Your ancient enemy reminded me that a magnifying glass can help you see things that are not visible to the naked eye,' said Houdini. 'I think that's what we need.'

For the next few hours, the time-thieves and Houdini scrutinised every inch of the picture once again, but this time with the aid of the magnifying glass. Outside the sun moved from east to west, with the Eiffel Tower on the horizon acting like the pointer of a sundial, marking time that they didn't have. With the arrival of Henry Faulds – or rather, Arthur John Priest – and his threat to find the fingerprints of the guilty, the net was closing.

Because there was only one magnifying glass, the time-thieves took it in turns to look, for an hour at a time, while the others rested and ate. Houdini, when it wasn't his turn, dozed on the sofa, his pocket handkerchief over his eyes. And at some point that afternoon, a strange alchemy occurred. The time-thieves and Houdini began to love the painting. *Mona Lisa* was no longer a muddy dame hanging in the dark corner of a grand gallery. She was a miracle of a thousand brushstrokes, making up the most fascinating and secretive woman any of them had ever seen. By the evening they were all, if not as smitten as Vincenzo, a little in love.

But the sun was beginning to lower, and they hadn't found anything, even with the help of the magnifying glass.

'Let's go right back to the beginning,' said Konstantin, stretching his aching limbs. 'I'll get my sketchbook. We need to read that riddle again.' He retrieved the sketchbook where he'd scribbled down Vincenzo's translation of the *Codex* riddle, and read the thing aloud.

The saviour of the world is in her smile,

The saviour of the world is in her eyes,

The saviour of the world is behind her back.

If you would find what you now lack,

The answer lies in just one dame

The Mona Lisa is her name.

'Well, there's our answer,' said Aidan.

'How d'you mean?' asked Luna.

'Well,' Aidan replied, 'there's no point fiddling about with any other bits of the picture but the ones that are mentioned in the riddle. Smile, eyes, behind her back. Done.'

'Most of the picture is behind her back,' grumbled Konstantin. 'But all right. Let's give it a go.'

The *Mona Lisa*'s smile, as they might have expected, told them absolutely nothing. Everyone had a good look with the magnifying glass, but the secretive expression had no hidden marks or special runes.

The eyes, however, were a different matter. Luna, for it was her turn, peered deep into the left eye with the magnifying glass. The fact that the sun was setting actually helped – the light was less glaring, and she was able to see the tiny marks which resolved in front of her keen eyes.

'There's something here,' she said. 'I can just make it out. It's an I – no, an L, and a V.'

'Let's have a look.' Aidan practically shoved her out of the way, and even Konstantin, in his more polite manner, jostled for position. Even an exhausted Houdini rose from the couch and came to look. 'Oh *yes!*'

The letters were tiny. 'The brush he used must have been no wider than a single hair,' said Houdini.

'LV,' said Konstantin. 'What does it mean?'

'Roman numerals!' exclaimed Luna, struck by inspiration. 'Just like the ones on a clock. So what would that mean… L is fifty, isn't it, and V is five. Fifty-five!' She was flushed with triumph, thinking herself very clever. But her victory was short-lived.

'Is it not more likely,' said Houdini gently, 'that those are just initials?'

'Ah yes,' said Luna, feeling a bit squashed. 'Of course. **L**eonardo da **V**inci.'

'Grand,' said Aidan, throwing up his hands. 'It's a signature. Probably just Leonardo's little joke. He's just messing with us.'

'I've seen an L and a V like that before,' said Konstantin, looking again.

'We've all seen an L and a V before,' scoffed Luna.

'No, I mean just like that,' said Konstantin. 'LV. Like they are almost joined. I just can't think where.'

'Well, whether they are initials – which seems likely – or not,' said Houdini, 'if we've found some letters, there may be more.'

'Worth a try,' said Aidan, snatching the magnifying glass from Konstantin's hand. 'Bagsy I do the other eye.' He peered into the *Mona Lisa*'s right eye as closely as an apothecary. 'There's something here too,' he said, his voice taut with excitement. 'It looks like – half a butterfly.'

'You're joking,' said Luna. Now it was her turn to shove Aidan out of the way. 'He's right. It's a letter B.'

They all crowded round to look, and there, tiny but quite distinct, was a letter B in the highlight of the pupil.

'My go.' Konstantin took the magnifying glass. 'We've done the smile and the eyes, just as the riddle told us. Now for behind her back.'

Of course Konstantin's task took the longest of all, and he wasn't helped by the dying light as the sun set outside. All the others followed Houdini's example and had a catnap, curled up on the overstuffed chairs and sofas of the suite.

But the shout Konstantin let out when he found what he was looking for would have wakened the dead. In a trice they were all crowding round the picture.

'What?' said Aidan, speaking for everyone. 'What d'ye find?'

'Look,' said Konstantin. 'Here, under the second arch of the bridge.'

'I can't make it out,' said Houdini, taking over the magnifying glass. 'Is it more letters?'

'No,' said Konstantin. '*Numbers.*'

Luna had a try. 'Looks like a 7… and a… a 2.'

'72,' said Aidan. 'Clear as mud. Anything else?'

'Isn't that enough?' said Konstantin, sounding exhausted. Then he answered the question. 'No. There's nothing else hidden in that picture. I'd stake my life on it.'

'I hope there's no need to go that far,' said Houdini. 'Let's collate all our findings.' He grabbed Konstantin's sketchbook, found a blank page and scribbled a diagram. He drew the two eyes of the *Mona Lisa* and put LV in the left and B in the right. Then he drew the bridge with the four little arches, and under the furthermost arch to the right he wrote the number 72. 'Well, writing them down is the easy bit. Now we have to work out what they mean.'

'All right,' said Konstantin, who suddenly didn't feel tired at all. 'A B on its own doesn't mean much. The number, we are pretty sure, is a number. But the initials are definitely Leonardo's initials. Just like on the...' He stopped. 'On the *Codex Arundel*.'

'Are you all right?' Aidan waved his hand in front of his friend's face. Konstantin's grey eyes had gone glassy-looking.

'He's having a funny turn.'

'No,' said Konstantin, holding up his forefinger. 'No. It's the *sketchbook*.'

'What's the sketchbook?' said Houdini, holding up the book he'd been scribbling in.

'No, not that one. Leonardo's sketchbook.' Konstantin unlocked the safe and grabbed the priceless volume. 'We call the sketchbook the *Codex Arundel* because it was found in a castle in Arundel. But that wasn't what Leonardo called it. He had a different name for it... Not even a word... more... *two letters*.'

He turned Leonardo's sketchbook round to face them. There were only two letters on the front.

'LV!' his audience chorused.

'That's right,' said Konstantin, his pale cheeks flushing. 'His initials. I knew I'd seen them written down like that before, like they were almost joined. I'd seen them *here*. On the front of Leonardo's *own sketchbook*.'

'Quick. Let's flip through it,' urged Aidan.

'No,' said Luna forcefully. 'Page 72.'

'Of course!' They were silenced by this inescapable logic. Konstantin, with shaking hands, leafed through the numbered pages. When he reached page 72 he stopped. On the page was an exquisite drawing of a landscape – and not just any landscape. It was the exact landscape,

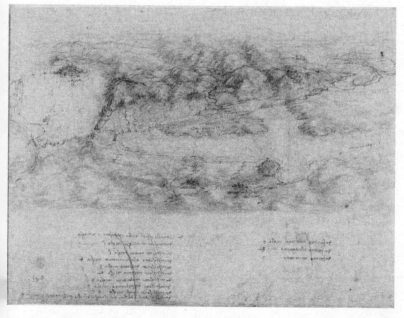

down to the last detail, that was behind the *Mona Lisa*'s back.

There, exquisitely sketched in centuries-old sepia ink, were the sharp, craggy mountains. The trees, in full spring leaf. The winding river, emptying into a lake, and over the almost dry fork in the river, a bridge with four arches.

'We're such dunderheads,' exclaimed Aidan. 'I can't believe we didn't see this before.'

'To be fair, we only really leafed through it at the start, and since then it's been in the safe,' said Luna. 'I liked all the drawings of people, but I probably just blew past this. I'm not really one for landscapes.'

'Yes,' mused Houdini. 'This is a quite different drawing. All the mechanical drawings are from Leonardo's fertile brain. But this has a different feel altogether.'

'Different how?' asked Konstantin.

'This...' Houdini felt for the words. 'This is something he is seeing with his own eyes. This is a life drawing. He was actually *here*. This is a *place*.' He looked up, his eyes taking on that shimmering, magical look. 'We just need to know where this is. Because I would bet you every sovereign in that safe that the *Salvator Mundi* is hidden there.'

'Well, look,' said Luna, pointing. 'There's writing on the page. All these notes, see? It probably says where it is.'

'All in mirror writing, though,' said Konstantin.

'That's not the issue,' said Luna. 'To read that, all you need is a mirror. But to *interpret* it we need...' She looked up. 'You know what we need? An Italian.'

'It's late,' said Houdini, checking his pocket watch. 'Vincenzo will be at home.'

'If only we knew where he lived,' lamented Luna.

'We do,' said Houdini. 'Remember? I had to drop off the magic Sol Tinctura glass at his house so he could take it to the Louvre and put it on the *Mona Lisa*. He lives at 5 rue de L'Hôpital Saint-Louis.'

Aidan jumped to his feet. 'Then what are we waiting for?'

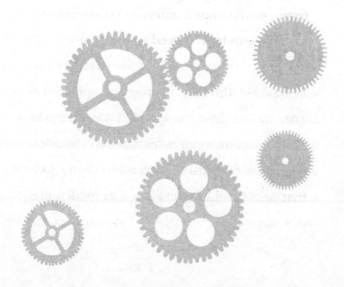

26 AUGUST 1911
7 p.m.

Vincenzo's apartment in the rue de L'Hôpital was actually a single room.

The scene was like a painting. There was a bottle of wine on a table next to a solitary glass. A blue china plate, bearing the rind of a cheese and a crust of bread, told the tale of a simple supper. Another bottle, long emptied, had been repurposed as a candlestick. A single white candle, stuck into the bottleneck, lit the whole room, and was melting down the glass, making a sculpture of wax. In one corner was a sagging bed, and in the other was a basin of water in place of a sink, with shaving equipment next to it, a ragged towel, and a small cracked mirror propped up by a few shabby books. The place was small and squalid and sad. Little wonder, thought the time-thieves, that Vincenzo had loved to spend time with them in the finest suite of the Hotel du Louvre.

Vincenzo, when they entered, sprang up in surprise. He was in his shirtsleeves and bare feet, obviously preparing to go to bed, and was touchingly pleased to see his visitors. The way he attempted to tidy up his little home made them like him even more.

'I cannot offer you refreshment,' he said, 'nor even a chair. Miss Luna, if you take mine, we gentlemen can sit on the bed.'

So they arranged themselves like that, and after a little pause Houdini said, 'We don't require any refreshment; all we need is a little information. Could we ask you if you know where this is?'

He produced the *Codex Arundel* and opened it to the page that held the landscape.

Vincenzo peered at the drawing in the candlelight. He narrowed his dark eyes and shook his head. 'I feel like I know it like I know my own home. It is so familiar, I feel like I could step into the page and walk around. But I don't know where I know it from.'

'Then allow me to enlighten you,' said Houdini. 'This is the background to the *Mona Lisa*.'

'Of course!' Vincenzo hit his forehead with his hand. 'How did I not know it at once? I must have looked on it a thousand times.' He began to leaf through the pages, gazing at the wonderful diagrams, the drawings and the scribbled mirror writing in the flickering candlelight. 'This is Leonardo's sketchbook – the one with the poem in it, yes? The one you had me translate?'

'Yes,' said Houdini.

'Where did you find this?' Vincenzo asked.

'Don't be angry,' said Luna, 'but it is from the British Museum.'

Vincenzo gave a little snort. 'So Leonardo's work is British now, is it?'

Luna laid a hand on his arm. 'We wish we could give this to you. We really do. But if you can tell us where the landscape is,' she said, gently turning back to page 72, 'we can at least give you the *Mona Lisa* back. We only need her to help us find… something else.'

'So you don't know where this landscape is?' asked Aidan.

'No,' said Vincenzo. 'But I think it must say in the notes underneath.'

'Could you translate them?' asked Houdini.

Vincenzo placed his hand on his heart. 'Of course. It would be my honour to read the master's own hand.'

'We would pay you well,' the magician promised.

Vincenzo shook his dark head. 'You are already giving me the *Mona Lisa*. That is payment enough.' He rose from the bed and grabbed the cracked mirror from the corner of the room. Luna vacated his chair so he could sit at the table, and held the *Codex Arundel* as close as she dared to the candle. Vincenzo positioned the mirror so he could read the mirror text. Slowly he read:

Una vista a volo d'uccello del Valdichiana

'What does that mean?' asked Aidan breathlessly.

'It means… how would you say it? A bird's-eye view of the Valdichiana.'

They all wanted to ask, but Konstantin got there first. 'What's the Valdichiana?'

'It is a beautiful valley in Tuscany, right in the heart of my country,' said Vincenzo. 'It runs from north to south between the plain of Arezzo and the plain of Orvieto. It is about a hundred kilometres long.'

'A *hundred* kilometres long!' groaned Aidan. 'Finding something there would be like finding a needle in a haystack.'

'But this drawing is of a specific bit,' said Vincenzo comfortingly. 'It has notable features like the mountains and the river and the bridge. It should not be so hard to pinpoint.'

Konstantin pointed at the drawing. 'There's a faint B over this river where the bridge is. We were wondering what the B stands for.'

'B for bridge!' shouted Luna, loud enough to wake a dog in the neighbouring apartment, who started to bark excitedly.

'Don't be a muttonhead, Duch,' said Aidan. 'Bridge in Italian won't necessarily begin with a B.'

'He's right,' Vincenzo agreed, but more politely. 'Bridge in Italian is *ponte*, so it begins with a P. But you're right too, *signorina*,' he said to a chastened Luna. 'This B seems to indicate the bridge.' He got up again and took one of the tatty books from his shelf. 'If the drawing is of the Valdichiana, then it might help to look at some of the local features.'

'What's that?' asked Aidan.

'An atlas of Italy. A book of maps.' He held the volume to the light. The covers were hanging off and the pages looked chewed. The book was obviously much loved. 'This is my bedtime reading. I read it before I go to sleep, as a child might read a fairy tale. Italy is my magic kingdom.'

The well-worn book fell open at a particular page, just as a story book might fall open at a favourite tale. 'This is Dumenza,' Vincenzo said, with a sigh in his voice. 'My home. One day I'll see it again.' He laid his hand briefly and tenderly on the page, then became business like and began to leaf through the book. 'The Valdichiana – or Chiana Valley – is just outside Florence. So it will be on the Tuscany page of the atlas. Here.' He turned to the right page, and the time-thieves and Houdini crowded over the page.

'Here is the Valdichiana. So what we are looking for is a river and a lake, just as in the drawing. Here is the major river of the valley, the Chiana, which flows through Arezzo. Just beyond Arezzo, the Chiana canal flows into a lake.' He followed the course of the river with his forefinger. 'And here you can see that the stream divides, just as it does in the painting. The right fork was stopped, by a dam designed by Leonardo himself, to create a water source for Castiglion, the fortress on the hill. The riverbed was almost dry but still a bridge stood there, which used to span the river.' He peered at the name pointed by the little arches. 'Il Ponte Buriano.'

'The Buriano Bridge!' shouted Konstantin, setting off next door's dog again.

'*Sì*,' said Vincenzo, snapping the book shut in triumph. 'The B you mentioned is not for bridge but for Buriano. Whatever you seek is at the Buriano Bridge, just outside Arezzo.'

Houdini clapped Vincenzo on the shoulder. 'My friend, you have told us all we needed to know.' He looked at the others. 'I think we are ready to let the *Mona Lisa* go home.'

Vincenzo's dark eyes burned in the light of the candle and his face split into an enormous smile. 'You mean it? I can take *La Gioconda* back to Florence?'

The time-thieves smiled at each other and then at him. 'Yes!' they shouted in unison, joined in their joy by a volley of barking from the neighbour's dog.

Vincenzo jumped up and kissed each of them in turn, on both cheeks. 'Madonna. I cannot believe it is true!'

Houdini said, 'This is no trick. Come to the Hotel du Louvre tomorrow after work with your portfolio. We will have a new suit of clothes for you, and we will arrange safe passage to Italy for you. Konstantin here has been to the port already – he'll get you a ticket, won't you, Konstantin?'

'It would be my pleasure,' said Konstantin, still smiling.

Vincenzo sat down on the bed again, as if his legs would no longer support him. He shook his head as if dazed. 'I cannot believe it. I cannot believe we pulled it off. I cannot believe *La Gioconda* is coming home.'

Then, as sudden as a thunderclap, the flimsy door was battered in, and the room was full of people, harsh lamplight, shouting voices and the dove-grey uniforms of gendarmes.

The time-thieves, Houdini and Vincenzo jumped to their feet in alarm. The little bedsit was so full that there was no space for Arthur John Priest to enter the room. In his detective disguise as Henry Faulds, he stood at the doorway to make his dreadful pronouncement. 'Vincenzo Peruggia, you are under arrest for the theft of the *Mona Lisa*.'

26 AUGUST 1911
7.45 p.m.

For a moment no one moved; the time-thieves were rooted to the spot with terror.

Then Houdini stepped forward. 'Sir, my associates and I happened to be at your fingerprint demonstration today. This man is innocent. He was the glazier who placed the glass on the *Mona Lisa*. His fingerprints had every right to be on that frame.'

'Indeed,' said Arthur John Priest, his watchglass eye flashing malevolently in the lamplight. 'But do they have a right to be on *this*?'

He stepped forward and threw an object on the little table.

It took the time-thieves and Houdini a couple of seconds to realise what it was. But then the dreadful realisation dawned.

It was the doorknob to the storeroom of the Louvre.

The conspirators were struck dumb. Vincenzo, his arms held in the vice-like grip of two gendarmes, looked from left to right as if hunted.

'Our Scotland Yard agents have determined that the *Mona Lisa* was actually stolen from the stores the day *after* she was taken from the gallery,' said Arthur John Priest. 'The thief was apprehended in the stores, where the *Mona Lisa*'s broken glass and frame were found. He contrived to create some sort of Pepper's Ghost phenomenon to scare the gendarmes away.' His single eye looked scornfully at the gendarmes, who hung their heads in shame. They were the ones who had been scared away by the hologram of Professor Lorenz. 'However, the officers did have the presence of mind to lock the door of the storeroom after them as they fled. But the thief managed to take off the door handle and effect his escape. His mistake was to throw the doorknob over some railings in the rue de Rivoli, where my agents found it.' He nodded smugly. 'The fingerprints on the handle are clear as day, and they match both the prints on the *Mona Lisa*'s frame and the set of prints I took from *you, signor*.'

He turned to the gendarmes. 'Put him in handcuffs. Mr Peruggia, you're coming with us – and if I were you, I'd get yourself an *avocat*.'

'An avocado?' said Aidan, surprised.

Arthur John Priest withered him with a look. 'A lawyer.'

Vincenzo was bundled out of the room, protesting loudly in Italian. The remaining police started to pull the little room apart, looking for the missing *Mona Lisa*, and Konstantin had the presence of mind to hide the *Codex Arundel* beneath his greatcoat. He was just in time, for one of the gendarmes grabbed the atlas of Italy, preparing to tear it cover from cover in his search for evidence, but Houdini stepped in. 'That's mine,' he said, and the officer, clearly feeling the little man's air of authority, surrendered the book at once.

'Indeed,' said Arthur John Priest, overhearing. 'And might I ask what you are doing in the house of a known criminal?'

'He's not a…' began Luna. Aidan trod heavily on her foot and she stopped.

Houdini said smoothly. 'As I said to you, my friends and I happened to be at your fingerprint demonstration in the Louvre. It was clear from his speech that he was Italian so we made the gentleman's acquaintance after the display – as you may have seen – and I asked him if he would accept a commission to translate an Italian book for me.'

Arthur John Priest's eye narrowed. 'What Italian book?'

There was an awful pause. Then Aidan, inspired, said, 'Why, *this* book, of course!'

He tapped the atlas in Houdini's hand.

'That's right,' said the magician, catching on immediately. 'My associates and I are planning a trip to Italy. Signor Peruggia was translating this atlas for us, telling us the best routes, recommending landmarks that must not be missed.' He stared at the 'detective', his silver eyes unblinking.

'I see,' said Arthur John Priest, sounding wholly unconvinced. 'I would hate for you to try any of your tricks with me, Mr Houdini.'

Luna's heart sank. So Arthur John Priest did know who Houdini was, and what he did for a living. The 'detective' turned to go, then turned back with a flourish of his checked cape. 'Obviously, if you are travelling to Italy, I won't be seeing you around here again.'

'Trust me,' said Houdini, 'we'll be gone in the nick of time.'

Outside in the rue de L'Hôpital, the time-thieves and Houdini joined the little crowd that had gathered to see the notorious criminal be carted away. Vincenzo was thrown into the back of a police carriage pulled by four black horses. The carriage was as black as the horses, with grim-looking bars on the single window.

Konstantin, since he had the best command of French, was shoved forward to talk to one of the officers.

'Find out where they're going,' urged Luna. '*Quick!*'

Konstantin caught at the gendarme's coat just as he was jumping on to the driver's box. 'Please sir, where are you taking him?'

The gendarme looked down at Konstantin as if he was something nasty on his shoe. 'We are taking him to the commissariat in Denfert-Rochereau.'

'You're taking him out of town?' exclaimed Konstantin in a panic.

'What are you talking about, boy?' sneered the gendarme. 'Denfert-Rochereau is a suburb of the city. It's in the fourteenth *arrondissement*. We need to take him somewhere out of the centre of Paris to question him.' The gendarme jerked his head at the police carriage. 'Your friend back there is the most wanted man in the world.'

27 AUGUST 1911
8 a.m.

The next morning found the time-thieves and Houdini standing across the road from the commissariat, the police station at Denfert-Rochereau.

It was a squat, broad building with iron bars at the windows. It was grey, imposing and looked a little bit like a fortress. Two gendarmes in their dove-grey uniforms were posted at the door.

The travellers had slept little, worrying about Vincenzo, so they had taken a carriage at dawn to Paris's fourteenth district. Now, as they stood on the pavement where the taxi had dropped them, a nearby church bell struck eight times. They gazed at Vincenzo's prison.

'We have to get him out of there,' said Luna.

'No, we don't,' said Houdini. 'Quite the contrary.'

'We can't just let him rot.'

'I've no intention of letting him rot,' said Houdini sniffily. 'But we're not getting him out either. That's what they expect. We're going to get him further *in*.'

The three time-thieves looked at him, open-mouthed. Aidan, who always felt most able to challenge Houdini, said, 'What are you talking about?'

'I'm developing a trick,' said Houdini, 'and as always, when I'm planning, I don't want to say more until I know I'm right about something.'

'Right about what?'

'That police station is built on top of something, and I have a hunch about what it is. I don't know any French,' said Houdini. 'But I think I know that word.'

He pointed to a nearby street sign. In ornamental letters, it said:

CATACOMBS

'*I* don't know that one,' said Konstantin. 'What does it mean?'

Houdini's shimmering eyes took on a faraway look. 'In Budapest there is a beautiful castle. And underneath the castle, the *katakombák*. The words are similar enough. Catacombs.'

'What are catacombs?' asked Luna.

'Subterranean tunnels,' said Houdini. 'Let's find out if I'm right.'

There was a little bakery opposite the commissariat, emitting the heavenly twin smells of freshly baked bread and croissants. Houdini marched in, and a little brass bell bounced and tinkled on a brass coil above the door. The time-thieves joined the snaking morning queue. 'What are we doing?' asked Konstantin.

'*I'm* not doing anything,' murmured Houdini. 'No French, remember? But you are going to ask for a box of croissants. Twenty will do it. And have them wrapped.'

This request stretched even Konstantin's French, but fortunately he was served by the baker's daughter, who was charmed by the young man with the halting French. She packed the croissants in a pretty box, stuck on a label and tied the parcel with a pretty pink ribbon. For the charming young man, she swiped a scissor blade down the ribbons to make them into special curlicues.

'One more thing,' said Houdini in Konstantin's ear. 'An apron. We'll give it back.'

Konstantin rolled his eyes, but turned once again to the baker's daughter and made the polite request. The obliging girl took off her own apron and handed it to the handsome customer.

The time-thieves gathered on the pavement outside. 'Now what?' asked Konstantin.

'Now,' said Houdini, 'you deliver the croissants to our friends in the police station.' He seemed to think again. 'No, not you. Aidan.'

'Hero of the working classes,' sighed Aidan, holding out his hand for the apron, 'that's me.' But he tied it on with good grace.

'Take off your cap and turn it backwards,' said Luna, beginning to see the plan, 'and give me your jacket and roll up your sleeves. There. Much more like a baker's boy.'

'Give the croissants to the desk sergeant,' instructed Houdini. 'But then, if possible, I want you to get "lost" on the way out. I want you to find a stairway and go down it as far as it will go. Get to the very bottom and find out what's in the cellars. Then leave as fast as you can. Got that?'

Aidan, his eyes very blue, nodded.

'And here,' said Houdini. He opened his hand to reveal a little pile of flour, which he patted on to Aidan's face.

'I don't think you'll see any of the arresting officers, as they were on the night shift. But just in case they are still hanging around, we don't want them recognising you from Vincenzo's apartment.'

'I didn't even see you pick that flour up,' said Konstantin. Houdini flashed a smile.

'Prestidigitation,' he said.

'I thought you didn't know any French,' said Aidan, sneezing the flour out of his nose.

'I don't,' said Houdini. 'It's Latin. It means "nimble fingers". Let's go.'

27 AUGUST 1911
8.30 a.m.

Aidan approached the police station, his heart thudding beneath the baker's apron. He thought it perfectly possible that he would be stopped at the door and get no further. And indeed, one of the gendarmes held out his truncheon across Aidan's body.

'*Arrêt*,' he said.

In answer Aidan held up the box. The incredible smell of the freshly baked croissants wafted from the packaging. This deception might not exactly be one of Houdini's tricks, but the pastries certainly seemed to have a magical effect on the policeman. He lowered his truncheon and jerked his head towards the police station. He smiled slightly and muttered something that Aidan didn't understand, but if he was a betting man he would have guessed the gendarme said, 'Tell them to save some for me.'

Aidan crossed the threshold of the police station, his eyes adjusting to the dimness after the brightness outside. There was a short corridor leading to a reception desk, but he could see, just to his left, a little iron staircase leading down. He carried on and went up to the reception desk. He dumped the box in front of the desk sergeant in a little cloud of flour, and uttered the one French word he knew. 'Croissants.'

The desk sergeant's eyes brightened greedily. '*Merci*,' he growled and then made a motion with his hand which very clearly meant 'go away'.

Aidan went, but not very far. He went carefully down the iron staircase, making sure that his hobnail boots didn't make too much sound on the stairs.

When he arrived at the next floor down, it soon became clear that he had reached the jail. There was a wide passageway with iron bars at either side, the air was damp and foetid, and the walls were silvery with moisture. Aidan walked quietly down the corridor, keeping carefully to the middle in order to stay the maximum distance away from the occupants of the cells. Despite his determination not to look right or left, Aidan could not help catching a glimpse of the prisoners. Some were curled in a ball in the corners of the dank and grimy rooms, some were stretched out on their beds of straw, and some – who Aidan guessed had been hauled in for drunken behaviour – were rattling their bars like apes in the zoological gardens and bellowing angrily. But despite the row, Aidan was less afraid of the prisoners than of meeting another gendarme down here. Yet this floor seemed to be entirely unguarded. He supposed that, since all the prisoners were handcuffed and the cells locked, there was no need for the gendarmes to be down here. And perhaps they didn't want to be down here any more than the inmates did.

At the very end of the dim, dripping passageway was a cell that was clearly reserved for the worst offenders. The bars were reinforced, there was a heavy-duty padlock on the clasp, and the cell was almost completely dark. Just as Aidan was wondering which hardened criminal lurked in the shadows of the cell, he heard a familiar voice. 'Aidan!'

Aidan pressed himself to the bars of the cell. 'Vincenzo?'

A figure loomed out of the dark. It had not even been twelve hours since Aidan had seen Vincenzo in his own apartment, but he was already a changed man. His white glazier's smock was filthy, and hung loosely. His face was drawn and his eyes hollow, like a Death's-head

Hawkmoth. He'd obviously spent the night listening to the drunken shouts and the soft weeping of the prisoners, torturing himself about what might happen to him. Even his moustaches, instead of turning up at the ends, drooped hopelessly. Aidan felt horribly guilty that they'd got Vincenzo mixed up in their Butterfly Mission.

Two dirty hands reached out to him from the bars, to be obstructed by the sturdy steel handcuffs that met the iron of the bars with a clang.

'I am so happy to see you, my friend,' said Vincenzo in a heartfelt whisper.

Aidan squeezed the hands that Vincenzo held out to him. 'We are going to get you out of there,' he promised. 'But for now, I need to ask you a question. Is this the bottom floor? Or are there stairs downwards?'

Vincenzo looked confused by this question, but seemed to catch the urgency in Aidan's voice. 'There is another stair,' he said, pointing to the left, 'in the darkest corner – here. No one seems to go down there. They seem somehow… afraid.'

Aidan peered into the blackness and could just make out a little door. It bore a sign of one word which Aidan, who had never been taught, could not read. Had it not been for Vincenzo he would have missed the door entirely.

He squeezed the filthy hands again. 'We'll be back for you. I promise.' And then he broke away.

Aidan felt his way to the door. He suspected it would be locked – but it wasn't. It opened silently inwards and he found himself at the top of a stone staircase. The walls were slimy with moss, and there was an ancient, stone-like smell that Aidan's memory somehow associated with churchyards. That, and the fact that Vincenzo had warned him that there was something to be afraid of, made him shiver. He felt in his pocket for something engineers always carried, because they were well used to being in dark tunnels – a tinderbox. He struck a match and felt the immediate comfort of light as the stairway illuminated. Carefully, carefully, he began to descend. He could feel himself going down into the very depths of the Earth. Eventually his boots struck a flatter surface of paving instead of stairs. He was in a small cellar which seemed older, by several centuries, than the building above. It was littered with discarded rubbish – old files, chairs with missing legs, broken barrels. Something greasy and furry with a long tail ran over his boot and scuttled away from the light.

In the darkest corner was another door, made of ancient and rotting wood. One of the barrels was partially blocking the door, and Aidan pushed it out of the way. His match died and he lit another, remembering the time he had been trapped with his fellow time-thieves in the Puzzle Chamber of Thutmoses. Now, as then, he did not enjoy those few seconds of darkness before he could strike the next light on his tinderbox. He pulled at the door and some of the rotting wood actually came away in his hand, making a hole big enough to get through.

He found himself in a stone corridor, but this time the space was large and grand. And, carved on the stone doorway before him, was another sign. He could not read what it said either, but he could see by the formation of the letters that they were very old. He had a strong, strange sense that they were a warning. His hand holding the match seemed to shake all by itself, and Aidan steeled himself to walk through the doorway, holding the light high so he could see.

What he saw there made his insides turn liquid with terror.

And then the match went out.

Luna, Konstantin and Houdini stood anxiously on the corner opposite the police station, watching and waiting. Luna was especially anxious. She found Aidan annoying, just as much as she enjoyed his company, and she supposed that was what it was like having a brother, but that description didn't seem to fit what she felt. What she did know was that the prospect of anything happening to him was appalling. What if Aidan was found poking around and got himself arrested? What if he was locked up, just like Vincenzo?

After what seemed like an age, Aidan shot through the door of the commissariat, looking as if the devil was after him. He pelted across the road, a little cloud of flour trailing behind him, and nearly got run over by a cart. When he joined the others, the flour had gone from his face but his complexion was still strangely white. Luna, weak with relief, cannoned into him and gave him the most enormous hug.

'Steady on, Duch,' he panted. 'I'm all right.' He looked at the others over Luna's head. 'You won't believe what's down there.'

'What?' said Luna, disentangling herself.

'Skulls,' said Aidan. 'Loads and loads of human skulls.'

27 AUGUST 1911
9 a.m.

After returning the baker's apron, the time-thieves and Houdini went to look for somewhere to have breakfast. 'I'm starving after that little adventure,' declared Aidan.

They found a little café on the corner, in sight of the police station, and sat outside in the morning sun. Once they were stuffing themselves with bread and croissants and hot chocolate, Aidan, between bites and sips, described his visit to the police station. Houdini wanted to know every detail of the building, and where everything was, so Aidan told him all about the reception desk, and the spiral staircase to the cells, and the stone staircase to the cellars. Luna and Konstantin wanted to know every detail of how their friend Vincenzo was doing, and were concerned to hear about his troubling appearance.

But of course, what everybody most wanted to know was about the skulls.

'There are hundreds of them,' said Aidan. 'Thousands even. Piled high, all the way along this underground passageway. Then my match went out, and I can tell you, I wasn't about to light another one. I just hot-footed it out of there as fast as I could.'

'Ah,' said Houdini, and the unaccountable little man was actually *smiling*. 'I suspected as much. The *katakombák* in Budapest, the tunnels under the castle, are full of graves. Catacombs are underground cemeteries.'

'Well, in that case thanks for the warning,' said Aidan drily. 'Those skellingtons scared the bejeezus out of me.'

'Well,' conceded Houdini, 'that was bad for you, but good for us. I think that if the catacombs are full of skeletons, that's wonderful.'

'How come?' asked Luna.

'Because it's unlikely that anyone would want to go down there, even the sturdiest policeman.'

'That's exactly what Vincenzo says. He says no one's been near that door since he got there. He says they're afraid. And I can't say I'm surprised.'

'All right,' said Konstantin, brushing croissant crumbs from his greatcoat. 'So we know there is a way down to the catacombs.' He turned to Houdini. 'Now explain this trick of yours. How are you going to make Vincenzo Peruggia vanish? What did you mean when you said you were not going to get him out, you were going to get him further in?'

Houdini paused before answering. Then he said, 'In my stage show I do a trick called the Vanishing Lady. You may remember it.'

Indeed the time-thieves did.

'I am taking you into my utmost confidence when I tell you that the lady never vanishes at all. The box in which she is enclosed is a trick cabinet with a false back. The lady does not really vanish. She's in the cabinet all the time, just further in. I merely create a misdirection elsewhere on the stage – a dove, an explosion or' – he looked at Aidan – 'a box of croissants, and when everyone is looking elsewhere I restore the lady.'

'Just like the *Mona Lisa*!' burst out Luna. 'She wasn't really gone. She was in the Louvre the whole time, and we took her the *next* day when no one was looking.'

'Precisely, my dear,' said Houdini.

'So we get Vincenzo out of jail,' said Konstantin slowly, 'by hiding him deeper inside the jail?'

'Exactly,' said Houdini. 'The front door will be guarded twenty-four hours a day. You saw it yourself, Aidan. Two gendarmes, all the time. So we don't bring Vincenzo out into the daylight. We send him down into the dark.'

27 AUGUST 1911
10.30 a.m.

After breakfast the boys were instructed to stay at the café. 'Konstantin, you went to the bakery,' said Houdini. 'Aidan, you took the croissants to the police. So Luna,' he smiled, 'it's your turn to do some work. Come on.'

They crossed the road together and entered the police station. Houdini led Luna down the passageway that Aidan had described, and went straight up to the reception desk to address the sergeant sitting behind it. 'You speak English?'

'Yes.'

'I want to visit the thief of the *Mona Lisa*.'

'Not a chance. No press. Those are my orders.'

'I'm not a journalist. Signor Peruggia was working for me as a translator. He is helping me to interpret some… ancient Italian texts. I urgently need to conclude my business with him.'

'Who's she, then?'

'His daughter.'

The sergeant assessed Luna with a doubtful eye. 'Doesn't look much like him.'

'Mother was a redhead,' said Houdini glibly.

The desk sergeant said nothing for a moment.

'Look, have a heart, won't you?' wheedled Houdini. 'Haven't you any children? Mouths to feed?'

'Nope,' said the desk sergeant, and went back to his newspaper.

Houdini leant over the desk. 'No other… *expenses*?'

The sergeant took the hint. He looked up from the newsprint, the light of greed in his eyes.

Houdini pushed a golden sovereign across the desk and left it there.

The desk sergeant removed his hat and placed it over the sovereign. 'I suppose there's no harm in a family visit. I'm a compassionate man.'

'I knew it as soon as I saw you,' flattered Houdini.

'Plus your frien[d]

and I have the keys [to his]

cell, so he can't exactl[y...]

at his belt. 'I'll have to [...]

all right?'

'Perfectly,' said Houdin[i]

'I don't think he's danger[ous...]

more... sad.' He came around [...]

led them down the spiral stair[...] described

to the cells. He walked them dow[n] the dank passageway,

ignoring the catcalls of the other prisoners, to the very

darkest reaches, where the grimmest cell was located. He

unlocked the door of this awful cage and Houdini and

Luna stepped into the dim and the damp.

'Five minutes,' said the sergeant. 'No more.' And then

he went back to his desk. Once the sound of the jingling

keys had receded, Vincenzo loomed out of the dark.

'My dear friends.' He embraced them both as well

as he could in the heavy cuffs. 'I knew you wouldn't

desert me.'

Luna noticed with sorrow, just as Aidan had, how much

their friend had altered overnight. She had thought his

bedsit a simple place, but his cell was even more sparse,

with only a bed, a chair and a chamber pot. In an echo

once again offered Luna his

ini sat on the bed.

searched my apartment,' he murmured.

said Luna. 'They were doing it while we were

'Of course there is nothing to find. But I've been thinking – because of our association they might well search your hotel suite. You should move the *Mona Lisa*.'

'She'll be gone by tonight,' Houdini assured him. 'And so will you. Luna, be good enough to watch the passageway for me.'

Luna stood and went to the bars of the cell, watching for the officer's return. Houdini lowered his voice still more. 'When we have left you, wait until nightfall so that your escape is not connected to us. This is important – not for our sake, but for yours, as we must be at liberty in order to help you. There is a church near here, and you can hear its bell from here. We heard it on the street this morning. When that bell tolls midnight, leave this cell, but do not go up into the light. You must go down into the dark. Enter the little door to your left of your cell and go down the stairs you will find there. There is a disused cellar, and another ruined door. Go through that door and you will find the underground catacombs. They are full of skulls and skeletons. Gather your courage and hide among the bones.'

Vincenzo swallowed and crossed himself, but he did not protest.

'It will not be a nice place to spend a night. But that's the point. No one in their right mind would hide in a pile of bones. But no one in their right mind would look there either. Tonight, also at midnight, we will enter the catacombs at the visitor entrance and bring you a new suit of clothes, and your travel documents.'

'But what about my papers? I can't travel as Vincenzo Peruggia. They'll be looking for me at all the ports and stations.'

'You'll be travelling with my identity,' said the magician. 'You'll be Mr Harry Houdini.'

'Then what about you?'

Houdini smiled a secret smile, a little like the *Mona Lisa*'s. 'I have another way home.'

Luna heard the jingling of the keys in the dark. Their time was nearly up. 'The guard's coming,' she hissed.

'Wait,' said Vincenzo, clasping Houdini's arm. 'I am handcuffed and I am locked in a cell. How can I do as you ask?'

Houdini said, 'I've spent a career showing the world that a person can escape from anything if they really want to. Pull your hands apart.'

Vincenzo did so. The heavy cuffs parted and fell from his wrists with a clatter.

'When did you...? How did you...?' Vincenzo was flabbergasted.

'I'd put those back on if I were you,' said Houdini in reply. 'Just rest them on your wrists until your guard is gone.'

The sergeant was nearly upon them.

'But what about the door to the cell?' whispered Vincenzo.

Houdini put a finger to his lips, and Luna wasn't sure whether he had an answer to that particular conundrum or not.

'Time's up,' said the sergeant. 'You'd better get going, or it'll be my job on the line.'

They were halfway down the passageway, suffering the shouts and calls of the other prisoners, when Houdini turned to the sergeant. 'For one more sovereign, would you allow Luna here just a moment to say goodbye to her father, alone? The evidence you have against him seems pretty damning, and if he goes to prison God knows when she will see him again.'

The sergeant pocketed the coin Houdini offered. 'All right. *One* minute. But no more.'

Luna looked up at Houdini. She had kept deliberately mute in the presence of the sergeant, as she was supposed to be Italian, but that meant she was unable to ask the magician what on earth he thought he was doing.

'Give your papa my best,' said Houdini. He clasped her hand briefly – and dropped something cold and heavy into it.

Then Luna understood. She ran back to Vincenzo's cell, crying, 'Papa, Papa!'

The bemused prisoner came to the bars, but his puzzlement turned to delight when he realised he was being handed the key to his own cell.

Once again Vincenzo was almost speechless. 'But how… when?'

'Don't ask me,' said Luna, smiling. 'I don't know.' She looked back at the magician, who was busy distracting the desk sergeant. 'And he'll never tell.'

27 AUGUST 1911
NOON

The time-thieves and Houdini went back to the Hotel du Louvre to make their preparations for that night. 'This is the last time we'll be here,' said the magician as he led them into their room. 'The net is closing.'

Luna looked around the suite with a pang of sorrow. The Hotel du Louvre had been their home for the last two weeks and so much had happened here. But Houdini was businesslike. 'Luna and Konstantin,' he said, 'go and buy a suit of clothes for a gentleman. Vincenzo is the same size as me, fortunately.' He wrote down his own dimensions for the children. 'Make the check of the cloth as loud and noticeable as possible – just like the things I like to wear. And some shoes – shiny spats in a size 41. Again, as brash as possible.'

'Why so noticeable?' asked Konstantin.

'Because the best place to hide is in plain sight,' said Houdini. 'It's all about misdirection. Any decent magician will tell you that.'

'What about a hat?' asked Luna.

'Not necessary,' said Houdini. 'I never wear one, so nor will my doppelganger.'

Luna remembered the term with a jag of fear. Why should such a funny-sounding word make her afraid? Then she remembered. She'd heard it in the National Gallery, when Papa had been telling her about that strange and frightening painting, *How They Met Themselves*. She had a shiver of foreboding, but there was no time to explain her feelings. Konstantin, with a handful of sovereigns, was already halfway out of the door.

By the time they returned later that afternoon, with a suit of clothes they had bought on a fancy street called the Champs-Élysées, Houdini and Aidan had been busy.

The suite smelled strongly of sawdust and paint. A large box, constructed of new timber, stood in the middle of the room on an island of newspaper sheets. Aidan, looking happy, as he always did when he was building things, had a hammer in one hand and a paintbrush in the other.

On one side of the box, large theatrical letters shouted *THE GREAT HOUDINI!*

The shoppers, who had walked many a mile that afternoon, flopped down on the couch. 'What's the box all about?'

'It's not a box,' said Houdini. 'It's a trick cabinet. Fortunately, I have made many of these before. But rarely with so skilled a carpenter.' Aidan looked bashfully at the floor. 'As I explained yesterday, the purpose of a trick cabinet is to conceal something. A rabbit, a lady. Or in this case, a painting. Aidan?'

Aidan went to the wardrobe and brought forth the *Mona Lisa*. Houdini went into his bedroom and came back with two pillows. 'I asked for extra pillows three nights ago,' said Houdini. 'I had the feeling they would come in handy.' He began to tear them apart, stuffing handfuls of feathers into the very bottom of the box. Then, with Aidan's help, he slid the painting into the two pillow cases and laid the *Mona Lisa* on her feather bed. She fitted in the bottom of the box precisely, and Luna admired the workmanship that had taken place in their absence. Houdini proceeded to scatter the rest of the feathers on top. Finally Aidan brought a panel of wood and placed it over the painting.

'A false bottom,' said Houdini.

'What goes on top?' asked Konstantin.

'Once we'd bought the timber we found a lovely little magic shop in the Latin Quarter,' said Houdini, 'and bought some of the tools of my trade.' He threw in a jumble of things such as they'd first seen in his dressing room at the Egyptian Hall – stuffed doves, top hats, wands, juggling balls and playing cards. Once the box was full he placed on the very top some red cylinders that looked like small sticks of dynamite. 'Close her up, Aidan,' he said. 'And don't forget to trap the fuses in the lid.'

Aidan picked up another panel of wood and nailed the box firmly shut.

Once the banging had stopped and she could make herself heard, Luna said, 'Will she be all right? No one will steal her?'

'It's a chance we'll have to take,' said Houdini. 'But I don't think so. I have taken the liberty of posting a warning.' He led Luna and Konstantin round the other side of the box. There, in barely dry red paint, were the words:

CAUTION! HANDLE WITH CARE! CONTAINS STAGE EXPLOSIVES!

'I've put some flashbangs under the lid,' he said. 'If anyone opens it, they'll close it again fast enough.'

Konstantin eyed the box warily. 'We're not taking that thing to the catacombs, are we?'

'No,' said Houdini, leading him to the third side of the box, where an address was painted in neat black letters.

Port du Paris
2 Quai de La Tournelle
75015 Paris
France

'We will have the hotel deliver this to the port. Vincenzo will collect it in the morning, in his new persona as Harry Houdini. The only things we'll take to the catacombs are Vincenzo's new clothes and,' he tapped his pocket, 'my papers.'

'I don't get it,' said Konstantin. 'How do you know that the catacombs are open to the public?'

'There was a street sign,' said Houdini simply. 'You don't get street signs to things that don't have public access.'

'Yes, but surely they won't be open in the middle of the night?' argued Luna.

Houdini just looked at her meaningfully. 'Please,' he said. 'I've never met a door I cannot open.'

Luna remembered the cell door, and the handcuffs, and held her tongue.

There was a knock at the door. The time-thieves looked at one another in alarm.

'Don't worry,' said Houdini. 'I asked the porters to collect the box at seven. Which,' he glanced at his pocket watch, 'it now is. Ready? Have we got everything?'

The time-thieves looked around the suite which had been their home, to check they'd packed all their belongings. 'Ready,' they chorused.

Two porters in green hotel uniforms came into the room and carried away the box. The time-thieves and Houdini closed the door of their suite for the last time and followed the porters down to reception. Houdini gave strict instructions to the concierge about the delivery of his precious parcel, paid the bill and tipped the man heavily to see that the task was done.

Then they walked out of the door into the warm Parisian night – and not a moment too soon.

Two gendarmes, in their dove-grey uniforms, passed them in the doorway. As the time-thieves scuttled away, they could hear the policemen enquiring at the desk for a Monsieur Houdini. And, right under the policemen's noses, the box containing the *Mona Lisa* was carried out of the door and loaded safely on to a cart for the port.

27 AUGUST 1911
11.59 P.M.

The time travellers went for one last dinner at their favourite café on the bank of the Seine.

As so often before, they watched the sun set behind the great iron tower that stood sentinel over the city. But for once they couldn't really enjoy the delicious food and drink, nor the warm evening, nor the rose-gold sky, because all they could think about was Vincenzo. Vincenzo in his dank cell, Vincenzo creeping down the stairs and through the ruined cellar into the catacombs. Vincenzo among the numerous skulls Aidan had described, their hollow sockets staring at him in the half dark.

Or, even worse: another prisoner seeing the fugitive escape, raising the alarm, and the gendarmes running to capture their friend and lock him up so securely he would never be free again.

So it was with a great deal of trepidation that the time-thieves and Houdini took a cab to the place Denfert-Rochereau, just round the corner from the police station where Vincenzo was being held. There, just as Houdini had predicted, was the public entrance to the catacombs. It was a small black hut, like a witch's house. It looked terribly sinister. Houdini paid the carriage driver a gold sovereign to wait for them, however long they were, and another for the loan of the carriage lamp, which he unhooked from the driver's box. Then he led the time-thieves to the locked iron gates. Without a word, the magician laid both his hands around the sturdy padlock, as if cradling a crystal ball. Afterwards the time-thieves swore that the padlock actually began to glow, like a blacksmith's iron, but whether or not that was true it was definitely the case that the padlock just popped open.

They were inside the catacombs.

There was a smell of old stone and damp, which Aidan recognised from earlier in the day. And there was another smell too, one he couldn't recognise, a smell that made him afraid.

There was a stone staircase leading down into the dark. Houdini held the carriage lamp high and illuminated the way ahead. At the bottom of the stairs was a short passageway, leading to a stone doorway with something written above it in ancient letters.

'I saw one of these bits of writing this morning,' said Aidan, above the other entrance. 'What does it say?'

Konstantin stepped forward and squinted at the letters, which read:

ARRÊT! C'EST ICI L'EMPIRE DE LA MORT

'It says, Stop! Here is the Empire of the Dead.' He looked at the others, fearful but determined. 'Ready?'

'As we'll ever be,' said Aidan grimly. And they stepped over the threshold as if they were entering the gates of hell.

The time-thieves looked around with horror and wonder in equal parts. They had been on many adventures, but this was truly one of the most extraordinary and chilling places they had ever been.

The interiors of the tunnels were entirely made of bones – and not just piles of bones jumbled together. Entire walls of finger bones, pyramids of skulls, lattices of crossbones, all arranged in beautiful but macabre patterns.

'Where do they all come from?' wondered Luna aloud.

'Cemeteries. Plague pits,' said Houdini. 'From all over Paris, most probably.'

Konstantin, bringing up the rear, was furthest from the light and had the particularly terrifying position of feeling the bone-heavy dark closing behind him. And the tunnels seemed never-ending – they branched off, they turned back on themselves, a labyrinth of human remains. It seemed the time-thieves would never find the tunnel that led to the ancient cellars of the police station and Vincenzo.

'There must be *thousands* of bones,' marvelled Luna as they trudged down the seemingly endless tunnels.

'Try millions,' said Aidan grimly. 'Millions of dead.'

Konstantin shivered. Where had he heard that before? Millions dead. Then he remembered. Back in the Valley of the Kings, when he'd been talking to Lady Evelyn about the Great War. Millions of young men dead – an entire generation. As he walked, he felt like he was surrounded by the bodies of all those young men who were destined to die in a war that hadn't happened yet. Those who would perish on the battlefield in three years' time were gazing at him from empty eye sockets. To Konstantin, what he had learned about the past had become a dire warning for the future. So when one of the skulls whispered at him, he nearly jumped out of his skin.

'*Konstantin!*'

But it was all right. It wasn't one of the skulls but Vincenzo who addressed him, emerging from behind a great barrage of bones.

'All well?'

'I think so.' Vincenzo licked his lips nervously. 'I waited until they'd done their last cell check of the night. They come round at midnight. After that, I came down here.'

Luna considered what a dreadful and lonely hour he must have spent down here in the dark with all the bones.

By the light of the carriage lamp, and with the skulls observing them with their countless eyes, the time-thieves transformed Vincenzo Peruggia into Harry Houdini. The fugitive removed his old, prison-tattered clothes and put on the crisp shirt and loudly checked suit that Luna and Konstantin had bought. With the shiny spats on his feet, and his severely parted hair fluffed out on both sides like wings, he did indeed bear a passing resemblance to the magician.

'One more thing,' said Houdini. 'Your moustache.'

Vincenzo put his hand to his prized face furniture, his eyes wide.

'He's right,' urged Luna gently. 'It's the one thing that marks you out.'

'It will grow back in Italy,' said Konstantin comfortingly.

As if by magic Houdini produced his own shaving things from his pockets, taken from the hotel. He soaped up Vincenzo's top lip and shaved off his magnificent moustache. Once he'd wiped the foam away with his pocket handkerchief, Vincenzo's top lip looked positively naked. He wiggled it around. 'It feels strange.'

'But you look completely different,' said Aidan. 'So job's a good 'un.'

'Well, but Houdini ought to look different too,' said Luna. 'Here. Take off your jacket and roll up your sleeves. Now smooth your hair so it is more like Vincenzo's was. There.' With these small adjustments, the magician looked much less conspicuous.

'*Bene*,' said Vincenzo. 'So now what?'

'Now we go to the port,' said Houdini. 'The carriage is waiting. And you will be reunited with someone very precious to you.'

'Who?' asked Vincenzo.

'The *Mona Lisa*.'

And then came a dreadful sound. Footsteps, and shouts, from the direction of the police station. And a dreadful sight – the swinging beams of police lanterns.

'Gendarmes!' hissed Vincenzo. 'They must have done another check and discovered that I'd gone.'

'*Run*,' hissed Houdini.

This was easier said than done. The network of tunnels had been difficult enough to navigate when they had been walking calmly, but when they were fleeing for their freedom it was near impossible. The fugitives plunged down tunnel after tunnel: panicked, disorientated, checking, stopping, cannoning into each other, turning, like rats in a maze, all the time watched by the passionless, bloodless skulls and pursued by the relentless boots of the gendarmes.

At last they saw the doorway they had taken from the public entrance. They piled up the stairs and out into the night air. Luna, Konstantin and Houdini scrambled into the carriage and Aidan vaulted on to the box beside the driver to make room. The magician stuck his head out of the window and shouted, 'Another sovereign if you lose them! Go, *go*!'

The driver touched his hat and flicked his whip, and the horse leapt forward as if it had heard a gunshot. The carriage speeded away and the time-thieves craned out of the window, to see half a dozen gendarmes burst on to the pavement and run for the police carriages. A figure pushed through to the front of them and stood watching the fleeing taxi with a furious stance. The moonlight caught the watchglass eye of Arthur John Priest.

28 AUGUST 1911
2 a.m.

For a glorious moment, bowling through the square they'd just left, it seemed that the time-thieves would get away. But it was not long before the police carriages, all ringing bells and blowing whistles, were giving chase.

'You speak English?' bawled Aidan to the taxi driver over the clatter of hooves and carriage wheels.

'A little,' the driver yelled back.

'Can we outpace them?'

'Is very difficult to say,' answered the driver. 'The gendarmes use a pair of horses on their carriages. I only have Gulliame here.' He indicated his valiant grey horse. 'Also I am carrying five passengers, so that slows us down. But taxis are light, and – how would you say it – nimble. We might be all right.'

He urged Gulliame to go faster and the carriage careened across the Seine, the lights on the banks sparkling like a string of diamonds. Behind them the police carriages gained pace, and to the screeches of the bells and whistles was added a new sound – a gunshot. Aidan twisted around on the box to see a gendarme leaning out of one of the carriage windows. In his hand was a gleaming revolver.

'We need to go somewhere busy,' yelled Aidan, ducking the gunfire.

'I do not know this "busy",' the driver yelled back.

Aidan cursed inwardly at his lack of French – this wasn't the moment for a language barrier. 'Somewhere there are lots of taxis. It's our only chance to lose them. They are faster than us.' He thought desperately. 'If you want to lose a pig, you put him in a pig farm, yes?'

The driver nodded and smiled widely, seemingly enjoying himself. '*Oui. Je comprehend*. I know just the place.'

He hauled Gulliame's head around and the horse executed a screeching turn then headed towards the east of the city. The desperate chase continued through a few deserted streets, with the police carriages gaining all the time, until gradually the city began to look busier. And busier. Then positively crowded. And, incredibly a big red windmill, brightly lit, revolved high above a theatre which, even at this hour, was ablaze with lights. Better still, the street was crammed six deep with taxis just like the one they were in. Their heroic driver sped through a tiny gap in the traffic and their cab was lost among the multitude. The police carriages, far too wide to progress, were obliged to slow and stop. The time-thieves' taxi sped away – beyond the crowd and away from the red windmill and across the bridge to the dark, deserted island in the middle of the river.

'I knew that would work,' said the driver, screeching to a halt. 'A pig in a pig farm, *non*? You can always rely on it to be busy at the Moulin Rouge!'

Houdini apologised to the driver as they all clambered down, and paid him handsomely. The driver touched his hat once more and accepted the coins gratefully. 'I haven't had so much fun in years,' he said. '*Bonne chance!*'

'He said good luck,' said Konstantin as the cab drove away.

'We *were* lucky,' said Luna, 'that he found all those taxis.'

The five fugitives had been dropped by the magnificent cathedral of Notre Dame, and they looked up at the two great towers, incredible achievements in stone soaring into the predawn skies, as the great bells struck two, waking the roosting birds and sending them fluttering.

'Remember Homolle said that it would be easier to steal those two great towers from Notre Dame than take a painting from the Louvre?' said Luna, noticing that Vincenzo shifted uneasily at the mention of his old boss's name.

'Well, I'm glad we proved him wrong,' said Aidan.

'What now?' said Konstantin.

'We'll walk the rest of the way,' said Houdini. 'If your old acquaintance is still following us, they'll expect us to be in a carriage, not on foot. And I didn't want to lead them directly to the port. If they don't know where we're going they will have to spread their manpower between all the stations too. Konstantin, you've been a couple of times before. You be our general and lead us.'

Konstantin led them through Parisian streets silvered with the breaking day. At every corner, they expected to see the one-eyed 'detective' who pursued them, but Arthur John Priest was nowhere to be seen.

As they reached the Port of Paris in the dawn light there was, however, another face that watched them from every lamppost, wall and doorway. It was Vincenzo himself, framed like the *Mona Lisa*, himself become a work of art. But his picture was not for admiration, but for identification. Bold black letters were printed at the top of each poster.

'It says: *WANTED! HAVE YOU SEEN THIS MAN?*' said Konstantin.

'Thank goodness you shaved your moustache,' said Luna to Vincenzo. 'You look nothing like yourself now.'

'Let's hope it's enough to get you through customs,' said Houdini. They shoved their way through the growing crowds and made their way to the vast steamer ship that was to take Vincenzo to Italy. It was already huffing out clouds of steam and raring to go. Passengers were making their way up the wooden gangways, and it seemed to the fugitives that everyone was looking at the flamboyant 'magician' with his wild hair and loudly checked suit. But no one approached them, and certainly no one seemed to associate this character with the wanted criminal in the posters.

'See?' said Houdini. 'I told you we hide best in plain sight.'

And at the customs house, when Vincenzo produced Houdini's papers and wrote the magician's signature on the required forms, the brightly painted trick cabinet that the magician and Aidan had made in the Hotel du Louvre was handed over to him without question or protest.

'Some sort of magician, are you?' asked the customs officer in halting English.

'The best sort,' replied Vincenzo. 'I am the Great Houdini.'

'If you say so,' said the officer, stamping the form dismissively.

Vincenzo regarded the box as he helped the boys carry it to the dock. 'What is it?'

'It contains your heart's desire,' said Houdini. 'Under the false bottom of the box, swaddled in feathers, lies the *Mona Lisa*. I gave you my word you could take her, and here she is.'

Vincenzo touched the box as if it contained a holy relic. 'Thank you,' he said in a heartfelt voice.

'And here,' said Konstantin. 'We managed to save this.' He took Vincenzo's beloved atlas from his greatcoat and gave it back to him.

Vincenzo looked at the book in his hands. 'I don't know what to say.'

Luna felt dangerously like crying. 'Where will you go?

'Florence first,' said Vincenzo. 'I will take a room in my favourite hotel – the Albergo Tripoli Italia in the centre of Florence. Dreaming of their feather beds got me through those dark hours in prison. Then I will donate the painting to the Uffizi. The *Mona Lisa* belongs in the finest gallery in the world.' He looked at them all in turn. 'You've all been so good to me. You have been friends to me when I had none. I will never forget you.'

'We won't forget you either,' said Konstantin, his voice wobbling perilously. 'I hope you get back to Dumenza.'

Vincenzo smiled a little sadly. 'One day. But I want to bring honour on my country first.'

'You've done that by returning the *Mona Lisa*,' said Luna. 'What more can you do?'

Vincenzo looked beyond them – beyond the ships' masts, beyond the horizon, as if he could see clouds gathering. 'They say there will be a war. A great war. If that happens, I will join the army.'

Konstantin swallowed. He knew 'they' were right. There *was* going to be a war. But what could he say? Don't go? That would sound insane. Instead he said, 'Take care of yourself.'

Vincenzo blinked once, turned away, then seemed to reconsider and turned back. 'You are the only people who have cared about me since I left my mother's house. So there's something you should know.' He looked at the ground. 'Monsieur Homolle – Theophile Homolle, the director of the Louvre…'

'The one who called you "dirty macaroni"?' said Konstantin angrily.

'The very one. I-I wasn't entirely straight with you. That day – the day that Homolle was angry with me – he thought I'd been blabbing about stealing the *Mona Lisa*. You thought it was your fault – that you'd got me into trouble,' he said to Houdini. 'But you hadn't. I *was* planning to steal it.'

'Well, you told us as much,' said the magician. 'That first night at dinner, remember?'

'Yes, but I didn't tell you the whole truth,' confessed Vincenzo. 'And if I'm never going to see you again, I would hate for you not to know what was really going on.'

'And what was really going on?' asked Houdini warily.

Vincenzo took a breath, as if he was about to dive into the sea. 'I was *hired* to steal the *Mona Lisa*. By him. By Theophile Homolle, the director of the Louvre.'

28 AUGUST 1911
6.45 a.m.

Luna's mouth dropped open as she attempted to digest this piece of information. The director of the Louvre had hired Vincenzo to steal a painting from his own gallery? 'But... *why?*'

Vincenzo shrugged expressively. 'I don't know. But I wonder if it has to do with what's been happening at the gallery. The flowers. The queues. The hysteria. The *Mona Lisa* is more valuable now she's gone than she was when she was there. Far more people are coming to gawk at the space where she used to hang, than came to gaze upon her face. I don't know. But what I do know,' said Vincenzo, hanging his head, 'that you deserve to know the truth. And now you know it, what have you to say?'

He looked up, like a dog expecting to be kicked. 'Have I ruined everything?'

There was a small silence, then Houdini broke it. 'Here is some coin,' he said, giving Vincenzo a handful of gold sovereigns. 'You may find you need help along the way. Let us start with finding a porter to take your property on board.'

Houdini clicked his fingers and a porter came running through the crowd. Vincenzo said, in surprise, 'You are still giving the *Mona Lisa* to me? After what I have told you?'

'Of course.' Houdini smiled. 'My word is the only thing you may believe about me. As I told you, we needed her only until we could discover the whereabouts of… something else, and you have done that for us. As far as I am concerned, she is ready to go home.'

The porter arrived and loaded the cabinet on to his trolley. Vincenzo, feeling that everything that he needed to say had been said, kissed them all on both cheeks, and turned to follow him.

As they'd done before with another Italian by the name of Guglielmo Marconi, the time-thieves waved and waved until Vincenzo could no longer be seen and the steamer was only a speck on the horizon.

As they turned away, Luna felt a hollow feeling in the pit of her stomach. But the bad feeling wasn't about Vincenzo. It was about Houdini.

'What's the matter, Duch?' said Aidan, falling into step with her as Houdini and Konstantin went ahead to find a taxi. 'You've got a face like a wet weekend. Everything's all right. Vincenzo got away.'

'I have a horrible feeling,' said Luna, feeling for the words, 'that Houdini doesn't exist. Look how famous he was becoming in 1894. But here, no one knows him. Remember, when he was signing the hotel register, and when he donated Chronos, we thought he was mad to use his real name. But no one knew who he was. Not even Homolle, the director of the museum. And now at customs, the officer didn't seem to know his name either.'

'So what do you think is going on?' asked Aidan.

'I think he *died*. Before this year. Before 1911.'

'How?'

'Probably doing one of his tricks,' said Luna. 'Remember the Chinese Water Torture Cell? None of us thought he was going to get out of there.'

'I think you've gone soft in the head,' said Aidan. 'We should be celebrating. Vincenzo got away, the *Mona Lisa*'s going home to Italy, and we're off to find the *Salvator Mundi*.'

'I suppose.'

By the time they got back to the Time Train in the rue de Rivoli, Luna had cheered up. Queues still snaked around the block, as all of Paris's population waited in line to see the gap where the *Mona Lisa* had once been.

'Vincenzo was right,' mused Houdini. 'The absence of something has become more of an attraction than the thing itself ever was.'

'Yes,' said Konstantin. 'And we haven't discussed our old friend Monsieur Homolle. Fancy trying to use Vincenzo like that – exploiting a vulnerable foreigner to steal the *Mona Lisa* for him! I won't forget that he called Vincenzo a "dirty macaroni". I'm glad his plan failed.'

'Homolle does feel like unfinished business,' said Aidan. 'Pity he's just going to get away with it.'

'Perhaps the loss of his precious painting is punishment enough,' said Houdini thoughtfully. 'And besides, we might be back in Paris one day.'

As they climbed into the Time Train, Aidan said, 'Where to? That Valdichiana place? Or that town beginning with A, where the Buriano Bridge is?'

'Arezzo?' said Houdini. 'No. Better say Florence. We may need some equipment to recover the painting, and we don't know how small Arezzo is. Florence is a city and will have everything we need.'

'Right you are, Captain,' said Aidan, saluting obligingly.

Konstantin was silent and thoughtful while Aidan set the levers for **FLORENCE – TUSCANY – 10 a.m. – 1911**. Then suddenly he blurted, 'Can we go later?'

Aidan turned. 'How d'you mean? Like, around noon? Or midnight?'

'No,' said Konstantin. 'I mean later in *time*.'

'How much later?'

'A couple of years.'

'A couple of *years*?' echoed Luna. 'Why?'

'I've been thinking about what Vincenzo said as we left him. That there's going to be a war and he wants to serve his country.' Konstantin looked at Houdini, his face pale and anxious. 'Look. We know what's coming. When we were in the Valley of the Kings our friend Abdel told us that there was a great war between 1914 and 1918. Then our other friend Lady Evelyn said that millions of young men died. I don't want Vincenzo to be one of those young men. We should have stopped him.'

Houdini looked unsure. 'We're meant to be saving a painting, not a person,' he said.

'Can't we do both? We did in Egypt. We saved Abdel. He was our friend too.'

Luna said slowly. 'He makes a good point. And if the *Salvator Mundi* has been hidden under the Buriano Bridge for three hundred years, another year or two won't matter.'

Houdini frowned slightly. 'So you want to get to Italy just *before* this great war, and stop Vincenzo from joining the army?'

Konstantin said, very definitely, 'Yes.'

Houdini nodded slowly. 'Very well. Aidan?'

Aidan shrugged. 'Fine by me.'

'All right then. Go for summer 1914,' said Konstantin. 'The war broke out on the 28th July. If you go for a week before that, we'll be in time.'

Aidan set the year to 1914 as he was bidden, and threw the brass lever forward. '*Adieu*, Paris,' said Konstantin as the Time Train gave a lurch. 'Or should it be *au revoir*?'

'What's the difference?' asked Luna, holding tight to the brass side rails.

'*Au revoir* means you're coming back,' said Konstantin, and the fine grey-blue buildings of the rue de Rivoli disintegrated into dust.

FLORENCE ITALY

21 July 1914

21 JULY 1914
10 a.m.

If Paris was a city of silver, Florence was a city of gold.

The streets were lined with ochre palaces, there was an old bridge made of stone as yellow as sunflowers, and a cathedral with a gilded bell of a dome loomed over it all. Green hills surrounded the city, studded with villas and churches like little nuggets of amber, and even the low river glittered brightly with borrowed sunlight.

Although the streets were crammed with horses and traps, there were still plenty of shiny machines honking and jostling for their position on the road. 'Motor cars again,' said Aidan. 'Even better ones, because it's three years later. The Time Train fits in nicely, like it did in Paris. Let's just leave it parked.'

'But take Chronos, like we did last time,' cautioned Konstantin, and Aidan freed the clockwork bird from the clock face on the console.

'What do we do first?' asked Luna. 'The *Salvator Mundi* or Vincenzo?'

'Let's secure the painting first and then that's done,' suggested Houdini. 'Then we'll head to Dumenza – I think it was in the north, according to Vincenzo's beloved atlas – and warn Vincenzo about the war. He'll be settled back in his home town by now for sure.'

'All right,' said Aidan. 'So where to?'

'Well, we'll need to get some equipment for our treasure hunt in Arezzo,' said Houdini, 'so we'll need somewhere to stay for a few days.'

'How about Vincenzo's favourite hotel?' suggested Luna. 'Remember, the one he dreamed of in prison?'

'The Albergo Tripoli Italia,' said Konstantin, who had a good memory for languages. 'Good idea.'

They walked through the ancient streets, the warm air ringing with bell song so loud they could feel it in their ribs. After asking two friendly citizens for directions, they found themselves entering the double doors of the Albergo Tripoli Italia.

Houdini rang the bell on the reception desk and a lady appeared from a back room.

'*Buongiorno*,' she said, sizing them up with a friendly glance. '*Francese? Inglese?*'

'English,' said Luna thankfully, and then, much to her surprise, the landlady beamed with pleasure and began to speak in a strong cockney accent. 'Gawd, it's good to see some proper English among all these eye-talians. Ever since I married my Luigi and moved out 'ere, I don't see no English 'ceptin the ones who come to stay. You're very welcome, young miss, and sirs.'

'We'd like some rooms for the week,' said Houdini.

'Rooms we got,' said the cockney signorina, turning the register around to face them and dipping a pen in the inkwell. 'Rooms we can do. Might I ask, begging your pardon, 'ow you 'eard of the Albergo Tripoli Italia? Always nice to know 'ow people find us.'

'Your hotel was recommended to us,' said Houdini as he took the pen. 'By our good friend Vincenzo Peruggia.'

'Aw, Vincenzo!' exclaimed the cockney signorina. 'Luverly fella.'

'He must have stayed here *years* ago,' said Houdini. 'You have an impressive memory, madam.'

'Gawd love ya,' said the lady, punching a surprised Houdini on the shoulder. ''E's 'ere now!'

'Now?' echoed Luna.

'Yes, dearie. Upstairs.'

'He is?'

'In Room 20. Funny thing. He booked a double room for two. Said 'e was spending 'is last night with 'is lady love – begging your pardon, dearie. But there ain't no lady with 'im that I saw. 'E was on his tod.'

'On his tod?' queried Konstantin. He did not know this expression.

'Yes, young sir – on 'is own.'

Houdini glanced at the time-thieves. 'May we visit Vincenzo?'

'Once you're guests, you can come and go how you like,' said the cockney signorina with a twinkle. 'Sign 'ere and 'ere.'

After they'd taken the rooms, the time-thieves and Houdini trotted up the carpeted stairs to Room 20 and knocked on the door just beneath the little brass number plaque.

There was a scuffling sound from inside, and a shouted instruction in Vincenzo's voice. '*Un momento, per favore!*'

After a long moment the door was opened a suspicious crack, and half of Vincenzo's face appeared.

'Vincenzo,' cried Luna. 'It's us!'

Vincenzo flung open the door, smiling widely. 'My dear friends,' he said. 'How I've missed you! It has been so long!'

Luna felt, once again, the incredible nature of time travel. It seemed remarkable that they were seeing Vincenzo again, a couple of hours after they had left him in Paris, but three years had passed for him. He looked a little thinner, his moustaches were neater and shorter, presumably in a more modern style, but he was the same Vincenzo. Never one for formality, he enfolded them all in a giant embrace. 'What are you doing in Florence?'

'Never mind us,' said Aidan, who was always straight to the point. 'What are *you* doing in Florence? And who's this lady love we've been hearing about?'

Vincenzo made sure the door was closed, then flicked back the coverlet of the bed. 'Here she is. I believe you all know her quite well.'

There, on the snowy white sheet, lay the *Mona Lisa*, glancing up calmly from her prone position, those magical eyes looking directly at them, that secret smile still in place.

'I thought you were room service,' said Vincenzo, 'so I hid her.'

'Vincenzo,' said Konstantin sternly. 'Why have you still got the *Mona Lisa*? I thought you were going to return her when we gave her back to you.'

Vincenzo sighed. 'Yes, it is true. But I wanted to keep her for a little while. Just her and me, before I give her back to the world. Once she is on the wall of the Uffizi Gallery she will not belong to me any more, but to Italy.'

'Well, she's enchanted you and no mistake,' said Houdini. 'I've spent my life in magic and I've never known anyone cast a spell such as this painted lady has over you.'

Vincenzo shrugged. 'It's true. But I am here now to do the right thing. I am determined to take *La Gioconda* to the Uffizi *today*.'

'Shall we come with you?' suggested Luna.

'I think we'd better,' said Konstantin, 'to make sure you actually give her back!'

'Besides,' said Aidan, 'it'd be grand to see you getting a hero's welcome after all this time.'

21 JULY 1914
11.15 a.m.

It was glorious walking through a sunlit Florence with Vincenzo. He had the *Mona Lisa* under his arm, wrapped tenderly in one of the hotel's sheets, and it was fun to look at the face of every friendly Florentine and think how amazed they would be if they knew that Vincenzo was about to return one of art's great masterpieces to her rightful home.

'Soon all these good people will know your name,' whispered Luna deliciously.

'She's right, you know.' Houdini smiled. 'On our way back you'll be carried through the streets in a victory parade.'

But Vincenzo looked increasingly glum. His fingers tightened on the painting, and it was clear he didn't want to be parted from *La Gioconda*.

Soon they were at the Uffizi Gallery, and it was quite a different building to the Louvre. It had huge, ancient arches with a queue of giant statues standing in the niches, and a small, single-file queue of humans at the door. Vincenzo went right to the front of the line and spoke to the guard. They had a brief exchange and then were waved through. 'What did you say to him?' asked Aidan.

'I said I had a painting to donate, and he said they don't see paintings without an appointment,' Vincenzo replied. 'I told him they'd see this one.' He led them up a flight of stone stairs. 'The director of the museum, a Signor Giovanni Poggi, is curating one of the upper galleries.'

The room they entered was quiet, and almost empty, apart from a tall, serious-young man making notes on a clipboard. He looked up as they entered.

Vincenzo said, 'Signor Poggi?'

'*Sì?*'

Vincenzo unwrapped the painting from its sheet and said something that they all understood. '*La Gioconda.*'

The serious young man looked at the *Mona Lisa*, then looked again. He picked up the panel and carried it to one of the windows, propping the painting on the sill in the golden morning light. He looked closely at the brushwork then stood back, looking completely amazed. He called to one of the guards who was seated by the door, and rattled out what seemed to be a roll-call of names. The guard disappeared and was back in a trice with a gaggle of people: more serious-looking men in dark suits who crowded round the painting, looking closely, taking off their glasses, putting them on again and nodding repeatedly. Then they all, as one, turned to look at Vincenzo.

The time-thieves began to shift their feet. This was not how it was supposed to go. They'd expected Vincenzo to be embraced, kissed on both cheeks, applauded – and yes, carried through the streets in a victory parade, just as Houdini had said. They hadn't expected these shuttered, unsmiling faces. The first man began to fire questions at Vincenzo like bullets. Vincenzo spread his hands, palms up, as if defending himself from the barrage, and answered in a humble voice. Luna caught the words 'Louvre', 'Leonardo' and 'Italia'.

'What are they saying?' hissed Luna, a feeling of foreboding rising in her.

'They are asking him where he got the painting,' said Konstantin, flapping his hand at her. 'Shhh, I want to listen.'

Just then another pair of actors entered the scene – two men in black uniforms with white sashes across the breast, red stripes down the trouser leg, and glossy feathers in their black hats. They marched over to Vincenzo and took hold of one arm each.

'Who are these chumps? What's happening?' asked Aidan.

Konstantin looked sick. 'Well, Aidan, what's happening is that for the second time in his life, Vincenzo is under arrest for the theft of the *Mona Lisa*.'

The words echoed around the glorious art gallery, resounding from the frescoed walls and the parquet floor. Age-old faces looked down from the gilt-framed pictures in disapproval at the scene – the young moustachioed Italian held fast by a brace of policemen, the oddly dressed young foreigners looking on, and Signor Giovanni Poggi of the Uffizi Gallery, holding on to the *Mona Lisa* as if he would never let her go again.

Vincenzo's parade through the centre of Florence was not at all as the time-thieves had expected. Their friend was practically dragged through the streets, protesting his innocence piteously. People stared all right, but not as they would stare as a homecoming hero. Of course, no one knew what kind of crime Vincenzo had committed; from his treatment, they assumed it was something terrible.

Mothers pulled their children into doorways, away from the gaze of this hardened criminal. A shoal of urchins followed them, catcalling and whistling, as the procession went from the shining golden parts of Florence to the poorer parts. Eventually the police came to a rough, square building with bars at the windows. Vincenzo was propelled through the entrance, and a studded door slammed shut in the time-thieves' faces.

Luna, who had had some success in the last jail she visited, was sent to plead with the guard at the entrance. She knocked and a little shutter opened in the massive door.

'Do you speak English?'

'Yes,' came the curt reply.

'Can we see the prisoner?'

The guard was all sweetness and light. 'Of course, *principessa*. All you like.'

This seemed hopeful. 'Thank you so much,' said Luna, smiling her politest smile. 'When?'

'At his trial, *principessa*,' growled the guard. 'There's a public gallery. You can see him then as much as you like.' And he slid the shutter closed with a snap.

22 JULY 1914
1 p.m.

Florence was in the grip of *Mona Lisa* fever.

Every stall sold prints or figurines of *La Gioconda*'s face. Her image was daubed on every street corner. And the queue to see the *Mona Lisa* swelled to thousands. Riots broke out in the streets around the Uffizi as the citizens flocked to see the world's most famous painting, missing for years and now back in its home town.

In the meantime, on the advice of the cockney signorina, who was most distressed to hear that her favourite client, Vincenzo, had been taken up by the police, the time-thieves and Houdini scoured the daily papers for news of the trial. And when at last the day came, they made sure they were seated in the front row of the public gallery of the Courts of Justice.

All thought of the *Salvator Mundi*, and finding Leonardo's other missing masterpiece, had gone from their minds. They only had one rescue mission – and that was to spring Vincenzo, once again, from jail.

Houdini was confident he could get Vincenzo out. 'It will be just like the police station in Paris,' he stated. 'Different country, different time, same principles. Padlocks and handcuffs will not have changed so much in a couple of years. It's escapology, pure and simple.' He rubbed his clean-shaven chin. 'We just need to find someone who can get us a visit with Vincenzo.'

Of course the time-thieves hardly understood a word of the trial. They could see that, just as in England, there was a judge, a lawyer for the prosecution, and a lawyer for the defence. They took to Vincenzo's defence lawyer at once: a young, nervous-looking man who kept pushing his spectacles up his nose. They liked him much better than the older, portly lawyer for the prosecution. And they made sure they applauded everything he uttered, even though they had no idea what he'd said.

And they weren't alone. The citizens were flying Italian flags and Florentine flags, and banners with Vincenzo's name painted on them — very obviously on his side. Even with the language barrier, it was clear that the public thought Vincenzo a hero. He had brought *La Gioconda* back to where she belonged, defeated the French and scored a huge victory for Italy. They too clapped when the counsel for the defence spoke, booed and hissed the prosecutor, and when Vincenzo took the stand they cheered him to the rafters.

Other witnesses were called, including the serious museum director from the Uffizi and a learned-looking gentleman who Konstantin claimed was an art expert. The art expert seemed to be in another trial entirely, for the word he uttered the most was 'Napoleon'. The testimonies went on for hours, and when the proceedings were finally over and the judge gave his verdict, the public in the gallery cried out in anger. They began chanting, throwing their flags and banners, and the clerks had to clear the court.

'What happened?' said Luna to Konstantin, who had been trying to follow the judge's words.

'It's bad,' he said, as they were jostled out of the gallery along with the rest of the protesting public. 'I didn't get all of it, but basically Vincenzo's going to jail for a very long time.'

As they spilled out on to the street, Houdini spotted a tall young man in robes walking around the side of the courtroom.

'The defence lawyer!' exclaimed the magician. 'That's our way in to Vincenzo. Let's waylay him.'

But others in the crowd had the same idea. Angry Florentines surrounded the young man, pulling at his billowing robes, throwing anything they had in their pockets at him, and berating him in angry voices. The time-thieves didn't need to know any Italian to understand that these people thought the lawyer had let their hero down, and that his weak defence of Vincenzo Peruggia had led to his imprisonment. Soon the hapless lawyer had been pushed to the ground, and disappeared beneath the furious mob.

Aidan didn't hesitate. He plunged into the fray, pulling bodies away from the young man, putting up his fists and dancing around like a boxer. 'Come on, then!' he shouted. 'I'll take on all of yous!'

The crowd, grumbling, dispersed at the sight of the tough-looking youngster, and Konstantin and Luna pulled the lawyer to his feet by the sleeves of the young man's legal gown.

'*Parle inglese?*' Konstantin asked.

'Yes,' gasped the young man, brushing himself down shakily. 'You saved me from a thorough beating,' he said to Aidan. 'How can I thank you?'

'Well…' His young champion grinned, remembering the slip-up he'd made in Paris. 'We need an avocado. And I think you just might fit the bill.'

22 JULY 1914
6.15 p.m.

In a very few moments the time-thieves and Houdini were seated in a Florentine bar with the young lawyer, whose name turned out to be Dottore Sandro Mattei.

'Doctor, eh?' said Aidan, impressed. 'Well, at least you can check your own wounds.' For the lawyer was bruised and grazed after his encounter with the public.

'That's not how it works,' said the young man ruefully. 'I'm a doctor of law. Lawyers in Italy are addressed as dottore.'

'Can we buy you a cup of coffee?' asked Houdini.

'After that trial,' said the young man glumly, 'I think I'll have something stronger.' He looked around nervously at the crowded bar. Florentines who were drowning their sorrows were already looking at him and pointing.

'Perhaps,' said Houdini gently, 'it would be wise to take off that robe you wear.'

'I'm not worthy of it anyway,' said Sandro, shrugging his arms out of the sleeves and hanging the thing carelessly over the back of his chair. He clenched his fist and banged it on the table. 'Damn it all. I've failed Vincenzo and my country.'

'Nonsense,' said Luna kindly. 'All is not lost.'

Once the waiter had brought wine for the gentlemen and lemonade for the time-thieves, Houdini spoke again.

'Let us explain,' he said. 'We are friends of Vincenzo's, come all the way from Paris to help him. If you can get us in to see him, he will soon be free.'

The young lawyer took a gulp of wine. 'How is that possible?' he asked. 'The city of Florence just imprisoned him.'

'How long for?' asked Konstantin.

'Three years,' came the reply.

'Three *years*?' brayed Aidan, causing some of the drinkers to turn and look.

Sandro put his head in his hands. 'I know, I know. It's a disaster.'

Luna looked out at the beautiful square, at the giant statues, the golden dome of the cathedral and the pigeons wheeling above in the sunset sky, free and unshackled. It was terrible to think of Vincenzo locked away from all this, from his beloved Italy, mouldering in a dark cell for three long years.

Houdini said, 'Could you tell us a little about what happened at the trial? We didn't understand a great deal. The people seemed to be so obviously on Vincenzo's side.'

'They are indeed,' said the lawyer glumly. 'All of Italy is on his side, including myself. That's why I took the case.'

'So what went wrong?' asked Luna, not meaning to be unkind.

'Things seemed to change when that art expert took the stand,' said Konstantin.

'Yes, what was all that Napoleon stuff about?' asked Aidan. 'What's Napoleon got to do with anything?'

Sandro lifted his head from his hands, as slowly as if it was made of stone. 'It was a legal point of ownership. Vincenzo thought that Napoleon, the great French general, stole the *Mona Lisa* from Italy when he invaded in 1797.'

'Yes, he said the same to us,' put in Luna. 'He thought he'd be doing nothing wrong by returning the painting to Italy.'

'Trouble is,' said Sandro, 'it isn't true. The expert the prosecution found, a Signor Alfredo Geri, says that the *Mona Lisa* was given to King Francis I of France by Leonardo da Vinci himself.'

The time-thieves digested this.

'So…' said Konstantin slowly, 'the *Mona Lisa* belonged to the French all along.'

'Since 1516, when her paint was barely dry,' said the lawyer. 'So Vincenzo had the right idea, but he did the wrong thing. The *Mona Lisa* was stolen from her rightful French owners, and now he's paying the price.'

The time-thieves and Houdini looked at each other, weighed down with guilt. They had done this. They had stolen the painting, and they had given it to Vincenzo to bring home to Italy. This had happened because of them.

Houdini said what they were all thinking. 'This was our fault. And we'll free Vincenzo if it's the last thing we do. May we see him? Once will be enough.'

Sandro Mattei looked at them all in turn. Then he got up and picked up his abandoned lawyer's gown. 'If you can succeed where I've failed, then you will do a service to all of Italy. Come on.'

22 JULY 1914
7 p.m.

It was growing dark, and Florence's pigeons were preparing to roost rising up into the twilight sky. Sandro led the time-thieves away from the beautiful part of the city across the river and into a terrifying slum, where hungry eyes watched them from doorways and beggars followed them like hounds.

Sandro led them into the courtyard of the huge dark building Vincenzo had been dragged to the day before. It could almost have been a monastery but for the horrid, keening cries issuing from the barred windows.

'Welcome to the Murate Prison,' said Sandro, 'Italy's most notorious jail, and Vincenzo's home for the next three years.'

The hideous place had that aroma of old stone and damp, which reminded Aidan sharply of the catacombs under the commissariat in Paris. 'Graveyards,' said Aidan. 'That's what it smells of.'

'You speak truer than you know, my friend,' said Sandro. 'Not many people leave the Murate alive. This way.'

The young lawyer led them down a colonnade of crumbling stone arches to the door with the barred hatch where Luna had spoken to the guard the day before. He rapped on the door and the hatch snapped back. Sandro spoke to the face at the window, giving his name and title, and pointing to the time-thieves and Houdini. They couldn't understand what he told the guard, but whatever it was, it worked. The door was unbolted and they were all ushered inside. As they passed through the portal, Luna could see Houdini examining the locks with a practised eye.

Inside, the sense of the monastery the Murate had once been was even stronger. There was an ancient stone passageway with doors leading off to each side, oak doors bound with iron. Luna almost expected the spectres of long-dead monks to bar their way, but the reality was much worse – there were living men locked behind each door, and the Murate now represented not heaven but hell. A guard unlocked one of the doors, handed a candle to

Dottore Mattei, and the time-thieves and Houdini crowded inside the cell with a depressing sense of familiarity. For the second time, in a different year and a different country, Vincenzo was in prison for the same crime.

At first they could hardly see him by the light of the single candle the guard had left, but then his shape resolved out of the gloom. He was seated on a mattress of straw, his hands shackled to each other and the wall. There was nowhere to sit, so the time travellers and the lawyer stood in a semi-circle.

Houdini waited until the door had closed. 'Vincenzo, my friend,' he whispered, 'we've come to get you out of here.'

There was a long silence. Then Vincenzo looked up at Houdini, and spoke a single word. 'No.'

Houdini was so surprised, he actually took a step back. 'What do you mean, no?'

Vincenzo smiled bitterly. 'I know you, my magical friend. I know you will have been looking at the locks ever since you entered this place. On the front door, on my door. How many, what type? And now you're looking at my shackles. How are they secured? How can they be sprung?' He shook his head. 'I bless you, and I thank you, but no. No tricks, no escapology. Not this time.'

Luna sat by him on the prickly straw and took Vincenzo's shackled hands. 'But… *why?*'

The prisoner turned to her. 'This is my country. Do you think I want to spend the rest of my life looking over my shoulder as a fugitive from Italian justice? No. The only honourable action is to serve my time. If I could be freed by legal means, that would be different. But the law is the law.'

The law is the law. Konstantin thought about this. 'How about it, Dottore Mattei? Are there any legal routes we could take?'

'Well,' said the lawyer, shifting his feet on the stone floor. 'We could lodge an appeal. But we don't have any grounds.'

'Grounds?'

'Reasons,' explained the young man. 'Vincenzo's case doesn't fit any of them.'

'And what,' asked Houdini, 'would give him grounds for an appeal?'

Dottore Mattei ticked the reasons off on his fingers. 'Miscarriage of justice. Mistrial. New evidence or doubts cast on the mental capacity of the prisoner at the time the crime was committed.'

'Well now, wait a minute,' Konstantin held up his forefinger. 'What about the last one?'

Sandro goggled at him. 'You want to cast doubt on my client's mental capacity?'

'No, of course not,' said Konstantin. 'But we could, you know, play it up for the courts. We said just the other day that the *Mona Lisa* had enchanted him.'

'I am here, you know,' grumbled Vincenzo.

'I mean, not to put too fine a point on it, the man's in love with a painting,' said Aidan, as if he hadn't spoken. 'That's what my old ma would call "doolally".'

The light of the candle seemed to flare in Dottore Mattei's eyes. He wagged his own finger at Aidan. 'You know, you might be on to something there.'

'He is,' said Konstantin. 'In my country there are some very clever doctors who deal with the science of the mind and behaviour, a field known as psychology. Foremost of those is Mr Sigmund Freud.'

'Ah. I know of Professor Freud, of course,' said the lawyer.

'Freud would say,' Konstantin continued, 'that Vincenzo had developed an attachment to the *Mona Lisa* almost as if she were a human woman, and therefore he was not responsible for his actions in regard to the painting.'

'Hello,' said Vincenzo, waving his shackled hands until the chains clanked. 'Is no one going to ask me about this?

Perhaps I don't want to be freed if people are going to think I'm mad.'

'Not mad,' said Luna. 'Just… romantic. I mean, you kept her by your side for years. Can you deny that you were bewitched by the *Mona Lisa*?'

'Anyone might know of my regard for her,' said Vincenzo stiffly.

'Well, there you are,' said Luna. 'Surely you don't want to live here for the next three years?' She licked her lips. 'The Dottore said people rarely get out of the Murate alive,' she whispered dramatically. 'They get sick and *die* here. Surely you want to see Dumenza again – and your family?'

Vincenzo sighed. 'All right,' he said. 'Go on.'

'What you say would certainly amount to grounds for an appeal,' said Dottore Mattei to Konstantin. 'But none of those doctors are here. What we need is an expert witness to testify to Vincenzo's state of mind.'

'What if,' said Konstantin, slowly turning to the magician, 'what if you *are* able to help him escape, Mr Houdini? But not with your escapology tricks. Instead you would use every other piece of magic at the Great Houdini's disposal.' He waved his long hands in front of his face, as if he was painting a phantom canvas in the air.

'Your acting talent, your ability to engage an audience, your showmanship. And, most significant of all, the one crucial weapon in your arsenal that you have not used for years.'

'And what's that?' asked Houdini, intrigued.

Konstantin smiled. 'Your authentic self.'

24 JULY 1914
7 p.m.

A few days later found the time-thieves once again sitting in the public gallery of Florence's Courts of Justice. Vincenzo's appeal had been successfully launched, and the court was once again gathered to hear the case for the defence. There was the same cast of characters: Dottore Sandro Mattei standing on one side of the court, the portly lawyer for the prosecution standing on the other, and in the middle the learned judge. The public gallery was crammed with Florentines who were, again, all too obviously on Vincenzo's side, with their banners and slogans and flags. The only thing that was different was that Houdini wasn't sitting with his fellow time travellers. And that was for a very good reason.

The judge called the court to order, and the time-thieves braced themselves for another few hours of not understanding most of what was said. But this was different too.

'Ladies and gentlemen of the gallery and members of the court,' the judge began in his gravelly voice, 'we are gathered here today to hear the appeal of Vincenzo Pietro Peruggia, recently sentenced to three years in prison for the theft of the *Mona Lisa*.'

Under the cover of loud boos from the gallery, Aidan leant forward and murmured to the others, 'Either I've gone doolally, or I can understand Italian.'

'Me too,' whispered Luna.

'Just wait.' Konstantin smiled.

'Today our proceedings are a little different, for they will be conducted in English. This is because we will be hearing from an expert witness who does not speak Italian, so we have settled upon English as our only mutual language. Dottore Mattei, have the goodness to call the witness.'

The young lawyer stepped forward. 'If it pleases the court, I call Professor Ehrich Weisz.'

The great double doors of the courtroom were thrown open and Houdini walked in, but he looked quite different from the man the time-thieves knew.

In place of one of his garish checked outfits, he wore a sober three-piece suit in charcoal grey, procured from a Florentine tailor. His hair, usually so wild and crinkly, with those flyaway wings on either side of his head, was parted severely on the side and smoothed down with pomade. He wore little round glasses to veil his silvery eyes, and he had painted on a neat little beard and moustache with the assistance of the cockney signorina's mascara. With the addition of a white laboratory coat over his clothes, he looked every inch a man of medicine.

The strange magic of Houdini's stage presence began to work at once. The watchers in the gallery, who had been chatting and translating for each other during the judge's address, abruptly fell silent and leant forward attentively. What was this odd little man about to say?

'Professor, will you state your name and profession for the court?'

'Of course. My name is Professor Ehrich Weisz, ant I am a neurologist and psychoanalyst at the University of Budapest.'

Aidan noticed that Houdini was speaking in the strong Hungarian accent that he'd employed when Aidan had first met him on the rail tracks of King's Cross. He knew the change of accent indicated that the magician was putting on a performance.

'Have you brought the required copies of your medical qualifications?'

'I had indeed.' Houdini passed a sheaf of papers to the clerk of the court, who showed them first to the prosecution and then to the judge.

Luna remembered Houdini typing the certificates only yesterday in the hotel room, and stamping them with a seal he had carved from a bar of hotel soap.

'Do you think they will fool anyone?' Konstantin had asked.

'Please,' Houdini had replied. 'I've been making stage props for years. Do you really think I can't falsify a couple of medical certificates?'

And indeed, the judge seemed to accept the documents without question. 'Impressive,' he said. 'Dottore Mattei, you may begin your examination of the witness.'

The young lawyer stepped forward with the notes he and Houdini had prepared over long hours and many glasses of wine in the hotel room. His hand shook slightly, but his voice was strong. 'Professor Weisz, could you tell me how you first became acquainted with the prisoner?'

'I was visiting Paris during my university's summer vacation in August 1911. As a lover of Leonardo I had gone to see the *Mona Lisa* in the Louvre, and there I met Vincenzo Peruggia looking at the same work.'

'And you met more than once?' asked the lawyer.

'Yes,' answered the 'professor'. 'I went back to the gallery a number of times during my visit, and each time he was there, staring at the *Mona Lisa* like a man bewitched.'

'And then?'

'We fell into conversation about the painting. He spoke of the *Mona Lisa*, or *La Gioconda* as I know your countrymen call her, as if she was a living woman.'

'And how did your acquaintance develop?'

'I was much interested in the prisoner's attachment to the picture, as it involves my own particular field of the study of the mind. So I asked him if he would allow me to buy him a drink, and share with me his attachment to the *Mona Lisa*.'

'And what followed?'

'I met the prisoner on a number of occasions during my visit. I made a study of him, and he was kind enough to answer my questions. I took copious case notes before returning to Hungary, and I now present these to the court.'

'If it pleases the court,' said Sandro Mattei, 'I will enter these case notes as Exhibit A. Since the theft of the *Mona Lisa* occurred in the middle of these sessions, Professor Weisz has offered us a unique glimpse into the exact state of mind of the prisoner when he stole the *Mona Lisa*. It is the defence's case that at the time Vincenzo Peruggia stole the *Mona Lisa* he was in the grip of a psychosis – a kind of temporary madness – which the professor here describes. '

The judge leafed through the notes that had been offered to him. 'These seem extremely thorough, but for the benefit of those in the court – including myself – who have not had your psychological training, could you try to sum up the nature of this "madness"?'

Houdini stood very still. Each of the time-thieves remembered him doing exactly this during his magic show, when he was preparing to perform a particularly impressive trick. 'I would say, in my professional opinion, that Vincenzo Peruggia is suffering from what we in the trade call a Lancelot complex.'

In the gallery Konstantin smiled to himself behind his hand. Keenly interested in knights of old, and battles, he had come up with this idea during those late-night discussions. To him the condition he'd invented seemed very believable, and much more plausible than some of the stuff he'd heard psychoanalysts come out with in his native Prussia.

Houdini took a breath. 'Imagine, if you will, the knights of King Arthur's round table, and in particular, his champion and bravest knight Lancelot. Lancelot's code of honour meant that he would do anything to rescue his lady love, Guinevere.' Houdini spoke very loudly and clearly, so that even those who were not too familiar with English would understand. 'Vincenzo truly thought that *La Gioconda* had been taken from her beloved home to a foreign country against her will, by an evil king, in this case Napoleon Bonaparte. If a damsel was in distress,' he turned to the gallery, 'which of us gentlemen would not wish to become a Lancelot, and rescue her? And if any gentleman ignored the call, would he really be worthy of the name?'

Luna thought it clever to appeal to the chivalry of the men present. She remembered what Lady Evelyn had said in Egypt – that, since the wreck of the *Titanic* (which, unbelievably, had sunk between their being in Paris in 1911 and arriving in Florence in 1914), young men had been more and more inclined to act with honour and chivalry.

'Besides Vincenzo's love for the *Mona Lisa*,' Houdini went on, 'there was another love, burning just as brightly as the first. And that was his love of his country.' Houdini turned to the public, playing to the gallery again as only he knew how. 'Ladies and gentlemen, Vincenzo Peruggia is a patriot. That means someone who loves his country. Go up and down this glorious land of yours, and you will not find a man who loves Italy more than he. And by returning the *Mona Lisa* to Florence, this man – this honourable man – found a way to unite those two great loves of his. He brought the object of his affections back to the country he adores. Yes, he enjoyed *La Gioconda*'s company for the intervening years since he left Paris, lived with her as a man might live with a wife. But then, despite his growing attachment, what did he do? He brought her back to Florence, her home, and gave her to the city. Considering his state of mind, this was a supreme sacrifice.'

'Thank you, Professor,' said the judge. 'That is very clear, and the court is grateful for your expert testimony. Let us hear from the prisoner. Signor Peruggia, have you anything to say in your defence?'

'Only this,' said Vincenzo. He stood very straight in the dock. 'War is coming. You have all read the news. Archduke Franz Ferdinand has recently been assassinated in Sarajevo, and the nations of Europe are choosing sides. The country I love may be about to be sad for a very long time.' Vincenzo looked up at the gallery and opened his arms to his watching countryman like an embrace. 'I think when I brought *La Gioconda* home, with her incredible smile, I put the smile back on Italy's face. That's all I wanted to do.'

At this, everyone in the public gallery leapt to their feet and erupted in applause, cheering fit to raise the roof and stamping their feet. They threw flags and flowers, which fluttered down to land at Vincenzo's feet. It took the judge some moments to restore the court to order, so that his verdict could be heard: Vincenzo Peruggia was to be released without a stain on his character.

The time-thieves and Houdini met around the corner from the courthouse, away from the crowds, and were soon joined by a jubilant-looking Dottore Mattei. Houdini shook the lawyer by the hand. 'Well done,' Houdini said in quite his normal voice. 'I hope you now feel worthy of the gown you wear.'

'I do,' said the delighted young man, his thin face flushed with victory. 'I think I will sleep in it from now on.'

'Here.' Houdini produced his purse. 'Please take these sovereigns in payment.'

Dottore Sandro Mattei looked at the golden coins that lay in Houdini's hand. 'Thank you, but I cannot.'

'But why?' asked the magician. 'You have earned them.'

'Oh, no doubt,' said the young man. 'But there are other reasons to do things rather than money.' He smiled. 'Let us just say that I love my country too.' And with a bow he allowed himself to be dragged off by a friendly Florentine mob who wanted to buy him a drink.

After another few moments Vincenzo was released from a side door, looking pale and rubbing his wrists where his handcuffs had been released – not by a magician this time, but by the officials of the Italian law. The time-thieves fell on him, embracing him delightedly and slapping him on the back. Vincenzo smiled and smiled, for the moment unable to speak.

'Where will you go now?' said Luna. 'Home to Dumenza?'

'Not yet,' said Vincenzo, his voice hoarse with emotion. 'I must go where the work is. And for me, that will not be easy.'

'Why?' asked Aidan.

'Because I am a thief. A hero, yes, but a confirmed thief. Who will employ me now?'

'Me,' said Houdini.

Vincenzo looked at him in surprise.

'We are going to Arezzo to look for a lost Leonardo, the *Salvator Mundi*, beneath the Buriano Bridge,' admitted Houdini. 'Apart from to see you, that's the reason we came to Tuscany. I could really use an Italian speaker, and a craftsman such as yourself. I will pay in gold sovereigns. What do you say?'

Vincenzo couldn't say anything, but enfolded Houdini in a massive hug.

25 JULY 1914

9 a.m.

Houdini decided they should leave Florence right away, as Vincenzo couldn't walk anywhere in the bounds of the city without an embrace or the offer of a drink – this was nice for a while, but it certainly didn't help when the time-thieves were trying to gather equipment for a top-secret expedition to find a lost Leonardo. The cockney signorina agreed to look after Houdini's 'motor car', which was parked outside the hotel, until his return. And, reassured that the Time Train would be safe, the three young people, a stage magician and the man who had stolen the *Mona Lisa* headed for the station to take a more conventional train to Arezzo, and from there took a carriage to the old hilltop town of Castiglion Fibocchi.

'Of course, the landscape might look very different now to the way it looked in the painting,' said Vincenzo, when the carriage had deposited them in the old stone town. 'There may have been houses built on the floodplain.'

'Well, so long as the bridge is still there,' said Aidan, 'that's all we need to worry about.'

'Well, let's see,' said Vincenzo. 'If we go to the old hilltop citadel, that will give us the exact view that Leonardo painted. This way.'

They climbed, puffing and panting, through the ancient and winding town, up the hill and to the top of the old fort, worrying with every step that the view would have changed out of all recognition. But they needn't have worried. The vista was almost exactly the same as it was in the *Mona Lisa*, and the time-thieves hopped around the ancient battlements, excitedly pointing out the features they knew so well.

'There's the lake!' cried Luna, pointing at a misty blue expanse in the middle distance.

'And the bridge!' yelled Aidan, standing perilously on the crumbling battlements. 'Look, you can even see the arches.'

'And the winding river!' shouted Konstantin, indicating a silvery ribbon snaking through the landscape. 'Oh, wait.' His face fell. 'This is not good.'

Houdini, too, walked to the edge of the ancient fort. 'What's the matter?'

'The river,' said Konstantin mournfully. 'It's back.'

In an instant Luna and Aidan were by his side. 'What d'you mean?'

'The river is a river again,' said Konstantin. 'It's not an almost dry riverbed. There's water. Look. It's glistening in the sun.'

They looked.

'If there's water under that bridge,' said Aidan uneasily, 'how the devil are we going to get at the *Salvator Mundi*?'

'We need to take a closer look,' said Vincenzo. 'It may just be a trickle, like it was in the painting.'

But it was not just a trickle. As the Buriano Bridge was a little way from Castiglion, Vincenzo found an obliging man with a horse and hay cart to take them there. The driver's eyes went as round as the sovereigns he was offered when he saw the glint of English gold. Soon they were actually crossing the Buriano Bridge, the horse's shoes clip-clopping on the stone. It felt very strange indeed to be inside a painting, to be actually crossing the four misty arches that were sketched in behind the *Mona Lisa*'s left shoulder.

'Stop!' called Houdini. 'That's far enough.' They all clambered down and he paid the driver, who touched his cap and left. The three time-thieves, Houdini and Vincenzo went to the balustrade and peered over the side of the bridge with dismay.

Even though it was summer, the river was in spate, and a deep torrent flowed through the ancient arches of the Buriano Bridge.

'*Damn*,' exclaimed Houdini. 'I had hoped that the river would still be dammed – no pun intended – and we would be able to walk underneath the second arch and find the painting.'

'If the *Salvator Mundi* is that precious, Leonardo wouldn't have made it easy for anyone who wanted to find it,' reasoned Luna. 'I bet he unleashed the river himself. There must be some kind of chamber under the second arch. It must have been almost dry when he hid it, and it's underwater now. He didn't want anyone to find it but himself, so he made the quest impossible.'

The word 'quest' had an immediate effect on Konstantin, almost as magical as one of Houdini's tricks. He immediately thought of knights of old, the clash of steel in battle, and the quest for the Holy Grail. 'Maybe not *impossible*,' he said. 'Let's go down to the river bank and get a better look.'

They all trooped around the side of the bridge and clambered down to the river, swishing through the dry summer grass that grew at the side of the river, and disturbing iridescent dragonflies on the tall reeds. But from the side of the river the prospect was even worse – the fast-flowing river reached over halfway up each arch, and the water curved around each bastion, choppy and difficult.

'Maybe all *is* lost.' Konstantin sighed. 'The water is too deep and fast. Even if it was possible to moor a boat under the arch, it would be impossible for a diver to hold his breath for long enough to dive down and find a hidden chamber. And only a fool would deliberately place himself underwater and risk drowning.'

'I've made a living doing exactly that,' said Houdini, 'in my Chinese Water Torture Cell. But no offence taken.'

The four time travellers and Vincenzo sat down on the river bank, dispirited. It seemed that this particular quest had come to an end. But as Luna sat down she spotted a bright butterfly that wheeled and fluttered sunwards. She caught a flash of a butter-yellow wing. 'It's a Silver-washed Fritillary,' she said glumly, thinking of all the butterflies

314

pinned on cards in her aunt's house and in the Butterfly Room of the Greenwich Observatory. 'I suppose we'll have to return to the Butterfly Club with nothing. Again.'

Aidan watched the butterfly rise into the blue Tuscan sky, his eyes narrowed against the sunlight. 'The Butterfly Club,' he repeated in a thoughtful voice. 'Hmm.'

Konstantin knew Aidan well enough by now to know that when he made that noise, like a purring engine, he was forming an idea. 'What is it?'

'Well,' said Aidan slowly, 'their mission is to search *forward* in time, yes? All this time we've been borrowing things from the future.' He took a deep breath, as if he was going to jump into the river right there and then. 'But what if we borrowed something from the past?'

'What do you mean?'

'Well, there's no doubt that Leonardo was one of the cleverest fellas of his age – of *any* age, come to that,' said Aidan. 'He wasn't just a painter, he was an inventor too. And one of the things he invented was the way to recover the *Salvator Mundi*. He's already given us the answer.'

Houdini turned to him, his eyes mirror-bright, as they always were when he was excited. 'The *Codex Arundel*.' It was almost a whisper.

'Bang on!' said Aidan.

'Slow down,' said Konstantin. 'What do you mean? What about the *Codex*?'

'First things first,' said Houdini, as if he hadn't spoken. 'Vincenzo, have the goodness to find us somewhere to stay for a week. This part of the mission will take a little longer than expected.'

Vincenzo nodded at once. 'Another hotel?'

'No,' said Houdini. 'Better to have our own villa, where people won't ask too many questions about banging and hammering and construction work.'

'I'll need some draughtsman's paper and pencils,' said Aidan, 'to do a few designs. I mean, they won't be Leonardo standard, but it will give us a better idea of what materials we need to buy.'

'Materials for what?' asked Luna. 'Constructing what?'

'Ah, that'd be telling,' said Aidan, winking at Houdini. 'I can't just *dive* in and tell you the incredible *depths* of my genius. You'll just have to hold your *breath* for a while longer.'

Houdini laughed, but Luna thought Aidan a know-it-all. 'You think you're clever, don't you?'

Annoyingly, Aidan just grinned. 'I know I am.'

Luna's Goodhart temper surfaced. She stamped her foot, which wasn't very easy to do on a steep riverbank. 'Oh, for goodness' sake, just tell us!'

Aidan relented. 'It's one of the things that first interested me about the *Codex Arundel*.' He looked at Houdini, who nodded. 'Over four hundred years ago Leonardo da Vinci made a design, complete and entire, for an underwater diving suit.'

25 JULY 1914
9 p.m.

The time travellers were fortunate that Vincenzo was with them, for they really couldn't have done without him. Speaking Italian, he arranged everything. It was Houdini's brainwave that Vincenzo should disguise himself as their butler. 'For there is no magic in the whole of my show,' said the magician, 'that can make a man as invisible as a servant.' In this humble persona Vincenzo rented a sizeable villa in the Tuscan hills. It had enough rooms for all of them and a barn attached to it where Houdini and Aidan could build in peace. Vincenzo took Aidan's beautifully drafted designs to Florence and bought all the materials they needed for the diving suit. And late into the night, when Aidan and Houdini were hard at work in the candlelit barn, he translated the mirror writing of the *Codex Arundel*, looking glass in hand, from Leonardo's original words. It was hard to believe that anything useful could be made from the intricate sepia drawings in the *Codex Arundel*. To Luna and Konstantin the designs for the diving suit just looked like squiggles – tubes and pipes and something that looked like the head of an octopus. But the instructions Vincenzo translated from the mirror writing were incredibly precise, and they could overhear details as if they were bizarre ingredients for the strangest recipe ever – cane tubes, pig leather, wineskins and cork.

In the master's text Aidan found not just instructions for how to build the diving suit, but part of the answer to the mystery of the missing painting. 'It seems as if Leonardo painted the *Salvator Mundi* for the French king too,' he said, looking up from the ancient writing, 'when the king was the ruler of Milan. But Leonardo thought the *Salvator Mundi* was his greatest work and didn't want to let the painting go to a private owner, even a king. He thought it had a bigger purpose in the world.'

'What kind of purpose?' asked Luna.

'Something religious,' said Vincenzo, and in the candlelight, reading from that ancient book, he looked quite monkish himself. 'He thought the painting had a mission, an almost spiritual power. He thought it could literally save the world. So he wanted it to be in a church or cathedral, not in the palace of a French king. So he hid it.'

'In the bridge?' asked Konstantin breathlessly.

'It doesn't say. But I think you had it right about the dam, *signorina* Luna. He quarrelled with the king, fled Milan with the painting and returned to his native Tuscany. On his way home Leonardo broke down the dam he'd built years before to create a water supply for the little town of Castiglion. The river became a river again.'

'Then what?' asked Aidan.

'Then Leonardo returned to Florence,' said Vincenzo. 'He painted one of his local models, Lisa Gherardini. He was very fond of the painting, which he called the *Mona Lisa* – he even used to carry it about with him. But the King of France had not forgotten that Leonardo owed him a painting, and Leonardo was obliged to give him the *Mona Lisa* in place of the *Salvator Mundi*. But *I* think that in the background of the *Mona Lisa*, for his own amusement, he painted the location of the *Salvator Mundi*'s hiding place – then wrote the riddle of its whereabouts in the *Codex Arundel*.' He looked up, his eyes full of candlelight. 'Leonardo *meant* for it to be found one day, but only by those who truly understand his work. By those who don't just look, but *see*.'

'Well, that might just be us,' said Aidan, 'if we ever finish this bally suit.'

26 JULY 1914
4 p.m.

There was not much Luna and Konstantin could do to help, so they were tasked with buying and preparing the food for the others. 'An army marches on its stomach,' said Konstantin. 'It's quite an important job, really.' Vincenzo purchased them some plain peasant clothes and they abandoned their Parisian pastels gratefully. Dressed as Italians, the pair walked into nearby Arezzo and perused the market stalls for local foods. They found Italian food just as fascinating as French, and learned the words for the different cheeses and breads – musical-sounding terms like mozzarella and ciabatta. One memorable market day they found pale, foot-long noodles known as spaghetti. They had no idea how to cook them but bought a bundle anyway simply because of their funny name. They skipped down the road making each other laugh, shouting, 'Spaghetti! Spaghetti!' in ridiculous voices.

At the bottom of the hill they pulled up short, the smiles falling from their faces and the laughter dying in their throats. For in front of Arezzo's church was a sinister black carriage. Four black horses with black feathered plumes on their heads stood in the traces, still as statues. The carriage was much longer than a hansom cab; there was no driver on the box, and the carriage windows were covered by a black curtain. Luna and Konstantin walked past the strange vehicle on their way to the villa, staring at the glossy black finish of the wood and the crystal-clear plate glass of the windows.

As they approached, the black curtain twitched.

Luna and Konstantin ran all the way down the hill as if the devil was after them. By the time they were at the villa, they'd outrun their fear and were laughing again, this time at themselves. 'Oof,' said Konstantin, folded over like a jack-knife. 'That gave me a fright!'

'Should we mention the carriage to the others?' panted Luna.

'No point,' said Konstantin. 'It was just a hearse. A funeral carriage. There would have been nothing inside it but the coffin of some poor unfortunate.'

'Then why did the curtain move?' said Luna.

'Must have been the wind,' said Konstantin. 'Nothing to do with us.'

Back in the barn the serious engineering work was going on, so Luna and Konstantin climbed high up into the ancient beams of the barn and peered down, lost in admiration, as Houdini and Aidan constructed Leonardo's diving suit. Houdini had spent years making stage illusions, so they knew he would be reasonably skilled, but it was Aidan who was the real revelation. They knew he'd put a pocket watch back together when he was ten, and they knew he'd worked on railways ever since, but they'd never actually seen him construct anything before. He pushed his goggles into his hair, so his black locks wouldn't fall in his face, narrowed his blue eyes with intense concentration, and got down on the hay-strewn floor to build his creation. His fingers were almost as dextrous as Houdini's as they worked, connecting pipes to washers, washers to metal plates, welding and screwing and hammering happily away.

'Gosh, he really knows machines inside and out, doesn't he?' said Luna with admiration.

Konstantin watched her watching Aidan. 'You like him, don't you?'

'Yes, of course,' she said in surprise. 'But I like you too.'

'Even though I'm...damaged?'

Luna looked at him. 'What *can* you mean?'

Konstantin sighed. 'I have a design fault. My heart failed, and had to be replaced by clockwork. *He* can make anything, build anything, fix anything. I wish he could fix *me*.'

'Everyone has different skills,' said Luna comfortingly. 'You have too.'

'Like what?'

'You're the one of the bravest people I know.'

Konstantin looked at her sideways. 'Really?'

'Yes, you went into the future with no fear at all. You always volunteer to go first in any sticky situation. You stood up to that... that time terrorist Arthur John Priest in Egypt, and again in Paris. And you've got the future inside you, ticking away – you're the first of your kind. You're not damaged.' She laid her hand on his arm. 'If anything, you're *better* than us. You're part-human, part-machine. You're a superhuman, the very first one. It takes courage to be the pathfinder.'

Konstantin looked a little more cheerful, then he said, 'You said *one* of the bravest people you know. Who's the other? It's Aidan, isn't it?' He looked back down at his friend. 'I wish I could be like Aidan...' It sounded silly as soon as he said it, but it was the closest thing he could think of to how he felt. 'As brave as him.'

Luna suddenly saw how it was. 'Konstantin,' she said. 'Are you *jealous* of Aidan?'

He was silent.

'You do *like* him, don't you?'

'Of course,' said Konstantin. 'He's my brother. My time brother. I just wish he wasn't so... *annoying*.'

She laughed. 'Me too.'

Eventually, famished and thirsty, the craftsmen had to stop for dinner. They had decided it was too risky to keep a servant, so it was up to Luna and Konstantin to provide the meals, as they weren't involved in the actual invention. That night they cooked the amusingly named spaghetti for dinner, with some tomatoes and basil and the cheese with the equally funny name. There was also soft bread and olive oil, spicy salami and sweet grapes. The grown-ups had wine, scarlet as a Red Admiral butterfly, each bottle nestled in its own little basket. As they ate, Vincenzo told them about the international situation, as he bought a newspaper every day. Storm clouds were gathering, he said, and Europe was on the brink of war.

'It may not happen, though,' he said soothingly, seeing the time-thieves' frightened faces. 'War is always a last resort.'

'Maybe he's right,' said Luna later as she and Konstantin washed the plates. 'Maybe something *will* happen to prevent the war. Remember, it hasn't happened yet.'

'I don't know,' said Konstantin doubtfully. 'When we were on the *Titanic*, we concluded that we couldn't stop really *big* things from happening. I think the point of the Butterfly Effect is that you can change a *small* thing, and that can have far-reaching consequences. We changed the fate of hundreds of passengers just by putting a radio back. We probably can't stop the Great War, but we can stop Vincenzo going to war, and I'm going to make sure we do that.'

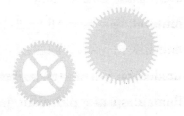

28 JULY 1914
11 p.m.

'Come on – it looks like they've finished.'

It was two nights later. Luna jumped down from the beam in the barn, and Konstantin did too, just as the engineers held up Leonardo's invention to the light.

'It looks like a creature from a nightmare,' considered Luna.

Konstantin said, 'A creature from the deep, more like.'

Aidan grinned. 'She's not very pretty, is she?'

He was right. The suit had a helmet of pig leather, with a face mask with windows for the eyes made of repurposed motoring goggles. All kinds of pieces of apparatus were attached to it, via a lengthy tube, and the whole thing was stitched on to a kind of leather coat, which gave it a scarily human aspect – part-man, part-machine, the kind Luna had spoken about to Konstantin. 'I know this design is from the past,' she said, walking all the way around it, 'but it kind of looks like it's from the future.'

'Oh, totally,' said Aidan. 'In days to come they'll use this kind of technology to go into other inhospitable environments, like space.'

Luna laughed. Aidan was always teasing her about things like that, and this was clearly a joke. As if a human could ever walk in space! 'How *does* it work?'

'These are cane tubes joined by leather. They are reinforced with steel rings to stop the pipes being crushed by the water pressure. They're attached to the face mask at one end, and at the other to this cork float,' he indicated a bell-shaped block, 'to keep the openings above water. The leather coat has a pouch to hold this wineskin which contains the air the diver needs. And look…' He pointed to another smaller funnelled bottle. 'This one is for – well, you know.' He blushed.

'Urination,' put in Houdini politely. 'That was my idea. I'll tell you from doing escapology, if you need to go, you need to go.'

'We'll test the suit in the horse trough,' said Aidan professionally, 'but she looks pretty watertight to me. I reckon she'll do the job.'

'Speaking of which,' said Luna, 'who *is* going to do the job?'

'I would love to,' said Konstantin truthfully, looking longingly at the suit, 'but I never learned to swim. I was always too sick.'

'And we shouldn't risk your clockwork heart anyway,' said Aidan. 'Imagine if you rusted.'

'I never learned either,' said Luna sadly. Young ladies of her class were discouraged from messing around in water. 'How about you, Houdini? You spend your life upside down in water.'

The magician shook his head. 'But sadly, I never learned to swim.'

'*I* can swim,' said Vincenzo proudly.

'*No,*' they all chorused.

'You've just got out of prison,' said Aidan. 'If you're caught nicking another Leonardo, they'll bang you back in as soon as they look at you.' He looked round at them all. 'I suppose that leaves me, then.'

Luna's stomach seemed to plunge into her boots. She really, really, didn't want Aidan to do it. 'Can you even swim?'

'Like an otter, Duch.' He grinned.

In the morning they tested the suit in the horse trough next to the barn. It worked very well. 'No leaks,' gasped Aidan when he took off the helmet, his hair still bone-dry. They helped him out of the trough in the heavy suit, and water streamed on to the flagstones. 'The float seems to keep the airways open.'

But Houdini, who was well used to testing and re-testing tricks, shook his head. 'But this is *still* water,' he said. 'If we use the floats in that fast-flowing river they'll be halfway to Florence in no time.'

'You're right,' said Aidan, peeling off the leather suit. 'Tell you what. This suit was clearly designed for a man diving alone. But since you're all going to be there as my support team, we should run the breathing tube up *over* the Buriano Bridge. Then you lot can be up there keeping the airway clear while I'm down below.'

'Will the tube hold you?'

'Not on its own,' said Aidan, 'but if we tether me with a strong piece of cart rope too, that'll take the pressure off the pipe.'

While the suit was drying on the washing line, looking like the shed skin of a most peculiar creature, Houdini taught Aidan about being underwater.

'All right,' said the magician. 'What's the most important organ in the matter of holding your breath?'

Aidan didn't even have to think about that. 'The lungs, surely.'

'Wrong,' said Houdini. 'It's the *mind*. Much of the battle, when holding one's breath, is mental. To know, logically, that your body can persist on the oxygen already available to it. To ignore outright the mind and body's compulsion to breathe.'

He went on to share his secrets with Aidan – how to pant like a dog to fill the lungs before immersion, how to breathe slowly and effectively once in the suit, how to allow the body to relax, since it was effort which wasted oxygen, and how to control the instinct to panic if his air supply was interrupted.

'Remember,' he said, 'if you black out, it doesn't matter how deep the water is. You'll still die.'

'Thanks a million,' said Aidan drily.

'Want to try it?'

'Why not?'

In one of the stranger afternoons of his life, Aidan spent the rest of the day plunging in and out of the horse trough in the stable yard, practising holding his breath. 'How long can *you* hold your breath?' he asked Houdini.

'My record is three minutes and thirty seconds, when I was doing the Chinese Water Torture Cell on Coney Island,' said Houdini modestly.

'Jesus, Mary and Joseph!' exclaimed Aidan. 'That's a long old stretch. You could boil an egg in that time.'

'That's nothing,' said Houdini. 'There are pearl fishers in the Indian Ocean who can hold their breath for twenty minutes.'

'Twenty minutes!' exclaimed Aidan. He shook his wet head so that diamond droplets fell on the cobbles. 'That's a lot of eggs.'

Using the techniques Houdini taught him, he gradually extended the time he could hold his breath while Houdini timed him with his pocket watch. He managed a very creditable two minutes before it was time to join the others for dinner.

'Remember, this stuff is only useful if your air supply fails,' said Houdini as they walked back into the house. 'But I'm rather hoping that won't happen.'

'You and me both,' said Aidan.

'But it's always good to have a back-up plan when you're dealing with water. And if anything goes wrong, pull sharply on the rope three times,' Houdini said. 'That's the signal I always use. Then we'll pull you up at once.'

Aidan nodded. 'Got it.'

They'd all decided that twilight was the best time for the dive. They needed the cover of darkness so as not to arouse anyone's suspicion, but Aidan still reckoned he'd need a bit of light to see what was down there. 'There's got to be some sort of chamber or cubby hole,' he said, 'and I need to see it to get into it.'

Vincenzo hired a horse and cart and they drove to the Buriano Bridge just as the sun was setting. Leonardo's landscape looked heart-breaking in the rose-gold light, and the Tuscan hills were the same hue as a Holly Blue butterfly. Vincenzo tied up the horse on the bridge and Aidan carried the suit down to the bank. Soberly, his fellow time-thieves helped him put it on. There was very little chatter now, and no joking at all. As the sun lowered, the only sound was the roosting birds and the clatter of the horse's hooves as it shifted on the stone bridge. Bright butterflies danced around the bizarre leathery suit, as if wishing Aidan luck.

Houdini checked that all the connecting points of the suit were secure, just as his Chinese assistants had done for him in the Egyptian Hall in London. Then he took the breathing tube up the bank and fed it over the parapet of the bridge. Last of all Vincenzo threw down the rope, as thick as Luna's wrist, which was securely tethered to the cart at one end. He then took out a fishing rod and tackle – they had decided that he should sit on the bridge wall, covering the rope, and pretend to be fishing. Vincenzo had even brought that day's newspaper to read, just as a fisherman might while waiting for a bite. Down on the bank, Konstantin passed the other end of the rope round Aidan's waist and tied it with a competent-looking military knot.

Luna could not keep the worry from her face. Aidan smiled at her. The smile was more for Luna than for him, for his stomach felt most peculiar.

'Chin up, Duch,' he said. 'I'll see you in no time.'

Then he waded down into the river.

29 JULY 1914
9.30 p.m.

Once he was fully submerged in the surprisingly cold water, Aidan's first instinct was to panic. It seemed so unbelievable that a person could breathe underwater. He wanted to gasp, to gulp air, to cry out, but he made a superhuman effort to slow his breathing and relax.

'Trust Leonardo,' he said to himself, over and over like a prayer. 'Trust Leonardo.' The rope held him admirably, the breathing tube remained clear, and the suit barely leaked at all. But there was another problem. At first Aidan could see nothing through his goggles. The water was reasonably clear, but the river's flow was quite fast, and he felt disorientated. But once he'd got used to the direction of the current, his eyes got used to underwater vision and he was able to swim towards the second arch of the bridge. His leather gloves touched something solid and he could see the square stone blocks of the arch. Now what? The last rays of the sun helpfully sent a shaft of light through the greenish water, but all the blocks looked exactly the same: rectangular and robust, grown over with centuries of algae and lichen.

As the sun faded he searched desperately for something – anything – that might indicate an underwater chamber. Exhausted by constantly fighting the current, he clung to the bridge for a moment and closed his eyes. As his hands clung and his body drifted, he sent a silent plea to a long-dead genius. 'Leonardo da Vinci,' he said. 'I could do with a little help right now.'

Suddenly the rushing water and the bridge disappeared, and Aidan was warm and dry and back in the suite at the Hotel du Louvre with his fellow time-thieves, gazing and gazing at the *Mona Lisa*, searching for any little clue as to the whereabouts of the *Salvator Mundi*. His vision honed into her eye, that pupil golden as amber, suddenly huge, with the letters **LV** for Leonardo da Vinci inscribed in tiny letters in the highlight. And then, the left eye.

There was the number **72**, and the letter **B**.

'72B, 72B,' muttered Aidan to himself, his voice unnaturally loud inside the diving helmet. He grasped the stones of the bridge and pulled himself down, down, as far as the breathing tube would go. He counted two stones up from the riverbed and seven stones along. But no amount of pushing and pulling would shift the stone he'd arrived at. 'Too deep,' he said to himself; his own voice was a comfort. He began again. He counted seven stones up from the riverbed, and two stones along. The stone he landed on this time looked different from the others.

Aidan's heart began to speed. He felt around the face of the stone, through the moss and slimy algae, and found a series of ridges and curves. Slowly, unbelievably, he traced their outline. They described a letter.

The letter B.

His pulse pounding in his ears, he frantically began to clear the moss from around the edges of the letter. The B was in the middle of a massive block, and if the block could somehow be pushed inside it would let a man through. The B was the key – it *had* to be.

Aidan gathered the last of his strength and pushed at the stone letter. The B, incredibly, moved inwards about an inch, and triggered some sort of age-old mechanism. With a tremendous grating sound which told that it had not been moved for centuries, the entire block shifted inward, leaving a man-sized hole to swim through. Aidan manoeuvred his body through the gap and then almost deafened himself with a shout of triumph that resounded within the helmet.

He'd found it – the underwater chamber!

But his triumph was short-lived, and the cry died in his throat.

Something was wrong.

He couldn't breathe.

29 JULY 1914
9.30 p.m.

When Luna and Konstantin scrambled back up to the bridge, Houdini went down to the river bank, to be ready to haul Aidan out if need be. The two remaining time-thieves leant precariously over the balustrade, trying and failing to see how their missing member was getting on. Vincenzo sat on the guide rope to make sure it was secured and didn't shift. He was giving a very good impression of a night fisherman. He'd got a little squashed hat and gabardine coat from somewhere, and was holding his rod over the water so the line and bait dangled in the stream. At all times, the three of them made sure that Aidan's breathing tube, which threaded over the parapet on to the bridge, was clear and unimpeded.

It was late, and the place was lonely, so they didn't expect to see anyone pass over the bridge. So when hooves and carriage wheels sounded in the twilight, they were not unduly worried. They had their cover story of a local man fishing with his children. But as Luna looked down the road, her blood chilled and she grabbed Konstantin's sleeve. There, approaching in the moonrise, was the sinister black carriage they'd seen in Arezzo. The black horses seemed to move in a fluid, slowed-down motion, their feathered plumes bobbing, the lacquered sides of the carriage reflecting the moon like water.

This time there was a driver on the box, clad all in black and wearing a broad black hat. He pulled the four horses to a halt on the crown of the bridge. The tall figure clambered down, looked down interestedly at Vincenzo's fishing line, and asked pleasantly, 'Any luck?' He spoke in English, with a broad Southampton accent.

Luna peered beneath the stranger's hat. The brightening moon caught a flash of watchglass. 'Arthur John Priest,' she whispered with dread. 'What are *you* doing here?'

Arthur John Priest turned and leant on the parapet. He looked at all three of them in turn. 'Same as you,' he said. 'A spot of fishing. Although you might describe me as a fisher of men. Funny phrase, that, isn't it? Almost biblical.

I wonder who else was described as that?' He looked about him. 'Such a shame Nadia isn't here. She always knew her scripture, our Nadia.'

No one moved, no one said a word.

'Ah well.' Arthur John Priest shrugged theatrically. 'I'll just have to tell you myself, won't I? The fisher of men was Jesus.' He looked at them. 'Our Saviour. The Saviour of the World. Or, as our fisherman friend might say, the *Salvator Mundi*.'

Suddenly everyone on that bridge knew that Arthur John Priest was there for the same reason as they were – to recover Leonardo's priceless masterpiece. Luna realised that the hearse was just the right size for carrying away a large canvas, just as their own cart was.

Arthur John Priest seemed to enjoy their discomfort. 'That's what you're doing here, isn't it? Fishing for treasure. Up to no good.'

'Speak for yourself,' said Konstantin through his teeth. 'We're the ones *doing* good.'

'According to whom?' said Arthur John Priest politely. 'The Butterfly Club? They've got a pretty broad definition of what's "good", if you ask me.'

'I wasn't asking you,' said Konstantin bravely.

Arthur John Priest flashed his yellow teeth in an unpleasant smile. 'Of course, Daddy can do no wrong, can he? The great doctor Tanius Kass. Absolutely infallible, isn't he? Except when it comes to matters of the *heart*.'

Konstantin was pale in the moonlight. 'What are you talking about?'

Arthur John Priest jerked his head at Luna. 'Ask her,' he said. 'She's already worked out that dear Auntie Grace isn't quite the philanthropist that she makes out.'

Luna swallowed. Was their ancient enemy confirming what she'd begun to think – that the Butterfly Club's motives were not exactly pure?

Vincenzo, who hadn't really been following any of this, shifted his weight on the bridge wall. Of course, he was pinned to the spot and couldn't move: not only was he anchoring the guide rope, but he was also keeping Aidan's breathing tube in place.

'*Signore*,' he said gently, 'we don't want any trouble. We are just fishing – we have every right to be here. We wish you a good evening, and perhaps you would be good enough to go on your way.'

Arthur John Priest put his hand to his throat in mock shock, as if he was clutching a string of pearls. 'But of *course*,' he said. 'I'll be on my way. I apologise if I gave offence. The last thing I'd want to do is to put my *foot* in it.' He laughed. 'Or rather, *on* it.'

And deliberately, precisely, Arthur John Priest placed his heavy boot over Aidan's breathing tube.

29 JULY 1914
9.45 p.m.

Aidan knew at once that he was in trouble.

As soon as he'd entered the secret chamber the air in the breathing tube had abruptly stopped, and he was gasping for air. He schooled himself not to panic. What had Houdini said? Panic uses oxygen. He remembered the wineskin of spare air and transferred his mouth to the back-up breathing tube. He quickly calculated whether he had enough air in the wineskin to get to the surface. If he'd been in the river there might have been – but now he was inside the bridge, and he had no idea if the water filled the arch. Designed to buy valuable seconds for a diver to reach the surface, the wineskin was of little use if you were trapped in a watery prison. With the aid of the fishing lamp he tried to get his bearings – the only way he might survive was if he managed to get back through the hole, but the water in the bridge was cloudy with centuries of silt and he couldn't find the opening again. His lungs felt as if they would burst. He tried to recall all that Houdini had said. Three minutes was the longest the magician had managed to hold his breath, but for a person who had not trained his lungs it was nearer one to two. Hopelessly he moved his mouth back to the breathing tube, but it was no good – it was completely blocked.

In those last seconds of consciousness his life flashed before his eyes in sepia scenes like those photograms they had at the fair. The little house in Ireland, his six sisters packed into one bed like sardines. Swapping his petticoats for breeches. The watch he'd put together at the age of ten, its innards spilling over the kitchen table, chain splayed out like a tail, a slain mechanical mouse. His ma cutting his hair off, the black silky stuff falling on the flagstones, every lock that fell feeling like a link of chain that had once held him fast. Then working with his da on the railways, the iron rails under his boots, the road to anywhere he wanted to go. And then the time-thieves, the happiest days of his life, on the *Titanic*, in Egypt, in Paris. Konstantin. *Luna*. He knew he would never see them again. Spots danced before his eyes, where the sepia pictures had been. Aidan felt his muscles relax, and consciousness begin to slip away.

On the top of the bridge Konstantin faced Arthur John Priest as if they were a couple of gunfighters.

No one spoke, and Vincenzo and Luna watched on, rooted to the spot. The seconds ticked away inside Konstantin's chest, every one representing one of Aidan's heartbeats as he struggled for breath in the suit that could become his coffin.

Until this moment, Konstantin would have loved to be in that suit. Naturally a boy of action, he'd felt so useless and second-rate standing by while Aidan was doing all the heroics. But now Aidan was in danger, all his resentment vanished. He felt afraid, but simultaneously full to the brim with the courage that Luna claimed he had. His clockwork heart was racing dangerously, but he had no thought for his own safety. He stepped forward, and with an enormous shove, the strength of the superhuman that Luna had told him he was, he pushed Arthur John Priest over the side of the Buriano Bridge.

29 JULY 1914
9.50 p.m.

The air came back to Aidan in a rush, jerking him awake. Gratefully he began to suck at the tube like a lamb at a feeding bottle, feeling the beautiful, blessed air fill his lungs and revive his limbs. Now he had a choice. Badly frightened, he had half a mind to find his way out of the bridge, tug on the guide rope three times and be hauled to the surface. But he was already inside the bridge, and he had a Butterfly Mission to complete. Raising the fishing lamp, he swam upwards in the dark, and in just a few seconds his head broke the surface of the water.

Ignoring the irony that he'd been a few feet from fresh air all along, he looked around. As the water streamed from his goggles he could see that he was in a square stone chamber, half filled with water. The lower parts of the walls were green and slimy, where the level of the river had risen and fallen over the centuries, in flood and spate. But high up, near the top of the bridge where the arch curved, the walls were dry as bone. And there, as if in a strange, underwater art gallery, something hung on the wall.

The something was almost the same size as the *Mona Lisa*, but was wrapped in dark cured leather. There was a sheen on the leather, as if it had been waxed for further waterproofing.

This had to be it.

This had to be the *Salvator Mundi*.

Aidan knew it would be a mistake to attempt to unwrap the package here, for he'd have to get it through the river water first. He unhooked the package from the stones. It was surprisingly heavy – a panel, he guessed, not a canvas. He took a deep breath and plunged into the depths once more.

The bulk of the package weighed him down helpfully and he sank back down to the bottom of the bridge – seven stones up and two along. For a moment he panicked about getting the panel through the opening, but

Leonardo had known what he was doing. The painting fitted – *just* – through the gap, and Aidan was once more in the rushing river. Clinging to the leather parcel and battling the current, he tugged three times, sharply, on the guide rope.

29 JULY 1914
11 p.m.

Arthur John Priest toppled backwards over the bridge, clutching at the air as he fell. He landed with an enormous splash in the river. The current carried him downstream at once, and Luna and Konstantin flew to the balustrade, joining Vincenzo in peering down into the torrent.

'Do you think he's dead?' gasped Luna.

'Not he,' said Konstantin. 'He's survived three shipwrecks and a world war. I think he'll be fine.' He was feeling most peculiar, as if something was squeezing his chest. It felt as if it was he, not Aidan, who had a rope around him. He supposed he'd pulled a muscle shoving that fiend over the bridge. 'What do we do now? Pull Aidan up?'

'I don't know,' said Luna. 'If he's just about to find the *Salvator Mundi* he'll be terribly angry if we haul him up like a fish.'

'And there is another problem,' said Vincenzo. 'If he has found some sort of chamber and is inside it, pulling on the guide rope might dislodge the breathing tube. Then he'll be trapped.'

'I don't know,' said Konstantin, rubbing his aching chest. 'That wretch had his foot on the pipe for a few minutes. What if he's unconscious? Then we're just leaving him to die.'

They looked at one another, appalled. It was a terrible few moments, as they wondered whether action or inaction would be more dangerous for Aidan. But just as they were unable to wait a second longer there was a sudden, unmistakable tug on the guide rope. Then another, and another.

Leaving Vincenzo to anchor the lines on the bridge, the time-thieves rushed down to the river bank, holding on to the guide rope as they went. 'The signal!' gasped Luna to a waiting Houdini. 'Get him out!'

Houdini lent his stocky strength to the effort and the three of them hauled Aidan to the bank. It was like landing an enormous leathery fish. He was streaming water, enormously heavy in the bulky suit and had the added weight of the package – it felt like an impossible task. Konstantin felt as if his chest muscles were tearing apart. But as soon as Aidan reached the bank he was able to help them by hauling himself up, and soon they had him and the package clear of the torrent, and were helping him out of his leathery skin.

Once free, he lay gasping on the bank like a landed fish, gulping the summer night air.

Luna knelt by him. 'Are you all right?'

He grinned his trademark grin, eyes still closed. 'Yes,' he breathed, like a sigh of relief. He sat up and then began, shakily, to get to his feet.

Konstantin clutched his clockwork heart in relief, feeling for the familiar tick and tock. But something was wrong. There was nothing there – not the feeling, and not the sound. The summer stars started to spin around him and, as Aidan stood up, he fell to the ground.

Now, in a heartbeat, the situation was reversed. Luna knelt by Konstantin's side; Aidan stood over him, with Houdini looking on.

'Jesus, Mary and Joseph!' exclaimed Aidan. 'He just dropped! D'ye think his heart gave out?'

'Yes,' said Luna. 'Arthur John Priest was standing on your breathing tube and Konstantin pushed him off the bridge. But the excitement must have been too much for him.' Frantically she loosened Konstantin's collar and fanned his ghost-pale face. She looked desperately at Houdini, the only grown-up on the river bank. 'What do we do?'

'Don't look at me,' said the magician, looking rattled for once. 'I've been revived before, many times, but I've never done the reviving.'

'Well, I don't know what to do!' she cried in desperation. 'Konstantin was the doctor's son. I've got no idea how to revive a person.' She slapped his cheeks in turn, first gently, then more firmly, and shook him by the shoulder.

Aidan knelt too, and laid his hand over Luna's to stop her. 'Maybe that's just it. Maybe we have to think about him not as a person, but as a machine.'

Luna looked up at him pleadingly. 'Then what would you do to a machine?'

'Stand back,' said Aidan. Luna rolled clear and Aidan knelt over Konstantin, one knee on either side. He clasped his hands together into one fist, raised them over his head, and brought them down in the middle of Konstantin's chest in a heavy blow. Konstantin coughed once then began to gasp and splutter as if it was he, not Aidan, who had been underwater. Aidan laid his ear to Konstantin's heart. 'Ticking,' he said, his voice steeped in relief. 'We're all right.'

Luna looked at him, aghast. 'What,' she said, 'was that?'

'Kinesis.' Aidan grinned. 'Most machines respond to a sharp jolt to their moving parts. Otherwise known as a bleedin' good thump.'

Konstantin's eyelids flickered and then opened. He looked at Aidan and smiled weakly. 'You saved me.'

Aidan helped him to sit up. 'Sounds like you saved me first. So let's call it quits.'

Luna's own heart was so full she couldn't speak. Silently she did what she'd always wanted to do but had never dared – she folded them both in the most enormous hug.

Considering that you could never be quite sure when Arthur John Priest would pop up again, the time-thieves decided against opening the precious package at the Buriano Bridge. They piled into the back of the cart with the package, Houdini climbed up the front, and Vincenzo drove them home to the villa.

They took the parcel into the barn, and lit every lamp they had. It seemed right that they should open the package in the middle of a circle of candles, because the unwrapping of the panel seemed like an almost religious experience. For a moment they all sat, gazing at the parcel, which had been wrapped by Leonardo himself. Houdini nodded at Aidan. 'Go on,' he said. 'You risked your life for this. You should be the one who opens it.'

As Aidan fumbled with the leather ties of the package, the butterflies stirred in his stomach once more. What if they unwrapped a blank panel of wood? What if other adventurers, in the intervening centuries, had found the *Salvator Mundi* and replaced it with a dummy package? What if the panel had been damaged by flood water and damp over the years?

He unwrapped the waxed leather with a shaking hand, smoothing away the wrappings, then the layers of canvas beneath, then lastly a wad of flock wool.

It was all right.

Underneath, untouched by time, was a pristine panel with a golden sheen of varnish. It was a picture, head and shoulders, of Jesus. He was holding one hand high in a blessing, and in the other he held a beautifully painted crystal sphere.

'*Il Salvator Mundi*,' breathed Vincenzo.

Houdini nodded solemnly. 'The Saviour of the World.'

They all gazed at the figure, and the figure gazed back. He looked God-like, but at the same time oddly human –

even familiar. He was wearing a robe banded in bronze, his brown hair hung about his face, his hazel eyes followed the viewer around the room, and his mouth was set in a secret smile.

Aidan looked at his fellow time-thieves. 'Jesus, Mary and Joseph,' he exclaimed.

'Well, he's *one* of those,' joked Luna. 'What's up?'

'Don't you recognise him?'

They looked again.

'It's the *Mona Lisa*.' He turned to Vincenzo. 'You see it, don't you, Vincenzo?'

Vincenzo, who'd spent longer gazing at the *Mona Lisa* than anybody except Leonardo, nodded, as if in a dream. 'Yes,' he said. 'It's the same person. The same model, certainly.'

'But… but…' said Luna. 'This is a man. The *Mona Lisa* is a woman.'

'Sometimes,' said Aidan quietly, 'the distinction is quite blurred.'

'What's he holding?' wondered Konstantin, peering closely at the crystal sphere.

Luna thought about all they had been through to get to this point, and of the gathering clouds on the horizon. 'I think,' she said, 'it's the future.'

Houdini turned to Vincenzo. 'This one *does* belong in Italy.'

'No,' said Vincenzo. 'I've changed my mind about that. Leonardo was right. Art belongs to the world.' He smiled at them all, rather sadly. 'You are the ones who discovered it. Take it.'

Luna looked at the others. 'We can't.'

'No,' said Vincenzo. 'There's something you don't know.' He took a newspaper from his coat – the paper he'd taken as part of his cover as a fisherman, the paper he hadn't had time to read until now. He unfolded it. 'Look.'

They gazed at the headline. The huge black letters took up almost all of the front page. They read:

LA GUERRA È DICHIARATA!

Aidan, no wiser, asked, 'What does it mean?'

'War is declared,' said Vincenzo soberly. 'Take the *Salvator Mundi*. Show it to everyone.' He looked up from the headline that would change the world. 'If ever the world needed a saviour, it's now.'

30 JULY 1914
3.30 p.m.

O f course, no one could think of anything but the outbreak of war, so when a vehicle turned up in the centre of Florence to take the *Mona Lisa* back to Paris, Giovanni Poggi of the Uffizi Gallery felt nothing but relief.

He'd been worrying about how to return the painting across a land border after the hostilities had begun, and was most grateful that the Louvre had thought of it all for him. Granted, the truck they'd sent was more like a train than a van, and the delivery men in smocks and flat caps seemed very young, but he supposed most of the older men had already joined the army. He was intending to himself. And, for that matter, perhaps all the decent vehicles had been commandeered for the army too. Anyway, what did it matter what the truck or the delivery men looked like? The conservator they sent with it, with the crinkly hair and the funny accent and the bright silvery eyes, seemed to know all about the painting, and he certainly knew about the personnel at the Louvre, stating that he had been sent by Monsieur Theophile Homolle, the director of that great gallery, and his deputy Georges Benedite.

'So that's all right,' said Luna, who had been hiding in the back of the Time Train with Vincenzo while the boys and Houdini had gone to collect the picture.

'Yes,' said Konstantin, flinging his cap into the back. 'It was much easier stealing the *Mona Lisa* the second time than the first.'

Konstantin looked round at Vincenzo. 'What will you do now?'

Vincenzo looked solemn. 'All I ever wanted to do was bring honour on my country,' he said. 'I still have one more chance to do that.'

'No,' said Konstantin, knowing what he was going to say.

'Yes,' said Vincenzo, with determination. 'I am going to join the Italian army. They need soldiers, and I will stand up and be counted.'

Konstantin felt the tears rising dangerously in his throat. He swallowed them down. 'Be careful,' he implored. 'You have no idea how bad it's going to get.'

'I will,' promised Vincenzo. He took his leave from them all in turn. The final, and perhaps the hardest, farewell of all was to the *Mona Lisa* herself. He leant over the back seat of the Time Train and kissed the *Mona Lisa* on the lips. '*Arrivederci*,' he said tenderly. 'Time to go home.'

It was an awful wrench to watch him walk away through the golden Florentine square, scattering pigeons as he walked. The great friend they had made was heading into such an uncertain future. Aidan, sitting at the console of the Time Train, began to twiddle knobs and switch switches, because he had a horrible feeling that if he didn't keep himself busy he might cry. 'Now what?' he said – his usual question, but this time delivered in an artificially bright voice.

Luna answered his question with another. 'What do we always do?' she said. 'We put the *Mona Lisa* back.'

30 JULY 1914
3.30 p.m.

Despite the grave international situation, the Louvre was busier than they'd ever seen it. It was even busier than on those crowded days following the theft of the *Mona Lisa*, when the whole of Paris had gathered to see what was going on.

Once again queues snaked around the block, tailing back as far as they could see. The time-thieves, wobbly from time travel, followed the crowd, and, taking advantage of the boys' delivery uniforms, walked right to the front of the winding queue. The snake led into the Salon Carré, the coffee-and-bronze gallery they knew so well. And when they got to the front of the queue: nothing. Just a space, cordoned off by a red silken rope placed in a square on brass stands. Each member of the crowd, when they reached the front, gawped at the gap for some moments, then moved on.

'What are they looking at?' wondered Aidan.

'A space,' said Konstantin. 'They've come to see the place where the *Mona Lisa* used to hang.'

'*All these years later?*' said Luna.

'Evidently,' said Houdini.

'Someone's making a bundle of money,' observed Aidan. 'At this rate Homolle won't want her back.'

'Oh, he will,' said Luna, who'd formed a dark notion of what was going on. 'Let's go and see the museum director.'

'You mean Monsieur Homolle?' said Aidan.

'Well, but it won't still be him,' said Konstantin. 'Way back at the start of this, the professor told us he was only museum director until 1911.'

But when they knocked on the door of the museum director's office, Theophile Homolle was there, sitting behind the desk. He didn't seem at all surprised to see them. He looked up from his desk as if he'd just seen them minutes ago, rather than years.

'Ah,' he said with great satisfaction. 'I wondered when you'd all come walking back through this door.'

'Well,' said Konstantin. 'You'll never guess what we're bringing you this time.'

Homolle sat back in his chair and regarded them all. 'Oh, I think I will,' he said. 'You've come to return the *Mona Lisa*, which you stole in the first place.'

The time-thieves gaped at him. 'So you knew all along?'

'Of course,' he said, as if it was the most natural thing in the world. 'It was all arranged. With Mr William Holman Hunt. I would let you steal the painting, I would be sacked from my position here, but I would be well rewarded with 10 per cent of the Louvre's admission fees for the rest of my life. The Louvre keeps 80 per cent of the gate, and everybody's happy.'

Aidan couldn't read, but he was excellent with numbers. 'So, 10 per cent for you, 80 per cent for the Louvre.' He narrowed his blue eyes. 'Who gets the other 10 per cent?'

Homolle smiled. It was not a pleasant sight. 'How do you say? *Le Club Des Papillons*.'

None of them needed a translation for those final words.

'The Butterfly Club,' they groaned, with one voice.

'*Exactement*.' Homolle smiled smugly. 'They told me you'd be happy to steal the painting, but that you would eventually return it.'

'Money,' spat Luna. 'It always comes back to money.'

'That is how the world turns.' Homolle shrugged expressively. 'Well, it has been a pleasure to see you all, but I have much to do, so all that remains is for me to thank you for bringing the *Mona Lisa* back home – and increasing her value in the intervening years by several million times.' He looked at the painting greedily, without any of the pure love with which Vincenzo had said his farewells. 'I think we are going to need a new room especially for her. Wait until the press get hold of this.' He rubbed his hands until his knuckles cracked. 'She'll be the sensation of the century.'

Deflated, the time-thieves walked back down the snaking lines of art lovers, wondering how all these people would feel if they knew that the *Mona Lisa* was now back within the walls of the Louvre.

As they settled glumly back into the Time Train they all sat for a moment, not speaking. It was Luna who broke the silence 'We've been taken for fools.'

'How d'you mean?' asked Konstantin.

'You remember when we were in London, and we went to see Houdini at the Egyptian Hall, and I said I was surprised that the Butterfly Club were sending us on any more missions, because the last two times, whatever they've asked us to get, we've either left it alone or put it back?'

'Yes.'

'Well, we did the same here. They *knew* we would. William Holman Hunt and the Butterfly Club knew we would eventually conclude that the *Mona Lisa* belonged in France. Morals, that's our problem,' she grumbled. 'We always do the right thing. And they banked on that.'

'I've been played too,' said Houdini ruefully. 'They knew the Great Houdini would not be able to resist the challenge to make the *Mona Lisa* disappear. They played on my ego like a violin.'

'And meanwhile, in the intervening years, we've made an unknown painting into a priceless masterpiece.' Luna huffed out a frustrated sigh. 'I hope no one goes to see the mouldy thing.'

'I bet they will, though,' said Aidan grimly.

'I'd give my right arm to know what happens in the future,' said Konstantin. 'Shall we ask the professor?'

'Not here,' cautioned Aidan. 'Too public.'

Then the two boys looked at each other, eyes shining.

'Well, since we're here…'

'Five more years?'

'Seems about right.'

'Wait, what are you—?' Luna realised what they were thinking, but it was too late.

As quick as a cat, Aidan set the dials and threw the lever, and the street disappeared.

THE LOUVRE
PARIS

30 JULY 1919

30 JULY 1919
4 p.m.

The rue de Rivoli reappeared again, almost unchanged. Some of the paint looked newer, some older, hemlines were shorter, and the weather was duller. But everything was much the same as the time-thieves staggered out of the Time Train.

The crowds were just as big, but this time the Louvre was different. The queues did not lead into the Salon Carré but into an entirely different room. The time-thieves followed the queues to find that the *Mona Lisa* had been given her own gallery, with no other paintings to keep her company.

She looked like an icon that people had come to worship, rather than a painting of what had once been a living, breathing woman. She looked separate, solitary and very lonely. She still watched those who watched her,

her eyes following her viewers around the room, but her secret smile seemed to have dimmed. The time-thieves felt oddly deflated.

'So now we know,' said Houdini. 'Now we can go.'

'I suppose so,' said Konstantin. 'But I wish… I wish…'

'You wish what?'

'I wish we knew what happened to Vincenzo,' he said. 'I wish we knew if he'd survived the war.'

And then, as if he'd been conjured by the Great Houdini himself, Vincenzo Peruggia walked into the room. He was smartly dressed in a light grey suit with a knotted cravat, and he wore a straw hat. His moustaches were neater and shorter, he looked a little older, a little thinner, and there was grey in his dark hair. But he was very much alive, with all his limbs.

And he was *not* alone. He walked arm in arm with a lovely young woman. She wore an elegant bronze dress and a matching hat shaped like a bell. Her smooth brown hair fell to her shoulders, she had rather sallow skin and almond-shaped hazel eyes, and a small smile played about her lips. She looked a good deal like the *Mona Lisa*. The sharp-eyed Konstantin realised that they were wearing wedding rings, and that two people could not have looked happier.

Delighted, the time-thieves circled closer, waiting for the moment to make themselves known.

Signora Peruggia was speaking. She clutched her husband's arm and shivered deliciously, looking half afraid, half excited. 'Aren't you afraid they will recognise you, my love?'

'Not they,' said Vincenzo. 'It was a world away. And back then I wore a craftsman's smock, so I looked very different to the man you see now.' The couple stopped in front of Leonardo's masterpiece.

'There she is,' he said, with a sigh in his voice. 'My first love.' But instead of gazing lovingly at the *Mona Lisa* for hours on end, he turned quickly away from the painting to look into his wife's eyes. 'But her beauty is nothing to yours.' And they kissed in front of the painting, while the *Mona Lisa* smiled her blessing on them.

'She is immortal now,' said his wife.

'As am I,' boasted Vincenzo. 'The shingles on the roof of the Louvre will rot, but my name will remain famous. I'll always be the man who stole the *Mona Lisa*.' Then he added, in an undertone, 'With a little help from my friends.'

At this Konstantin would have rushed forward, but Houdini put out his arm. 'No,' he said.

'B-but…' Konstantin stuttered.

'Vincenzo never knew we were time travellers,' said the magician gently. 'Look at him. You can see everything you wanted to know. He survived the war. He's in love with a real woman, not a painting. And if you look more closely,' he coughed delicately, 'you will see that the Peruggias are creating a masterpiece of their own.'

Konstantin looked carefully at the front of Signora Peruggia's bronze dress. There was a definite, rounded curve to her belly. Of course, it wouldn't be the done thing to say anything out loud, but Konstantin understood: Vincenzo and his wife were going to have a baby.

'He's happy,' said Houdini. 'He's moved on. Leave him be.' And he led the time-thieves from the gallery.

Konstantin twisted around until the very last minute, looking at the man who stole the *Mona Lisa* until the crowd had swallowed him.

THE ROYAL OBSERVATORY LONDON

8 FEBRUARY 1894

8 FEBRUARY 1894
7 p.m.

The Time Train arrived on the brass meridian just as the clock in the Butterfly Room struck seven.

As always, following a time jump, the travellers sat still for a minute, allowing gravity to reassert itself and for their molecules to go back to the proper places. As soon as they were able, they all twisted around to make sure the *Salvator Mundi* had survived its trip through the decades. In a final, private viewing before it was given to the world, they admired once again the serene face of Jesus and the almost miraculous skill with which Leonardo had painted the crystal ball in which the future was held.

'Where will it go?' wondered Houdini.

'The British Museum, I suppose,' said Aidan. 'They always seem to be at the bottom of everything.'

'Or the National Gallery,' suggested Luna, 'since it's a painting. I went there a few weeks ago.' Actually, that wasn't right – time travel always got her in such a muddle. 'No: it was a few *days* ago. I saw Papa.'

'Well, at least it will be seen there,' said Konstantin. 'By thousands and thousands of people.'

They got out, feeling slightly wobbly. They had chosen Aidan, as they thought it was his right, to lift the painting from the back of the Time Train and present it to all the important ladies and gentlemen gathered in the twelve-sided room, in their stove-pipe hats and brightly coloured bonnets.

Aunt Grace and Dr Tanius Kass stepped forward, all smiles. They were accompanied by William Holman Hunt, his beard barely hiding his delighted grin.

'Well done,' said Aunt Grace, looking like the cat who'd got the cream. 'I predict this is by far the most valuable acquisition the Butterfly Club has ever had.'

The word 'valuable' set alarm bells ringing in Luna's mind. She watched William Holman Hunt greedily appraising the painting, brushstroke by priceless brushstroke.

'Where will it go?' she asked, as her aunt kissed her coolly on the cheek.

'Into a private collection for now,' said Aunt Grace. 'Is Sir Francis Cook here?'

Dr Tanius Kass, who was tenderly embracing his son, said, 'Yes, I think so. Sir Francis?'

Another elderly, bearded man stepped forward. *Really*, thought Luna, *lots of members of the Butterfly Club looked terribly similar*. Aunt Grace addressed the gentleman. 'Sir Francis, I assume you have a place for this masterpiece at Doughty House?'

'Indeed.' The gentleman bowed. 'I have recently built a Long Gallery at Doughty House – my estate in Richmond – to house my private art collection.'

'It will be for some years, if that will not inconvenience you.'

'Not at all,' Sir Francis replied obligingly.

Years. Luna had thought the *Salvator Mundi* would be on public display at once.

'But, madam, are you really willing to wait so long for a return on your investment?

'Not at all, Sir Francis. We will collect almost straightaway.'

'But how?' said Aidan, who was standing with his arm flung fondly around the shoulders of his father, Michael O'Connell.

'We have a rather audacious plan,' said Aunt Grace archly. 'We will travel forward to the turn of the millennium, and sell the *Salvator Mundi* at auction.'

Luna calculated how many years it was until 1900. 'That's six years.'

Aunt Grace's smile widened. 'My dear Luna. Not this millennium. The next.' She addressed the room. 'I'm speaking of the year 2000.'

A collective gasp rose from the ladies and gentlemen in the room. The butterflies stirred on their cards, and the time-thieves' mouths dropped open.

'Why wait that long? asked Konstantin, aghast.

'Because with every year it is lost, the painting assumes a greater value,' said Aunt Grace simply. 'Witness what happened to the *Mona Lisa*. We will sell the painting, ask to be paid in gold bars, and bring the bullion back here. It will be worth a fortune.'

'I thought we weren't supposed to travel beyond 1969,' said Luna. 'The professor said so. You never know what havoc we might wreak.'

'Fortune favours the brave, my dear,' said Aunt Grace. 'Fortune favours the brave.'

Aidan found his voice. 'Yes, but who would be brave enough – or doolally enough – to travel that far forward?'

'The man who dreamed up the plan. A man well known to you.'

They knew. They absolutely *knew* who would come walking through the double-clock door into the Butterfly Room, his opera cape stirring the wings of the pinned creatures nearest his entrance.

Arthur John Priest strode down the meridian line. He bowed politely to the company, and addressed Konstantin out of the corner of his mouth. 'You weren't expecting to see me again, were you, my little tin soldier?' he whispered harshly. 'Not when you pushed me over that bridge fit to drown me?'

Konstantin's blood turned to ice. 'What are you going to do to me?' he whispered.

'Oh, I'm not going to do anything,' said Arthur John Priest. 'I don't have to. It's that ticker of yours that'll be the death of you. The tin soldier's little lead heart. It gave out once, didn't it? Someday soon it won't start again.'

Aunt Grace was speaking. 'Mr Priest, Dr Kass and I will go over the particulars of your mission to the millennium. And speaking of time travel,' she subtly changed direction, 'we have a surprise for you. If the three of you go to Camden Lock tomorrow morning at ten, and ask for Mordecai Jones of Ink Inc., you will receive a gift of great significance.' Her smile widened. 'A little present from the Butterfly Club, in recognition of your sterling service to our cause.' She turned to Houdini. 'Mr Houdini, we are more grateful to you than we can ever express. But as you are such a busy man, our little society must trespass on your time no longer.'

Aunt Grace could not have been more polite, but her speech was, very clearly, a dismissal. Houdini had helped them, but he was not a member of the Butterfly Club, and it was time for him to go.

'I suppose this is *adieu*,' said Houdini to the time-thieves. His silvery eyes were mirrored with moisture. 'No, the other one. Konstantin, which French farewell means you will see someone again?'

Konstantin, momentarily himself again, smiled a little. '*Au revoir.*'

'Then it's *au revoir*, my young friends.' Solemnly, Houdini shook their hands. When he got to Aidan the young navvy plucked up the courage to say, 'Maybe we could come and see another of your magic shows one day?'

Houdini cocked an eyebrow. 'What's the magic word?'

'Abracadabra,' the three of them chorused.

'No.' Houdini smiled. 'Please.'

9 FEBRUARY 1894
9.59 a.m.

The next morning Luna pushed her way through the Friday crowds in Camden Market, still seething about the Butterfly Club's greedy tactics. She and her fellow time-thieves had been used, their sense of honour exploited, in the *Mona Lisa* affair. It had been a cynical plot to make a little-known painting more valuable, and in the meantime, the *Salvator Mundi*, a masterpiece that might help to heal a troubled world, was to be hidden from that world and kept in the private collection of the highest bidder. The Butterfly Club, not content with making a profit in their own age, would now look to the centuries to come, beyond the millennium, to fleece the future. Luna was not sure she could be a part of it all. She marched on furiously, almost oblivious to her surroundings, until she reminded herself that Camden was a notoriously dangerous part of London and a world away from the refined, leafy streets of Greenwich or Kensington. But there didn't seem to be too many thieves and vagabonds in the market that morning, just a cheerful crowd of housewives, maidservants and kitchen boys buying bits and pieces for their masters – vegetables, fruit, candles and shoe leather. And the welcome sight of Konstantin and Aidan, waiting by the lock.

Aidan, endlessly fascinated by how things worked, was sitting on the lock itself, hobnailed boots dangling over the canal. He was watching the lock-keeper open the sluice gates so the lock filled with water, allowing the canal boats to rise to the level of the next stretch of water. 'Bit slower than the Time Train, hey?' he said, by way of greeting.

Luna, who would normally be interested too, had no room in her head for anything but the *Salvator Mundi*. 'It wasn't meant to be tucked away,' she raged, without even a hello.

'What wasn't? asked Konstantin distractedly, turning away from the boats. He'd found it so hard, since yesterday, to think about anything but the clockwork ticking in his chest, wondering if and when it would cease.

'The Leonardo, silly,' said Luna, who knew nothing of Arthur John Priest's threat. 'It wasn't meant for profit. It was meant to help mankind. You heard Vincenzo. If ever the world needed a saviour, it was now. Then. Oh, you know what I mean.'

'My guess,' said Konstantin, 'is that Arthur John Priest offered to go to the far future and sell the *Salvator Mundi* as a way to suck up to the Butterfly Club. If his plan works, he'll make enough gold to make the Butterfly Club one of the richest organisations in the world.'

'Why would he want to help them, though?' asked Luna.

'You know him,' said Konstantin. 'He never wants to help anyone but himself. Perhaps he thinks that if he pulls this off, he'll be able to lead this enormously rich society, replacing your aunt. Then he'd be one of the most powerful players in the Empire, like the chairman of the East India Company. Or the Governor of the Bank of England. Or even the Prime Minister.'

Aidan shrugged. 'If that fiend wants to go forward to the year 2000, more fool him. I won't exactly cry if something horrible happens to him.'

'I suppose,' grumbled Luna. 'Come on, then. We'd better find Ink Inc.'

'Found it!' said Konstantin, pointing a pale finger.

There, just by the lock, was a shop front with the words *INK INC.* painted above the window in black gothic letters. In the window there were lots of designs painted on little cards – roses, birds, anchors and hearts. It might almost have been an art shop, but for another set of black letters below the window which read *TATTOO PARLOUR*.

'Jesus, Mary and Joseph,' exclaimed Aidan. 'I guess it's our turn to be inked.'

Somewhat reluctantly, they filed into the shop. Inside there was a dim stairway, and the roses, birds, anchors and hearts continued down the stairs, painted on the walls in a crowded scrawl.

At the bottom of the stairs was a small chamber, its walls covered with the same designs. It had no windows, but was lit by bright lamps, and the dark bulk of a figure sat beside what looked like a stretcher. The man almost blocked the light. He was enormous, and bald-headed, and he seemed an extension of the stairs and the walls in that the roses, birds, anchors and hearts continued on his flesh. He was decorated from head to toe with tattoos, and even his bald head was covered.

'Are you Mordecai Jones?' Aidan's voice didn't seem to work very well.

'I am.'

'Miss Grace Goodhart sent us.'

The tattooed giant had a surprisingly pleasant smile, with gappy teeth. 'Ah yes,' he said, unpinning a design from the wall. It was the same clockwork butterfly that adorned the wrists of the club members. 'The Butterfly Club. Don't get to do many of these.'

'Because they don't take many members?'

'Not so much that, dearie. It's because you have to have travelled in time to get the clockwork butterfly.' He selected a little glass bottle with a slick of blue-black ink in the bottom. 'When a sailor has travelled 5,000 nautical miles he traditionally gets a tattoo of a swallow. In your society, you get the clockwork butterfly tattoo when you have travelled fifty years in time.' He waved aloft a scary-looking needle apparatus. 'Ladies first?'

Konstantin looked at Aidan. 'Shouldn't one of us boys go first?'

'Well, that depends,' said Mordecai Jones with a dry chuckle. 'I've found the ladies are a bit tougher when it comes to the needle. You two might make more of a fuss, not less.'

Luna, trying very hard to be one of those strong women, still couldn't help saying, 'Is it going to hurt?'

The giant chuckled even louder. 'Of course it is.' Expertly he dipped his needle in the ink, chatting as he worked. It was hard to believe that such a large man, with his sausage-like fingers, could produce such intricate and delicate designs.

'Only exceptional people are accepted into the Butterfly Club. All sorts of folks, though. Last gent I did the clockwork butterfly for only had one eye. Roll up your sleeve, dearie.' Mordecai's strong hand held her forearm in a vice-like grip. 'And don't move.'

I can't do this, thought Luna. The tattoo, so permanent, would make her a fully paid-up and committed member of the Butterfly Club. She didn't know why she'd joined in the first place – she had never really had a choice; she'd literally been swept away in a journey across time. But at least to begin with they'd done some good. They'd saved the life of Guglielmo Marconi in 1912 – and in turn, his radio had saved the survivors of the doomed *Titanic*. And their intervention in the Valley of the Kings in 1922 had ensured that King Tutankhamun remained at rest in his native sands of Egypt. But the *Mona Lisa* mission had been different. They had saved no one – except perhaps Vincenzo. And they had made a lot of money for a lot of people who didn't deserve it. Luna Goodhart looked down at her naked wrist. Arthur John Priest had a butterfly tattoo; her father didn't. She knew which team she wanted to be on. With a supreme effort, before Mordecai Jones could draw so much as a blue-black dot, she pulled her arm away.

The tattoo artist looked up, his eyes kind. 'Don't worry,' he said. 'I was only 'aving a larf. It hurts for the first few minutes, then your body gets used to it.'

'No,' said Luna, 'it's not that I'm afraid of the tattoo. Well, not much. It's just…' She looked at her fellow time-thieves regretfully. 'I can't travel in time again.'

Aidan, looking sorry, said, 'But I want to.'

Konstantin, even paler than usual said, 'And I *have* to.'

'I don't expect you to come with me. And we will always be friends. No – more than that.' Suddenly Luna's voice wobbled perilously, and she knew she had to go or she'd cry. 'But I'm done with the Butterfly Club.'

And she ran up the decorated stairs into the light. As she passed a barrow of vegetables a Cabbage White detached itself from the wares and fluttered ahead of her, as if leading the way. Not knowing what else to do, Luna followed the butterfly, blindly pushing her way through the Camden crowds. Fortunately they were all strangers who didn't notice the red-haired girl crying, and wouldn't have cared if they had.

UNTIL NEXT TIME . . .

A NOTE ABOUT THE PEOPLE AND THINGS IN THE STORY

Ehrich Weisz, a.k.a. **Harry Houdini**, achieved worldwide fame as a magician and escapologist. His most famous trick was the Chinese Water Torture Cell, which involved him being wrapped in chains and suspended upside down in a glass tank of water. Because of the time it took him to escape (which he always did), Houdini learned to hold his breath for more than three minutes. Houdini was also famous for making things vanish, including, in 1918, an elephant – a skill that would come in terribly handy if he wanted to steal a painting...

Harry Houdini is still the most recognisable name in magic to this day.

The catacombs of Paris are a network of tunnels under the city, which house the remains of over six million people. Some of the skeletons date from the 12th century. A small section of the catacombs can be visited by tourists.

The ***Codex Arundel***, which includes the design for Leonardo da Vinci's diving suit, is now the property of the British Museum. It has been digitised and can be viewed online. In modern times the suit was actually built and tested by a diver named Jacquie Cozens. It worked.

Vincenzo Peruggia never returned to Italy after stealing the *Mona Lisa* from the Musée du Louvre. He did indeed throw the doorknob from the Louvre's storeroom over some railings, and early fingerprint technology connected the prints on the doorknob with the prints on the missing picture's frame. However, Vincenzo was not caught until 1913, when he showed the stolen painting to an Italian art dealer. He was tried in an Italian court, which agreed he'd stolen the *Mona Lisa* for patriotic reasons, but he was still sentenced to prison for one year and fifteen days. On his release he joined up to fight in World War I, but he survived and came home safely. He married and had a daughter, who he named Celestina. He died in France, sharing a country to the last with his first love, the *Mona Lisa*. Although convicts are not supposed to have memorials, a plaque was erected to Vincenzo Peruggia in 2010 in his home town of Dumenza, Italy. The man who stole the *Mona Lisa* is now considered a hero in his country.

The **Mona Lisa**, which was largely unknown at the time of her theft, was missing for more than two years. On her triumphant return to Paris, she became the most famous – and most visited – painting in history. Her worth cannot be estimated.

The **Salvator Mundi**, lost for centuries and then recovered, is thought by scholars to be a version of the *Mona Lisa*, possibly painted using the same model. It was sold in a private auction in 2017, for over $400 million, to an unknown buyer. No one knows for sure where the *Salvator Mundi* is now. It is once again lost, and hidden from public gaze. But it remains the most valuable painting in the world.

ACKNOWLEDGEMENTS

Thank you first and foremost to three wonderful women; Jane Harris, Felicity Alexander and Teresa Chris who made this series happen.

I'm also indebted to Felicity Alexander for her expert editing of the manuscript and to Jane Hammett and Lois Ware for their forensic copyediting and proofreading.

Two wonderful artists, designer Thy Bui and illustrator David Dean, really brought this book to life with their wonderful cover and part titles.

Thank you to the entire team at Welbeck Flame for helping The Butterfly Club series to fly, with such dedicated hard work and enthusiasm.

I inhaled so many books, films and documentaries about the Mona Lisa and Leonardo Da Vinci while writing this book, but one resource in particular was really invaluable. It is *Mona Lisa is Missing* on Amazon Prime, a documentary in which director Joe Medeiros undertakes a thorough investigation into the painting's disappearance, with a particularly sensitive look at the motivations of Vincenzo Perrugia.

If you get a chance, do go to the Musée Du Louvre in Paris and see the Mona Lisa for yourself. It's quite something to look in her eyes.

Finally some family. Thank you to Conrad and Ruby for knowing all the coolest butterfly names. My love of butterflies began in their company when they were little, in the caterpillar-shaped Butterfly House at London Zoo.

And last but never least, thank you to Sacha for always remembering to wind up my clockwork heart.

THE BUTTERFLY CLUB WILL RETURN IN THE TRIP TO THE MOON...

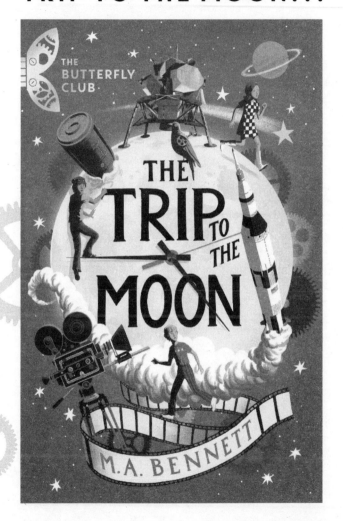

TURN THE PAGE FOR A PREVIEW

14 FEBRUARY 1894
11 p.m.

On Valentine's night, 1894, Konstantin Kass found it impossible to sleep.

He thought it pretty ironic that on a day when the whole nation was concerned with matters of the heart, he too could think about nothing but the little engine ticking inside his own chest. But he wasn't pining for some young *fräulein*, or wondering why he hadn't received one of the sickly cards the shops were suddenly full of, featuring lovesick shepherds or doves or cherubs. His worries were a little more serious, a little more life and death-y.

For Konstantin was genuinely concerned that his heart would stop.

He lay on his back, as he'd lain awake for hours now, just as he had last night. And the night before. And the night before that. In fact, ever since his clockwork heart had failed on the banks of the Arno river, right by the Buriano bridge, that night in 1914, he had been waiting for the inevitable. Arthur John Priest's prophecy that Konstantin's heart would one day stop, delivered in a vicious whisper back at the Butterfly Club, had entered his system like poison, and now infected every minute of his day. Konstantin laid his hand on his chest. The clockwork ticking was unmistakeably fainter, more irregular. At times it would seem to miss a beat, and Konstantin would have to wait for a sickening second that seemed like a lifetime, before the clockwork started again. But he knew that one day, it would not.

He wished Aidan were here. Aidan would know what to do. He'd never seen anyone understand machines like Aidan. He remembered those nights in Tuscany, sitting on a barn beam with Luna, watching Aidan recreate Leonardo da Vinci's diving suit in a miracle of engineering. Suddenly, ridiculously, he wondered if Luna had sent Aidan a Valentine's card. 'I need help,' he groaned aloud to himself, turned over and reached for the tinderbox.

He struck a light and touched it to the wick of the oil lamp on his bedside. As the match flared he caught sight of the butterfly tattoo on his wrist. Barely a week old, it had just about stopped hurting. It made him proud, proud to be a time traveller, proud to be part of something. He just wished Luna had got one. There was a Butterfly Club meeting tomorrow, on the 15th February, but he had to assume she wouldn't be there. She'd vowed never to travel in time again, and the thought made him sad, but he couldn't think about Luna now. His heart wouldn't let him – it ticked with more urgent matters.

Konstantin got up, and, wearing just his nightshirt, padded downstairs. The big house was quiet as the grave. His father and the servants were asleep, and through the windows he could see the big dark square of Horseguards Parade was empty. No prancing cavalry, nor marching infantry. Only a lone soldier stood awake and upright in his sentry box, keeping guard.

Holding the oil lamp high, Konstantin went down one flight of stairs, then another, then a third right down into the cellars. He took a key from a hiding place well known to him, and turned it in the door of a place he usually wasn't allowed to go.

It was the workshop of his father, Dr Tanius Kass.

14 FEBRUARY 1894
11.15 p.m.

It was a wonderful room with a wonderful Prussian name: a Wunderkammer, a Cabinet of Wonders. Whenever Konstantin had come down here to snoop before he had always enjoyed the experience, for the room was stuffed with his father's incredible inventions – automata, timepieces, clockwork devices, and brass cogs and springs lying around in little heaps like dragon treasure. Today, though he was too troubled to fiddle with the mechanisms or admire the workmanship. He was looking for something, anything that would indicate that his father had the necessary equipment to upgrade his failing heart.

That very heart nearly leapt out of his chest when he heard the door creak open behind him. His father, in a nightshirt and nightcap and also carrying an oil lamp, entered the room and shut the door behind him. He studied his son, but his eyes were troubled, not angry. 'Konstantin? Are you alright *liebe sohn*? What is the matter?'

Konstantin set down his own oil lamp on the workbench, and the little brass mechanisms gleamed in the light.

'It's my heart. Father, I think it's beginning to break.'

Doctor Kass set down his lamp too, and sighed. 'I knew this day would come. Machines, like people, fail in time. Fortunately, a machine can be improved and finessed.'

Konstantin looked around him at all the machinery. 'Is that something you can do?'

His father shook his head. 'No. I have a certain mechanical skill, which I inherited from your grandfather. He was a watchmaker in Königsberg, did you know that?'

Now Konstantin shook his head, mirroring his father. 'No I didn't know.'

'Your grandfather taught me what he knew about mechanics and clockwork, and then I became more interested in the workings of human beings. That's when I trained as a doctor.' He dropped a fond hand on his son's shoulder. 'I found the heart that ticks in your chest. But I did not make it.'

'Who did?'

'A very clever man called Otis Boykin. He invented a tiny machine called a Pacemaker. It is implanted in the body and stimulates the heart using electrical pulses, the same force that illuminates Mr Edison's electric lightbulb.'

Konstantin was lost. 'But...how is such a thing possible?'

'Now it would not be, of course,' said his father. 'But I met Mr Boykin in 1969.'

Konstantin was not at all surprised. He had suspected for a long time that his father had travelled far forward in time to save his son's life. Now Konstantin knew what he must do. 'Father. I think I have to go and see him.'

Doctor Kass sighed. 'I knew you were going to say that. But it is very dangerous to go so far into the future.'

'More dangerous than waiting to die?'

For a moment his father didn't reply. Then he said, 'we would have to convince the Butterfly Club to allow you to go on a special mission. There's a meeting tomorrow.'

WOULD YOU RISK
THE FUTURE TO
CHANGE THE PAST?